HEIRLOOM

EVENING TALES
FROM THE EAST

HEIRLOOM
EVENING TALES
FROM THE EAST

Mariam Behnam

OXFORD
UNIVERSITY PRESS

OXFORD

UNIVERSITY PRESS

Great Clarendon Street, Oxford OX2 6DP

Oxford University Press is a department of the University of Oxford.
It furthers the University's objective of excellence in research, scholarship,
and education by publishing worldwide in

Oxford New York

Athens Auckland Bangkok Bogotá Buenos Aires Calcutta
Cape Town Chennai Dar es Salaam Delhi Florence Hong Kong Istanbul
Karachi Kuala Lumpur Madrid Melbourne Mexico City Mumbai
Nairobi Paris São Paulo Shanghai Singapore Taipei Tokyo Toronto Warsaw
with associated companies in Berlin Ibadan

Oxford is a registered trade mark of Oxford University Press
in the UK and in certain other countries

© Oxford University Press 2001

The moral rights of the author have been asserted

First published 2001

ISBN 0 19 579329 3

Printed in Pakistan at
Mueid Packages, Karachi.
Published by
Ameena Saiyid, Oxford University Press
5-Bangalore Town, Sharae Faisal
PO Box 13033, Karachi-75350, Pakistan.

DEDICATION

To the Fikrees, my little friends of the old times and to my grandchildren who remind me of the difference between innocent fantasy and computerized dream-world!

CONTENTS

ABOUT THE AUTHOR

Mariam Behnam was born in southern Iran in the nineteen twenties. She belongs to an old and distinguished family of pearl merchants. She was brought up in Iran, Pakistan and the Gulf. Her education and ambitions led her to public service in Iran and diplomatic posts in Pakistan. During her career, she has served in several provinces of Iran, even in some rather remote areas, and has also been elevated to the post of Director General in the Ministry of Arts and Culture, Iran.

Her main previously published work is *Zelzelah*: A *Woman before her Time*. She has another work, *Naqshi as Doost* (The Role of a Friend), which was published in Lahore. Apart from this she has written several articles in Persian, Urdu and English on social welfare, culture, poetry and music of the subcontinent and the Gulf, which have been published in Dubai, Iran and Pakistan.

Zelzelah (which means 'earthquake') is the nickname her family gave her in childhood, because of her love for mischief and later when she grew older, because she refused to accept 'a woman's lot' in the conservative society around her. She was the second daughter of parents who wanted to have a son. Thus she grew up to be a rebellious, dynamic personality and in the process shook off some of the centuries old customs and traditions which marred the progress of women. *Zelzelah*, which is autobiographical, tells the story of an unusual woman, and also provides a rich and colourful insight into a civilization in transition.

Mariam Behnam left Iran in 1979 to join her extended family in Dubai, a place dear to her heart where she had often visited in the past, and the home of her ancestors for over a century.

She has become a citizen of the United Arab Emirates where she is a distinguished and respected figure actively involved in many social and charitable organizations. She lectures at various multi-national women's gatherings on a variety of subjects of interest to women and children. She encourages her audience to be aware of their inner strength as well as the importance of their role as mothers, not to hide behind closed doors, and to utilize their time constructively and effectively.

INTRODUCTION

O nce upon a time, as all good stories begin, life was full of wonder and imagination, for adults as well as for children. Long before the cinema took over the world of fantasy with ready-made dreams and television detailed wide-eyed wonderment with brutal reality, life was an endless merry-go-round of questions and answers, a daily stretching of the mind as the world around us washed over the world within us like the tide on the beach. Today's world cannot begin to understand yesterday's any more than yesterday's could have fathomed the developments which have taken place over the past several years. Those of us with memories going back that far can certainly testify to that. Never did we imagine that we would gain so much, nor lose so much in the process. Funnily enough, we also feel deep down that basically nothing has changed. We still laugh, we cry, we love and we hate. We need friends and human relationships to survive.

What we lacked in high fidelity sound and twenty-one inch picture quality, we made up for in ingenuity. Our religion did not allow the inclusion of theater or secular music so, instead, we told stories and recited poetry. We made up characters to suit the occasion. We read the classics, and endlessly debated their meaning. In essence, we lived our literature and the *literature* was our way of life.

Since time immemorial, in society on both sides of the Gulf, story-telling has been an important part of culture; even adults spent hours listening to their elders narrating these stories. I myself relished the role of story-teller to both young and old alike. I kept young friends enthralled for hours with stories which I owe primarily to my creative imagination. I was fond of retelling classical stories of empires, Sufis, old Chinese tales some of which I had read, some heard, and some created from the patterns of the classics. A good story is similar to an 'heirloom'. It should be treasured Nevertheless, I have never told a story in the same way twice and made full use of facial expressions and gestures to enthrall my audience.

Composing and reading poetry was very much in vogue from the 1920s, up to the late 1940s, and later. Recitations of the masters' poems were conducted amongst groups of men in their *majlis* as well as amongst the ladies. This was the closest we ever came to 'performing' but the effect was the same. I remember the response of my elders, particularly my grandparents, to my rhythmic and melodious recitations of classical and spiritual *qasidas* and *Masnavis* in praise of Allah and the Prophet [PBUH]. People around me felt that I possessed a good voice, and although I never trained professionally, I felt inspired to sing to myself, learn as much as possible, study hard, and gain a greater understanding of the classics. My talent did make me somewhat arrogant but at the same time it was a powerful boost to my self-confidence.

Poetry used to be a part of everyday life; it was not unusual for someone to quote an appropriate couplet in conversation and one's ability to do so was greatly admired. The elderly ladies of today in this part of the world remember idioms, anecdotes and classical verses from the poet-philosopher Sheikh Saadi and his books, *Gulestan* and *Boostan*; Hafiz Shirazi, whose books still adorn every house and whose verses are used as *'faal'*, a wish comes true with each verse. Sometimes one wonders how much the great poets and scholars have influenced our lives.

After half a century, when I revisited Bahrain, I was amazed to discover that no ladies' gathering was complete without the recitation of poetry. One lady begins with a *'Mashallah'* and recites a couplet and, whatever letter the couplet ends with, the next lady will use as the beginning of another two lines of verse, and so on. Lovely musical verses are sung with zest and joy, and the party exudes a lively aura of culture and learning.

The modern age arrived late for many people residing in the Middle East. In the 1920s, when bright young things on both sides of the Atlantic were kicking up their heels and doing the charleston, life remained unchanged in the towns and villages bordering the Gulf. Change was held back by the high walls and sturdy doors of tradition. When change finally arrived, it appeared initially as a trickle, gradually increasing to a torrent.

If television is the symbolic fruit of the modern era, then radio must be perceived as its seed. Radio came to us in the late 1920s in the guise of an old friend. There were several story-telling programmes, and children and adults alike were glued to the radio set.

There was a blind old man from Ajman who used to journey to Dubai to conduct business, riding on his donkey and accompanied by his teenaged son. He would travel for two full days and provided a rare treat for the children. We would all sit around him listening while he narrated stories and chanted. What stories. What treasures! We were transported to imaginary lands and relished every one of his tales. I later found out that he was illiterate, but to us, back in those days, he was a scholar whose capacity to remember thousands of couplets enthralled us. He greatly influenced me and I learnt from him the art of narration and developed a passion for composing and reciting poetry.

Many of my stories originate from the area bordering the Gulf, Lingah in the southern part of the coastal area of Iran to Dubai and Bahrain on the Arabian side. Culture, trade, and the thoroughfare between Lingah and Dubai, in particular, were so similar and the journeying between the two so frequent that one felt one lived in the same town. The later influences on these stories from Turkey, the subcontinent, Egypt, and the Gulf area arrived as a bonus with marriage and sojourn.

Today no one really has the time to narrate or listen to long stories or lectures, but we still read long and short stories. The stories compiled in this book are those that I can recall from the 1920s to the 1940s.

They range from fiction to folktales; some are moralistic stories of old masters. Some stories are my own creations, and some are based on real events.

There stories were initially heard and narrated in my mother tongue, Bastaki, the dialect I grew up with. Bastaki is primarily a flowing and rhythmic language and most suitable for recitations. I have endeavoured to preserve the easy flow of the stories but, unfortunately, some of this may have been lost through translation into English.

I have enjoyed putting this book together, and I do hope that it will give you as much pleasure as it has given me.

M. B.
Dubai, 2000

ABOU HASSAN AND THE KHALIFA

Many stories are told about the encounters that Khalifa Haroun Al Rashid had with his people while roaming the streets of Baghdad in disguise. Each of these tales is an example of his wisdom and the compassion he had for his people.

Abou Hassan was a young man who lived with his mother in Baghdad. His father was a wealthy merchant who had left him a vast fortune. The young man was intelligent, but he also loved the pleasures of life. So he invested half his fortune in estates and property and half he retained in order to have a good time, with all the numerous friends who had recently sprung up around him. Being generous by nature, Abou Hassan was always willing to help a friend in need, without ever verifying if the need was genuine or not. Needless to say, he squandered his wealth in a very short time and when the money was all gone, as it usually happens his new-found friends deserted him.

Abou Hassan was deeply grieved at the treachery of his comrades. But he resolved to start anew and live within the income from his property. He vowed that he would never make another friend and instead he would seek the company of strangers and having entertained them once, he would never see them again.

Thus, it came to pass that every evening he would sit by the bridge on the river Tigris and invite the first stranger who happened to cross it on his way to Baghdad. He would extend all hospitality and lay out a sumptuous meal for his guest. But in the morning he would bid his guest goodbye, never to see him again. This went on for quite some time.

One evening, the stranger that Abou Hassan invited was none other than the Khalifa Haroun Al Rashid, disguised as a merchant. It was the Khalifa's practice to wander around the city, in various disguises, and meet and talk to people to find out about their problems. In his opinion, his subjects would talk more freely to an ordinary man than to the Khalifa.

So the Khalifa accompanied Abou Hassan to his house and there they spent a very pleasant evening together. The Khalifa was very impressed by the hospitality, as well as the lively and intelligent personality of Abou Hassan and wanted to do something in return. But Abou Hassan would hear none of this, in fact he told him that when he left in the morning, it would be the last they would ever see of each other. The Khalifa was perplexed at the sudden change in the mood of his host.

'Why is it that you are such a generous host to strangers and yet shun their friendship?' he inquired.

'I have had bitter experiences with friends,' Abou Hassan replied, 'They were with me as long as I could entertain them and give them expensive gifts. As soon as they found out that I had nothing more to offer them, they abandoned me.'

The Khalifa, (remember that he was in disguise), was moved by this and said to Abou Hassan, 'I have some influence in the royal court and if there is anything you really want, I would probably be able to arrange it.'

At first Abou Hassan declined the offer, but on the Khalifa's insistence, he told him that there was one thing he wanted.

'What is that?'

'I would like to become Khalifa for one day,' Abou Hassan replied.

The ruler was taken aback and inquired why he made such a strange request.

'The reason' Abou Hassan told him is that 'I want to get rid of four evil men, who live in my neighborhood, and have made the lives of the townsmen really miserable with their vicious rumours and mischief. I also want to get rid of the *Emam* of *Jum'a*,' he continued, 'who aids these four evil men in spreading these vicious rumors and vitiating the atmosphere all around. We have petitioned against them to the Khalifa many times but to no avail. If I were Khalifa for one day, I would have them soundly beaten and then tied facing backwards on top of camels and drive them out of the town, in front of all the people. Everybody would be glad to get rid of these mischief-makers.'

The Khalifa was very amused at how serious the young man was about this. He was also glad that he had been able to gather information about these evil men who were creating problems in the neighbour-hood.

The Khalifa then suggested that they have one last cup of wine before retiring for the night. As Abou Hassan was filling the cup, the Khalifa managed to slip some sleeping potion into the wine. When Abou Hassan drank this he fell into a deep slumber. The Khalifa then ordered his servants to take him to the royal palace. There he was dressed in rich robes and put to sleep in the royal bed. The Khalifa then summoned his Grand Wazir, his aides, officials of his court, as well as the ladies of the palace. He instructed them, 'Make Abou Hassan believe that he is the Khalifa. I will hide and watch from behind the curtains.'

Abou Hassan got up the next morning after a sound sleep and found himself in a magnificent room with beautiful paintings, gold and porcelain vases and rich brocade curtains. He thought, 'Surely I am still asleep and dreaming of paradise.' Then his eyes fell on the people in the room, all bowing low in front of him and he was completely bewildered. To add to his confusion, the Grand Wazir entered the room and addressed him.

'Your Majesty, please get up and get dressed .The court is awaiting your presence.'

Needless to say the young man was aghast.

'Last night I was Abou Hassan, and now I am the Khalifa! Is this a dream? Something is really wrong here,' he said to the Wazir.

The Wazir, continuing the charade replied, 'Surely Your Majesty knows that he is the Khalifa of Baghdad, the Commander of the Faithful. Without you we would be nothing.'

The young man insisted that there must be some mistake; that he wasn't the Khalifa, that he was Abou Hassan.

'Come now, you must have had a bad dream. This Abou Hassan you keep talking about, is he the man in your dreams?' He asked with a very straight face.

Being an imaginative man, Abou Hassan decided to play along with whatever was happening. Servants brought in gold and silver pitchers full of scented water to wash his hands and feet and dressed him in magnificent robes of velvet and gold. He was then escorted to the grand hall and after a small ceremony, he was seated on the throne of Baghdad. The entire assembly bowed low before him and then stood with great reverence around him, awaiting his orders. All this made Abou Hassan think that maybe he really was the Khalifa after all. Then it occurred to him, 'This is what I had wished for. Now I have power over the entire land and can punish those evil men. I have been waiting for such an opportunity for a very long time,' he thought.

Aloud, he ordered his soldiers to go and bring the four evil men to him, '...the *Emam* of *Jum'a* knows who they are, and while you are at it bring him too, because he is the real ring leader.'

So the five men were presented before him and they were truly horrified when they saw who was sitting on the throne. It was none other than the young man they had tormented when he had lost his fortune. Abou Hassan ordered his soldiers to punish these men in exactly the same manner as he had told the Khalifa he would.

'Don't forget to have the town criers announce the spectacle first,' he added.

Abou Hassan then ordered the soldiers to go to the home of a certain Abou Hassan and give his mother a thousand gold coins. He wanted to make sure that his mother did not suffer any discomfort in his absence.

Abou Hassan then spent the rest of the day, feasting and having the best time he had ever had. He lay in the pavilion, with beautiful women playing music and singing to him. What lovely names they had—Mahjabeen and Aajlab. The food was delicious and so was the wine.

'Surely this is paradise,' he thought. Thus, the day went by very quickly, as it usually does when one is enjoying life! Night fell over the palace and soon it was time to retire. The 'Khalifa' took one last cup of wine. This last cup of wine had once again been laced with a sleep-inducing potion and while Abou Hassan slept the Khalifa's men quickly got him out of the royal robes, dressed him in his own clothes and took him back to his own house.

The next morning, as usual Abou Hassan was woken up by his mother.

'Where were you all of yesterday?' she asked, 'Your bed wasn't slept in and you remained away the whole day. I was worried sick about you.'

Abou Hassan shook himself out of his stupor and seeing his mother before him, asked her where he was and who she was. He refused to believe his mother when she told him that he was Abou Hassan and that she was his mother. He was the Khalifa of Baghdad! This couldn't be his home.

'Stop talking such nonsense. If the Khalifa hears this, then we will both be in real trouble,' his mother said, now really upset. 'Someone must have put a spell on you.'

She then showed him the bag of gold pieces that the Khalifa had sent her.

'Besides this, I have more good news. Son, you really missed a grand spectacle yesterday. Remember the petitions we sent to the Khalifa about those terrible men. Well, the Khalifa seems to have at last taken heed. He had those men soundly thrashed and sent out of town riding backwards on camelback.'

Abou Hassan kept on insisting that it was he who had done all that. His mother screamed at him to come to his senses.

'I am the Khalifa of Baghdad. I am! I am!' He kept insisting.

The neighbours heard the commotion and came to inquire if everything was all right. When they saw Abou Hassan insisting desperately that he was the Khalifa, they thought that he had lost his mind.

In those days the only cure for mental illness was to be locked up in the lunatic asylum. So Abou Hassan found himself locked up in prison for the insane. What a comedown from the opulence of the palace! But there, surrounded by people who were really mad, Abou Hassan slowly came to his senses and felt that perhaps what he had experienced was nothing more than a beautiful dream. When his mother came to see him, he told her that he realized his mistake and she took him home.

After all the excitement, Abou Hassan went back to his old habit of sitting by the bridge over the river Tigris, inviting strangers to spend the evening with him and never seeing them again. However, one evening, the first stranger to cross the bridge was once again the Khalifa Haroun Al Rashid, in the same disguise. When Abou Hassan saw him he covered his face and cried out, 'I don't want anything to do with you. The last time I took you home I ended up in a lunatic asylum.'

The Khalifa gently took him aside and convinced Abou Hassan to once again invite him so that he could spend a pleasant evening in his company. At the close of the evening, with the last glass of wine, the Khalifa once again drugged him and had him taken to the palace and put to sleep in the royal bed.

The next morning, when Abou Hassan awoke, he was delighted to find himself in the same circumstances. There was music and dancing and everyone referred to him once again as Khalifa. Overjoyed, he asked one of the ladies present to bite him, so that he would know that he was not dreaming. Everyone laughed at this and Abou Hassan realized that he was definitely not dreaming. The Khalifa who was watching this merriment from behind the curtain, could not contain himself and also burst out laughing thus revealing himself. Everyone stopped and bowed before the real Khalifa when he emerged from behind the screen.

'Why, you are the merchant I took home with me last evening,' Abou Hassan said astonished.

He began to apologize to the Khalifa, who stopped him and said, 'You are such a delightful young man that you are always welcome to the palace. Your honesty and simplicity has impressed me, as also your capacity to enjoy life to the fullest, without forgetting your duty to your fellowmen and your mother.'

The Khalifa then appointed Abou Hassan to a high position in his court. Abou Hassan did his work well and with great responsibility. He never forgot his duty to his mother. He married a lady of noble birth and— as end many stories of that era—they lived happily ever after.

GORGIN THE ARTIST

In days gone by, there was a strong tradition of story-telling. It is surprising how so much literature and poetry could originate from people who were not men of letters, at least not in the sense the term is used today.

Of particular interest are the stories narrated by Ali Muhammad, of Ajman, who was born blind. Needless to say he had never seen any colour or light, but the visual pictures he drew with his words were truly amazing. He even knew the Quran by heart. I am narrating one of his stories, which is intriguing, since it comes from one who had never seen the colours of nature.

Nearly two thousand years ago in a village, near the town of Kashan, lived an artist called Gorgin, with his wife and his son, Bahram. Gorgin was a painter who was much admired. People came from all over Iran and even from as far as the Gulf, to look at his work. IIe was highly respected and regarded by his friends and admirers. Bahram used to help his father and the two were inseparable.

Now, the Amir of the country, Miran, was kind-hearted and cared for his people. He lived in the town of Kashan. Despite the fact that he was the ruler, his house was so small that he was unable to hold proper audiences with his subjects and this made him feel isolated from his own people. One day a trusted friend of the Amir suggested, 'Why don't we build an auditorium in which people from all over the country can gather to meet you. You can then address them and take care of their grievances.' The Amir liked the idea, but was not sure of how he would arrange for the funds to build the auditorium.

'I do not want to spend money from the treasury for this building. That money is for the people.'

The friend came up with an idea, 'Amir, may you be blessed, you do not have to worry about the cost. The people of your kingdom will gladly contribute towards it.'

The Amir agreed to this idea, and consequently the town-criers went far and wide, informing all the citizens of the plan and requesting them for donations. Soon large quantities of contributions began to pour in and work began on the huge auditorium.

Gorgin and Bahram were delighted when they heard of the great hall being built by the people. They did not have any money to give, but wanted to donate what they could. So one day, when the auditorium was almost complete, they went to Kashan and requested an audience with the Amir. Miran had heard of Gorgin's great talent and called him in at once.

Gorgin said to the Amir, 'Your Highness, I am a painter and I would like your permission to paint the walls of the auditorium with the best pictures I can make. This is my son, Bahram, who helps me with my work.'

'I have heard of your talent. I give you permission to paint beautiful murals, both on the inside and the outside walls. When the people see your inspired paintings, they will forget their unhappiness and their grievances,' said the Amir, very pleased at the offer made by the artist.

Gorgin and Bahram wanted to create a mural which would be both beautiful and durable, and would stand till eternity, long after they were gone.

So the father and son went about gathering herbs, flowers and seeds, to make the paints they would need for this great project. You must remember that in those days there were no ready-made paints available. Craftsmen had to prepare their own formulae. Then they set about painting the murals. They worked day and night, creating beautiful images of paradise. Flowers, peacocks, gazelles—all seemed to come alive under the strokes of their brush. People would come from far and wide, for the sheer pleasure of watching the two at work. Sometimes the Amir would ride by and stop to gaze at the wondrous images created by the two artists. At last the mural was ready and the artists presented it proudly to the Amir and the people. Everyone clapped in appreciation of its beauty. The auditorium was then formally declared open.

After a few months had passed, Gorgin and Bahram visited Kashan, and Bahram went to have a look at their painting. A strong wind was blowing and it had started to rain. When Bahram saw the painting, he was shocked. The colours had started to run and had fused into one another. It seemed as though the animals and birds were shedding tears at having their beautiful coats and plumage spoilt by the rain. The painting on the outside wall was completely ruined.

He rushed back to his father, 'Father come quickly. The swans are crying and the pigeons are in tears. You have to come and see.'

'What is this gibberish, Bahram? Have you taken leave of your senses?' Gorgin replied, not being able to understand what his son was saying.

'Come and see father. The rain has destroyed our painting,' Bahram was close to tears.

When Gorgin reached the auditorium and saw the damage done by the rain, he was nonplussed. By this time quite a few people had gathered around and they began to taunt the father and son.

'Gorgin, is this what you wanted to preserve for eternity? Where has the red colour gone? Since when have flowers become black? Did you want to immortalize this weeping bird? What a waste.' They jeered.

'Please give me some time,' Gorgin said to the people gathered around, 'I will repair the damage and make sure this never happens again.'

Gorgin and Bahram were sad but they immediately started work on the wall again. They experimented with various methods to make paint which would not be damaged by the effect of rain or wind. After much effort they succeeded in repainting the wall, with material that would withstand the ravages of rain and wind.

But alas! Soon summer was upon them, and one day there was a knock on their door. The Amir's soldiers had brought a letter informing them that once again the walls of the auditorium had been ruined. On rushing there as fast as they could, Gorgin and Bahram saw a sight that brought tears to their eyes.

'Oh father look! Someone has broken the legs of the deer and the gazelle, and torn down the branches of the trees,' cried Bahram, tears pouring down his cheeks.

This time it was the sun, which had caused the damage. The entire wall had cracked into thousands of places. Humidity and steam from the heat of the sun, had aggravated the damage.

The Amir was extremely upset, 'A great deal of money collected by the people has gone into making the auditorium, and now it is ruined. Gorgin has to be punished for this waste,' he lamented.

'Arrest Gorgin and put him in prison, while I decide how to punish him.' He ordered.

'Please, Your Highness give us one more chance,' Bahram pleaded with the Amir, 'Together we promise to come up with a paint that will withstand both the rain and the sun.'

The kind-hearted Amir decided to give them one year to come up with a suitable paint.

Heartbroken, the father and son once again set about trying to develop a paint that would resist the ravages of nature. They spent hours in the jungle, collecting herbs, flowers, and whatever they thought would yield colour. They mixed and boiled the herbs, treated them with fire, but to no avail. Nothing they tried worked. Gorgin would often give up, but Bahram would persist.

'No my father, we cannot give up. Look at the sky. Its colour never changes. The colours of leaves and flowers don't run. And specially, nothing of the stone changes. Haven't you seen, when there is paint on a piece of stone, neither the sun nor the rain have any effect on it. When we have solved this mystery we will have the paint that we are looking for.' In his heart he knew there *was* an answer to the problem.

Thus the full cycle of the seasons passed, and then there came the knock on the door, which they had been dreading. The soldiers entered the house.

'The Amir wants to know if Gorgin has found the technique to make permanent colours?' They demanded.

'No, we have not found any solution to the problem.' Gorgin admitted.

'Then we have orders to arrest you and present you before the Amir for punishment,' replied the soldiers and led Gorgin away.

Bahram was totally dejected. Now his father would surely be hanged. He went and sat by the huge fire that they had kept going to treat the paints, and silently shed tears of grief. Suddenly his eyes fell upon something, which looked like bright, watery paint inside the fire. He pulled it out with a pair of tongs, and sure enough it was paint, that had spread on a kind of clay and had been cooked in the fire. Bahram washed this piece repeatedly, but the paint would not come off. At once Bahram knew he had finally found the answer. The paint had to be spread on clay and then put in the kiln to cook. This rendered the paint immune to both sun and rain.

Excited, Bahram rushed to Kashan to seek an audience with the Amir. He pleaded with the Amir to hear him out, to which the kind-hearted Amir consented.

Bahram explained to him, 'The pot of paint that my father made the day before he was arrested, has become as hard as stone, and the color as fast as the colour of the sky, which never changes.'

The Amir was skeptical, but agreed to give Gorgin and Bahram one week to prove that they could repair the walls with paint that would never spoil.

Bahram told his father that they had indeed discovered the secret of everlasting paint, and elaborated the technique.

Gorgin was not very enthusiastic. 'We can hardly put the entire wall in the kiln to be baked.' He pointed out.

But Bahram had the answer to this as well. 'We will spread the paint on small pieces of clay that we can bake in the kiln. Then with these pieces of clay, we will build the whole painting on the wall, thus recreating all the beautiful pictures that had been destroyed.'

Thus was born the art of tile-making or mosaic.

So Gorgin and Bahram succeeded in creating a medium which would last till eternity. Indeed, people may have forgotten the father and son, but the art they produced is still as beautiful and unchanging as the sky and the stone.

THE CROCODILE AND
THE MONKEY

This tale of the crocodile and the monkey is derived from the many tales of the wise and enlightened Bodhisattva who is believed to have returned to this world many times, in different incarnations. These stories invariably have a moral. One of the stories I remember, from the many we heard when we were children, was about the time when the Bodhisattva was said to have come back to life in the foothills of the mighty Himalayas, as a monkey. This was during the period when Bramadatta was king of Benaras.

The Bodhisattva in his new form grew to be big and strong. Indeed he seemed to be several heads taller than the other monkeys in the forest which was situated on the banks of the river Ganges. The river was the abode of several crocodiles. The biggest crocodile had a mate, who one day saw the big monkcy and from then on she was consumed with the desire to feast on his heart. She would look at the monkey's magnificent figure and regal looks when he came to the river to drink water, and think, 'If only I could eat his heart, I, too, would become as noble and dignified as him.'

One day, overcome by her craving, she said to her husband, 'I want to eat the heart of the king of the monkeys. You say you love me and would do anything for me. Well! I haven't asked you for anything for a long time. Now I want you to catch that monkey for me, so that I can eat his heart.'

'Good wife,' said the crocodile in a worried tone, 'We live in the water and he lives on dry land, how can I catch him? You are asking for the impossible.'

But his wife was not going to let her request go unheeded. 'I don't care. By hook or by crook, you have to catch him for me.'

She then began to mope and sulk and refused to talk to him. When that did not work, she used her feminine charms by weeping and sobbing, 'I cannot live without his heart. He must be caught. I want to be able to get close to him, and then I want to kill him and eat his heart. Please you have to do this for me or I will not be happy ever again.'

'Okay! Okay,' said the crocodile, totally exasperated with his wife's behavior, 'I have a plan. It just might work.'

One day, when the Bodhisattva was sitting near the bank of the river Ganges, the crocodile slid near him and addressed him in a very humble tone.

'Sir Monkey, I see you live here in this old place among these old trees. They don't bear much fruit and I can see that you are not eating too well. My heart bleeds for you.'

'Thank you for the concern, Sir Crocodile,' said the monkey, genuinely touched at the crocodile's concern, 'However, I am all right here.'

'But Sir, did you know that right across the river, on the opposite side is an orchard of fruit trees. From my watery abode I can see the branches laden with ripe luscious fruits. You ought to go there,' said the crocodile trying to tempt the monkey.

The monkey was delighted at the prospect of being in an orchard where there was an abundance of fruit.

'Lord Crocodile, you know that the Ganges is wide and very deep. I have no way of crossing it. How am I ever going to get across to the wondrous orchard you are talking about?' he asked.

'You need not worry. What are friends for after all. Whenever I think of you, deprived of the fruit, I feel depressed. I'll tell you what. Why don't you climb on to my broad back and I will swim across to the other bank with you. You can then eat all you want,' said the crocodile, driven to such cunning by his demanding wife.

'Thank you,' said the monkey, 'you are indeed a good friend. But will you also bring me back?'

'Yes, yes. Of course I will,' the crocodile was getting excited at the thought of his quarry walking into the trap.

So the monkey climbed on to the crocodile's back and together they set off. The crocodile swam very smoothly. Midstream, however, he plunged deep into the water, trying to submerge the monkey and drown him.

'Friend Crocodile, why are you trying to drown me? I thought we were friends,' cried the monkey.

'What friend? I am only trying to fulfil my beloved wife's desire to eat your heart. I can never refuse her anything. When you drown she can tear your heart out,' said the crocodile, now quite delighted that at last his wife would be happy.

'But Mr Crocodile what makes you think I have my heart with me?' said the monkey trying not to show his panic.

The crocodile stopped for a moment, 'What do you mean, you *don't* have your heart with you?'

'Don't you know? We monkeys never carry our hearts within us. Why it might get damaged when we swing from tree to tree,' replied the monkey.

'Then where do you keep it?' The crocodile was getting impatient.

'My heart is in that fig tree, near where I was sitting when you saw me,' said the monkey, pointing to a fig tree laden with fruit, 'It is invisible and you cannot see it. Each one of us knows our own heart and only we can find it.'

'If you show me where your heart is, then I will not have to kill you. All my wife wants is your heart,' said the crocodile, seemingly quite relieved, 'I will even take you back to the shore.'

'Okay, I will do this for you, so that your wife can be happy,' replied the monkey, Take me to the fig tree and I will point it out to you.'

The crocodile happily swam to the shore with the monkey on his back. Once they reached the shore, the monkey bounded off his back, climbed up to the highest branch of the fig tree and laughed loudly.

'Oh, you silly creature. You have such a big body, but a pea-sized brain. Did you really think that hearts can be kept on treetops.' The monkey then recited this verse:

Rose apple, bread fruit, mangoes too,
Across the water, there I see,
Enough of them, I want them not,
My figure is good enough for me.
Great is your body. But how small your wit.

The crocodile was miserable at being outwitted. But this was nothing compared to how wretched he felt later, when his wife heaped scorn on him, and continued to taunt him for the rest of their lives.

NEEKI

This is not just a story, but a true experience of a friend of mine. I feel that there is a lesson to be learnt from this tale of the power of 'neeki' or good deeds. Many poems and much prose, has been written on this subject—in Persian, Arabic, and other languages— because the theme is universal. If you do a good deed without expecting anything in return you will ultimately be rewarded. This is what we believe in and this is what we should practice. I shall try to narrate this story in the same manner as it was told to me.

I was on a trip to Europe. I had first stopped at London, to visit my sister, who was ill and in hospital and to attend to some personal matters as well. I then went to Paris, to take care of some business and after that I intended to return to Tehran, my homeland. This was the last phase of my trip and I had just enough money left to settle my hotel bills and buy some small presents for my family from the duty free shops at De'Gaulle airport.

The evening before I was due to leave Paris, I went out to do some sightseeing. On my way back, I saw a fellow countryman, who seemed very unwell and needed help badly. I tried to assist him as much as I could. Then I helped him to a taxi and took him to his flat. The place was in a very shabby condition. It seemed as though he lived by himself, with no one to look after him. I put him to bed, gave him something to eat and left some money for him, which would tide him over for a few days. I then took a taxi back to the hotel. When I reached for my bag to pay the taxi fare, I discovered, to my utter dismay that it was missing. I looked everywhere in the taxi but it just wasn't there. I rushed into the hotel and borrowed some money from the reception, to pay the cab.

Can you imagine my plight. Stranded in a foreign land with no money, no passport and no ticket? I had kept everything in my bag. I racked my brain for some clue to where I might have misplaced it, but to no avail. I had it with me in my countryman's flat, as I had taken money out of it to give to him and that had been my last stop. I was in deep trouble and had to come up with a solution fast as I was due to fly out the next morning at 6 am.

I borrowed some more money from the hotel and went to my embassy, but everything had closed since it was late in the evening. But by dint of good luck, I was able to see the Visa Consul. He said that he would arrange for a *se passe* (an out pass) which would enable me to leave the country without a passport. As for the ticket, the airline would issue me another one as my name was on their manifest, but they required two photographs with my application. Where in the world could I get those at this hour? And worst of all, I needed money to pay my hotel bill. The consul general expressed his inability to help with money. I felt panic rise within me and had visions of never

seeing my loved ones again and languishing in this country.

Then my luck seemed to change. Someone informed the embassy that my bag had been found and I could retrieve it from there. I was relieved. I quickly opened my bag to check if all my things were still there. I found my passport and documents, but, of course, all the money was missing.

Once again I took a taxi back to the hotel. Although the metro was cheaper I could not travel on that because I would have to pay cash and I didn't have any. Once more I swallowed my pride and asked the reception to pay the taxi. They obliged even though they looked at me strangely. In my room I began to think of all the people I knew in Paris who I could ask for help, but I couldn't get through to anyone. Now it was getting later in the night and time was running out. I was getting more and more nervous by the minute. My stomach felt like it was in a knot and the hunger pangs were not helping any. Then the phone rang and the front desk informed me that I had a visitor. The name did not seem at all familiar.

When I saw the man in the lobby, I did not recognize him at all. We exchanged greetings and sat down. He told me that he had heard that I was leaving for Tehran in the morning and he wanted a small favour from me. I jiggled my memory to try to place this man but could not. I said I would do whatever I could. He then told me that he had an elderly sister in Tehran, who was a widow and he wanted to send her some money, so that she could go to Mecca for pilgrimage. He gave me 15000 Francs to pass on to her and also gave me her address and phone number in Tehran. I could hardly believe my eyes. My hands shook as I took the money, but I kept my composure.

I immediately settled my hotel bill with the money. Of course, I would replace the amount once I was back home. Also, I still remember the dinner I had, it was the best meal I had ever tasted. The next morning I took my flight to Tehran and landed safe and sound back home. I was with my family and loved ones again.

The next day I rang up the elderly lady, so that I could go and give her the money her brother had entrusted me with. No one answered the phone so I went to her house. No one answered the door. A neighbour informed me that she had gone to Mecca, '...and she will never come back,' she added. I obviously thought that she had meant she had migrated there permanently. But the neighbour told me that she had died in a car accident on the way. The news was a shock for me.

Six years have passed since the incident. I have written several letters to the embassy in Paris, describing the man who gave me the money; asking if they could identify him and inform me of his whereabouts; so that I can return the money he entrusted to me—a total stranger. No one seems to know him. I want to return his money and condole with him on his beloved sister's death but, there seems to be no trace of him.

I firmly believe that the money was a gift from an angel, sent to help me in my time of need. I am holding on to the money and if in a couple of years I am still not able to locate the owner, then I will hand it over to charity, so that some other needy soul may be able to use it.

Thus my friend ended his story, leaving me with the firm belief that sometimes you get rewarded for a good deed almost immediately.

One day, when Amoo Feel, the elephant, had walked many miles, he felt tired and sought a place where he could rest. He found a beautiful, colourful spot beneath a large tree.

'I shall lie down here,' he thought, 'It looks cool, velvety and comfortable.' He lay down in the lovely nook, and as soon as he closed his eyes, he fell fast asleep. Little did he know that he was actually sleeping on a large patch of scented flowers. Now Amoo Feel was a gentle soul and had he known that he was destroying so many fragrant blossoms, he would never have done so. You see, Amoo Feel loved flowers and butterflies and all the lovely, tiny things that nature had to offer.

A little while later, a honey-bee flew by buzzing busily and heading for the flower bed where it drew nectar to make its honey. He was stunned to see such a huge mountain, completely covering his favorite patch. Indeed he had never seen such a humungous creature in his life. With much trepidation he approached the elephant's trunk and sat on it to have closer look. It looked even bigger from this close up. Then he flew and sat on one of the huge limbs wondering what to do. It seemed to him that this species of the animal kingdom was not very nice.

'It must be a really mean animal, to be so inconsiderate as to crush all our favourite flowers and deprive us of our sustenance.' The bee was getting angrier by the minute and even considered stinging the beast, but thought the better of it.

'I better go and inform the rest of the hive about this mountainous animal sleeping on our flowers,' he thought and away he flew to his hive.

'A strange creature has destroyed our flowers, and he is so big that even all of us put together would not equal the size of his fist,' the bee announced breathlessly to his fellows when he returned.

Hearing this alarming news, the entire bee community decided to go and see what their companion was talking about. As they approached the elephant they realized why the bee was so alarmed. In fact, they were awe-struck when they saw the size of the elephant. In a state of panic, they asked the queen what they should do.

The queen bee, after contemplating for some time said, 'If he gets up and shakes one hand we are all finished. We must be very careful.' She then thought for some time and said, 'Since it is not honourable to attack someone while they are sleeping, we must wait for him to wake up, to talk to him.'

Therefore, they all waited for the elephant to wake up,—and waited—and waited, but Amoo Feel was so deep in slumber he had no clue to the furor that he had caused. When a considerable amount of time had lapsed, the bees began getting impatient.

'We must try and wake him up soon,' the queen bee said, 'It is getting dark and we ought to be heading back to the hive.'

'But how do we do that?' Asked one of the bees.

'Let us try to call out to him,' replied the Queen.

But all the noise they could make collectively did not cause the elephant, lost in his dreams, to stir even one little bit. They even tried to sting him, '...my goodness his skin is as hard as a rock.'

They buzzed near him, and in fact tried every way they could think of to wake him up, to no avail. Then one of the bees had an idea.

'Here, let me try,' he said and went and gave Amoo Feel a sharp sting in one of his eyes.

'Oh! My eye! My eye! It's burning. What happened? What bit me?' said the elephant getting up with a start.

The bees were delighted that they had managed to wake up the huge mountain-like creature. 'Greetings, whoever you are,' said the bees to Amoo Feel.

Amoo Feel's eye was all red and swollen up, but even in his excruciating pain, he replied gently to the bees, 'I am Amoo Feel, the elephant; I was passing through the jungle, and feeling very tired I fell asleep here, in this lovely spot,' he explained.

'We don't care if you were tired. The fact of the matter is that you have destroyed our beautiful flowers, which were our means of sustenance. Flowers are to be admired. They represent nature's grace and beauty. They should not be crushed the way you have done,' the bees yelled angrily.

Hearing this, Amoo Feel realized the mistake he had made and became extremely sad. 'I did not realize the harm I was doing. I am truly very sorry for this and if there is any way I can make this up to you I would be happy to do so,' he said.

He addressed them in such a soft, kind tone that the bees were convinced that he had not done it deliberately. Realizing that he wasn't bad after all, the queen bee said to him, 'We are sorry we had to sting you, but there seemed no other way to wake you up. We feel we have misjudged you. We hope you will stay here and we can all be friends.'

Thereafter Amoo Feel and the bees became great friends. Wherever the elephant went, some of his new-found chums would be flying around him, talking and singing to him, and playing on his huge body. The elephant, however, still felt guilty about the flowers he had crushed, and constantly prayed that somehow, some miracle would occur to make the flowers bloom once again.

A few days later, a huge bear came into the jungle and attacked the beehive to steal their honey. The bees, frantically flew to Amoo Feel.

'Please help us. This big bear always destroys our hives and steals our honey,' they pleaded desperately.

'Don't worry, little friends. I will see who this bear is. I won't let him destroy your home.'

Being such a kind-hearted soul, he immediately ran to protect the beehive. The bear was creeping up to the tree, expecting that, as usual, stealing honey from the hive would be a simple matter. The tiny bees couldn't harm him and his shaggy coat protected him from their bites. He was shocked when he came face to face with the gigantic Amoo Feel. At first he stepped back aghast and then attacked Amoo Feel, biting him in his leg. Amoo Feel in a fit of rage, flung the bear away from the beehive and chased him out of the jungle.

The bees were delighted that their hive and the honey was saved. They flew up to Amoo Feel and kissed him gratefully, 'Thank you so much for being a true friend and risking your life to save ours.'

Then they saw that his leg was bleeding, 'Look at the great risk you put yourself to for our sake. You are badly injured.'

'Oh no! I deserve this for destroying your flowers. I just wish there was some way they would bloom again,' said Amoo Feel sadly.

The bees, however, were very thankful to Amoo Feel and they also prayed for a miracle that would cause the flowers to bloom again. Only then would their friend feel happy again. All of a sudden the sky began to darken with clouds and it started to rain. Amoo Feel's prayers had finally been answered. The rain caused the flowers to bloom once again and washed away all the blood and dirt from Amoo Feel's wound, thus healing it. All this made the bees and the elephant ecstatic, and they all danced joyously in the rain singing:

Oh wise Creator, let the rain pour
and wherever there is a flower, let it bloom.
We have no worries anymore,
and we are grateful to you.

'It is little Asma's first *rooza* (fast). Fatima, go to her house and be with her when she opens her fast,' said my *monkhali* grandmother.

She was a diminutive soul, but exercised great power over the family.

'Why all this fuss about Asma's first fast? Why is everyone so concerned? Has she climbed a mountain?' was naughty Mariam's comment, 'I too will be fasting tomorrow. Wake me up at *suhoor.*'

'Yes. Yes. We have heard *that* many times before. You are almost seven years old and it is high time you kept fast Zelzelah (earthquake) Bibi,' retorted *monkhali.*

'My name is Mariam, and I don't want to be called by that silly name you have given me.' This hot and cold war was an on-going process between my grandmother and me. Her word was law in the house and my arguments would often irritate her. She was used to being obeyed unquestioningly, and my perennial 'why' and 'how' put her off. But it amused me immensely.

'Well if you don't wake me up at *suhoor,* the *hil hilawi* will.'

Since in those days there was no radio, newspaper or even electricity, any news or announcements were carried by word of mouth or by special messengers. During *Ramadan* a man would go around the neighbourhood beating an empty hollow tin with a stick and calling people to arise from their slumber to prepare for their fast. These men were called *hil hilawi*. The *hilawi* would continue beating his tin outside the house, till he saw a flicker of light or signs of movement from within. We never saw them except on the *Eid* day, when they would go to each house in the neighbourhood to receive payment for their services. The *hilawi* were paid in cash or kind. They always beat the tins in a rhythmic pattern, and for us, this was part of the daily ritual of the Holy month.

'I will show *monkhali* that I have got what it takes to wake up before dawn and keep a real fast,' I said to myself, before going off to sleep.

I felt as if I'd hardly slept for a few minutes, when suddenly I heard someone shouting, 'Wake her up someone or she will be a real nuisance tomorrow. I know she will only last a few hours, but who is going to bear her tantrums?'

I jumped up and went and sat drowsily, with eyes half closed, at the elaborate *sofra*, stuffing myself so that I would be able to last the entire day's fast tomorrow. After having eaten my fill, I jumped back into bed to sleep, when my grandmother's voice beckoned me to read the Quran for a couple of hours. Whilst reading from the Holy Book, I waited patiently for the *Azaan Fajir* (the call for the morning prayers). When the *moazzen's* call came wafting through the first light of dawn, I said my prayers and went back to sleep. Lovely thoughts filled my heart, 'Tomorrow I will be the centre of attention. Everyone will pamper

me and treat me in a special way. Even *monkhali's* heart will soften towards me. I too will get a new dress just like Asma, for *futoor*. My friends will be invited and I will be showered with coins and sweets and the food will be delicious...' With this I drifted off to sleep.

I woke up early the next day feeling very excited, but the entire house was engulfed in silence. During this month the grownups slept late and usually all activity started around noontime. I was disappointed. Today was my big day and everyone was sleeping soundly, seemingly not giving it much importance. I ran to my maid Jamila's room and tried to wake her up. She and a few other personal attendants were privileged to have their sleeping quarters near those of the family. The rest were housed a bit further away from the main building.

Jamila hushed me up, 'Go back to sleep and do not make any noise. It is only 10 o'clock and *Bibi Gapi* (the mistress) will scold us for disturbing them.'

So much for the attention I was so sure of getting when I fasted!

The minutes crawled by and my restless soul waited impatiently for the special attention I was entitled to. By noontime the whole household was up and the routine work began. Today was Friday, so, much to my relief, there was no *maktab* to attend. It was extremely difficult to pass time until the evening. It almost felt like it would never come. The smell of food permeated the house and I kept asking *monkhali* what was the time?

'Good Lord, get away. This is the umpteenth time you have asked this question. Go and do something. Take out your embroidery or read the Quran. Just keep out of my way,' was her reply each time.

There was the usual sibling rivalry between my sister Fatima and myself during the day—sometimes our fights got quite nasty. She was a veteran at fasting, being older. The longest day of my life had begun and it seemed it would never end.

The entire afternoon was spent in preparation for the late evening feast, the *iftar*. One delectable dish after another of homemade sweets was being prepared not only for the family, but also for the many guests that always came. It was accepted as part of the hospitality of those bygone days, that guests would drop in without prior notice and they were always welcome. Nowadays, people usually send messages beforehand when they are coming. To me this seems to detract from the element of a pleasant surprise, and even the courtesy extended by hosts these days does not appear to be so whole-hearted.

Usually in our old house, the guests would first be served a cold drink, followed by tea, *qahwas*, alongwith fruit or sweets and whatever repast had been prepared. Several dishes were also prepared during *Ramadan*, to send around to friends and neighbours. The tradition still persists. The plates were never returned empty. The neighbours would reciprocate in a similar manner. Everyone tried to outdo the other by adding more variety and better presentation.

The main dish, *shoorba*, which is like the Arabic *harisa,* was cooked in large pots and had to be prepared by male servants. *Tandoori* (bread) was cooked in great quantity. Rice and other forms of curry were prepared in kitchens outside the living quarters, but savouries and delicacies, such as the *halwas*, traditional puddings and several assorted dishes, were prepared in the ladies quarters, by special maids and the mistress of the house. Usually the mistress would add the finishing touches of garnish and presentation.

On that special day, when I kept my first fast, I hovered around the elders and offered to decorate some of the *halwa.* I remember, in our household, as in others, all the crockery was round. There were huge round trays to carry several dishes, which were either, large or small, deep or flat; but always round in shape. I have preserved some century-old bowls and dishes, which are all round in shape.

Fasting has various effects on different people. Hunger and thirst irritates some people more than others. *Monkhali* was one of those people who, when she was busy during her fast, would often lose her temper and even use the stick of her hubble-bubble more frequently. So, when I got in her way, with my persistent demands to be allowed to help, she became very annoyed, 'Can't someone take this girl away? She is such a nuisance.'

But my great grand mother, whom we referred to as *monkhali gapi* advised her, 'She should be kept busy. Let her decorate some of the *halwa.* She needs attention. Can't you see she is ready to collapse.'

So ten plates of *halwa* were placed in front of me and I was bidden to do my best. I sat on the floor working along with the others outside the kitchen. Colourful mats were spread on the floor, on which we sat and worked. No job, inside or outside the kitchen, was ever performed on tables, always on the floor and the ladies sat on little stones or small, flat wooden stools.

Anyway, I tried to use my artistic skills and imagination to innovate on the traditional designs used to decorate *halwa*. Since all the dishes were round, the usual pattern was to have a center point with geometric patterns radiating around it. I tried to make leaves and branches starting from one side. *Monkhali gapi* had a pleasant nature, and encouraged me, 'Look at what the child has done. Not bad at all.'

To facilitate my effort, and of course, to attract more attention, I made a cone of thick paper and poured the coloured powder into it and started to make designs with that. For *rangina*, which is another *halwa* dish, made with dates, I used all kinds of peeled and ground nuts—almonds, pistachios and walnuts, to emphasize the design. All of a sudden, I felt important as more of the adults began to admire my handiwork. All *monkhali* could say was, 'Good, at least she is quiet.'

Now the beverages were being prepared for *iftar,* rose-water sherbet, lemon juice, *araq-e-bidameshk* and other locally made cold drinks. There was no such thing as ice or any modern cooling appliances. The best system we had to cool water was to keep it in narrow necked jars which were tightly closed. Matted ropes were wound around the jars, with a long loop around the neck and these jars were lowered deep into the well, for several hours. When these jars were pulled up at the time of *iftar*, the water was as cold as ice. When the jars or *koozas* as these were called, were being submerged, I added my own little one to the collection and planned to drink it all by myself during *iftar*.

As the evening wore on, my lips were becoming parched in the sweltering heat. My clothes were made of thick silk and I had on far too many layers of clothing. How I envied the maids, who wore only one loose, voile *thobe* and a *shaela* on their heads. They were lucky. The gold thread on my pantaloons felt tight around my ankles, and the gold embroidered, brocade, long-sleeved *kandooras*, and my bangles and necklace felt like shackles. But I was a *Bibi* and had to endure all this. Fortunately, apart from my dangling long plaits, I didn't have to wear anything on my head.

The time for *iftar* was approaching and with it the activities increased. Several *qalyoons* (a hubble bubble) were now being prepared. *Monkhali* was engrossed in preparing her *qalyoon* and when that was done, she was transformed and seemed to become happier. Once she wrapped her arms around her beloved *qalyoon*, she became positively angelic, laughing, joking and embracing the children.

My mother noticed how pale I looked and asked, 'My little girl, how are you feeling? There is not much time left. Go and put on your new green dress. I completed it today for your first *rooza*.'

Much to my delight, she informed me that Asma and two of my other friends were coming over for *iftar*.

Our house was a sprawling two-storied structure, with several wind towers and the winter quarters. Large houses usually had fifty rooms or more. The rooms always opened onto a courtyard. There was a *mosanni* (garden patch) in the center of the courtyard. The tops of the doors were adorned with arches of painted glass panels. The rooms were usually decorated with large, beautiful, colourful cushions placed at the end, with an embroidered silk *mokhada* (cushion) for the back and a big *sofra* in front. I was supposed to sit there to receive my little friends and open my fast with a *Bismillah*. But I kept thinking, 'Will the day ever end?' I rushed to the well to pull out the *kooza* jars, but the jars had already been removed and distributed around.

'You promised I could pull my own *kooza* out. My jar had a red coloured sign on it,' I howled in disappointment to Jamila. My *kooza* was lost and I was devastated. This was exactly the excuse I needed to burst into tears. I was hungry and thirsty, and all my dreams of being the centre of attention and pampered for doing something special, were shattered.

At last it was almost time for the *Azaan,* which would be the signal to break the fast. I spread my little *janemaz* (prayer mat) for my friends and myself. I rushed upstairs to peek through the holes. The *Masjid*-e-*Abbas* was very close to our house. My grandfather had built it. I watched the people heading towards the mosque and finally heard the *Azaan*. I ran downstairs and sat on my 'throne', like a bride amongst my friends, who had arrived a short while ago. The first date I put into my mouth tasted like fruit from paradise. A *kooza* was placed in front of me. I noticed it had a red patch on it. The delicious dishes were brought in to my *sofra* one by one, and I feasted my eyes on them before tasting them. Jamila showered me with coins and sweets, which is the traditional method of congratulating a child when they first complete reading the Holy Quran or, as in this case, keep their first fast. Everyone said *mabrook* to me and for a while I felt *very* important and behaved with proper decorum, suited to a young lady. But how long this lasted is left to your imagination.

Tales from ancient times almost always have an element of magic and the supernatural blended into the relative reality of the narrative. Inanimate objects begin to talk, wondrous events unfold and the art of the storyteller makes one believe that this really happened. Each story carries with it some grain of wisdom and a lesson in the power of kindness. The following story is such a tale and it originates in Azerbaijan.

Once upon a time there lived a King who was very proud of his strong and healthy body and took great pains to look after it. He was the picture of health and liked to be admired for his physique. But one day he fell sick with a mysterious illness for which there seemed no cure. You can imagine what a blow this was to him. He summoned all his astrologers, physicians and the other wise men of his kingdom and ordered them to find a cure, threatening them with dire consequences if they failed. After much deliberation they decided that the only remedy for the King's ailment was the cooked flesh of the son of the sea king. The sea king was a strange creature, half human and half fish—the proverbial merman of western folklore.

The *jarchees*, as the town criers were called, travelled all over the countryside, announcing that the

King would give half his kingdom to whoever would capture this creature. As word spread, all the able-bodied men of the kingdom went to the sea and cast their nets, but no one succeeded in catching this legendary son of the sea king. The King was getting weaker and weaker every day and becoming more and more anxious.

The King had a young son, Ilyas, who was very kindhearted and often tried to help all those whom his father treated unjustly. He was cared for by a wise and good old woman. She taught him never to hurt any living thing and to help the poor and needy. Ilyas would often go to the seashore to watch the fishermen cast their nets. One day, he went to the beach and finding it deserted, picked up one of the nets and cast it into the sea. When he began to haul it in it felt very heavy. He pulled it in with great difficulty and found the half-human, half-fish, sea creature everyone was trying to catch entangled in the net.

The strange creature was beautiful and spoke to Ilyas, imploring him, 'I know you want your father to get well and if you give me to him you will become a hero. But I am the only son of my father, the sea king, and he will die of grief if something happens to me. Please let me go and I will reward you with three pieces of advice, which will be of great help to you.'

Ilyas felt sorry for the young merman and released him. Before swimming off the creature said to Ilyas, 'The three pieces of advice I want to give you are: always stand up for the rights of your fellow men and yourself; only accept what is logical and thirdly, if

you lose something, don't be sad and resentful.' With these words he dived into the water and swam away gracefully.

Ilyas returned home and did not tell anybody about his encounter with the sea creature. But someone had seen it and reported it to the King at once who was furious. How could Ilyas do this to him? In a fit of rage he called the executioner and gave orders to behead Ilyas. But his courtiers loved the prince and prevailed upon the King not to execute his only son and forgive his youthful folly. So the King decided to banish him instead.

The old woman who had brought him up, was distraught. She did not want her beloved Ilyas to go, but feared that the King, in another fit of rage might change his mind and have him executed. So she tearfully bade him goodbye and before he left she gave him some advice.

'Now you will have to fend for yourself in this wide world, all alone,' she told him, 'Remember this rule to test a person's friendship it will help you in your journey: if you come across someone who wants to share something with you, see how he divides the item he wants to share. If he keeps the bigger portion for himself, such a man is greedy; if he takes the smaller portion and gives you the larger, then he is cunning and has some trick up his sleeve; but if he shares it equally, then he can be trusted.' With this she waved farewell.

The King's men put Ilyas in a small boat and cast him adrift, at the mercy of the seas. All he had to guide him were the wise words of the old woman as well as those of the sea creature. The small boat tossed him onto a distant shore and he continued his journey on foot. He wandered over mountains and deserts, meeting all kinds of people. He tested them in the manner he had been advised and found some were greedy, some devious and still others who proved trustworthy.

One day, he met a boy much the same age as himself. He too was travelling all alone. They struck up a friendship and Ilyas put him to the test with an apple. The youth went to great pains to divide the apple equally and Ilyas knew he had a friend for life. So the two wandered together and one day they came across a town and decided to stop there for the night. Before they went to sleep the boy said to Ilyas that he knew this place and would tell him something very interesting about it. But, first Ilyas must take an oath to share everything they acquired equally. Ilyas did so readily. Then his friend told him that in the morning he should go to the palace of the King of this land. The King had a beautiful daughter who had never spoken a word in her life, although she could hear perfectly well. The King had done everything possible to make her talk. '...Go to the palace and announce that you are a renowned physician and you will be able to make the princess talk. The King will undoubtedly tell you, that if you fail he will have you put to death. But do not be afraid. Accept the challenge.'

Ilyas was surprised that his friend had suggested such a dangerous mission, but he soon overcame his fear, as he trusted him, even with his life.

'When the king agrees to try you out, he will take you to a glass room where the princess sits,' the boy continued, 'There you will see a *shah-e-chiragh*. Greet this lamp and it will talk to you. Ask it to tell you the most interesting story it has heard and listen to it. Therein lies the cure for the princess' inability to speak. Report back to me all that passes.'

After this he told Ilyas to go to sleep, and not to worry and he advised Ilyas to proceed with the plan, even if he was not there when he woke the next morning.

So it came to pass and Ilyas found himself being escorted by the King to the princess. The King had promised him half his kingdom if he succeeded and if he failed he would be put to death. Sure enough, there in the glass room was the *Shah-e-chiragh* he was told about, in front of him. Ilyas greeted the lantern and asked it to narrate the most interesting story it had ever heard. Both the King and his daughter, Zulekha, were startled when the lamp replied. They listened intently to what it said.

'I am but a lamp that has hung here for years. I do not have a story to tell. However, I will ask you a riddle.

Two brothers lived together. One had a daughter and the other had a son, and the two were betrothed at birth. As the cousins grew up they developed a deep bond of love for each other. The boy's name was

Ahmed. His father contracted a fatal illness and died and the treatment left his family penniless. His uncle broke off the engagement, because now Ahmed was impoverished and he wanted a wealthy husband for his beautiful daughter. He married her to one of the richest merchants in town. Ahmed was heartbroken but could not do anything. But in the bridal chamber, the bride was unable to keep her tears in check and cried uncontrollably. The bridegroom was perplexed and insisted on knowing the reason for her sorrow. The bride told him, "You are a good and kind man and I have nothing against you. But I love my cousin and cannot bear to be parted from him." The bridegroom set her free to go to Ahmed, so off she went to look for her beloved in her bridal ensemble.

'In the meantime, the Governor of the city had issued orders that anyone found on the streets after dark was to be arrested. So the girl was taken into custody by the local *darogha*. In the morning she was presented before a magistrate, who heard her plea that she was going to her beloved Ahmed when she had been detained and implored that she be allowed to go.

In the meantime, the bridegroom had had a change of heart and wanted her back. The *darogha* also laid a claim on her, because he had kept her safe through the night. As for Ahmed, he had been betrothed to her in childhood and, of course, was the person she wanted to go to.' The *Shah-e-chiragh* now presented the dilemma.

'Who do you think deserves the girl?'

The King who always favoured the official view and was devoid of compassion, stated that she should go to the *darogha*, who found her. The King's minister was of the opinion that she should go back to the bridegroom, since she was his legally wedded wife. The King and the minister started to argue and created a commotion.

Suddenly, Zulekha who had been listening all this while, began to speak. 'You are both wrong,' she said, 'The *darogha* was only doing his duty in protecting the girl and does not deserve a reward for it. The bridegroom is entitled to compensation for the expenses he incurred on the wedding festivities. The girl rightly belongs to Ahmed, as matters of the heart are more important than other claims.'

Ilyas was overjoyed at the effect of the riddle on the princess. She had actually spoken. However, the King did not want to give up half his kingdom and also he was not satisfied that the princess had been fully cured. So he told him, 'Come back tomorrow and if you can make her speak a second time, then I will reward you with not only wealth, but also her hand in marriage.'

Ilyas went back to where he and the boy were staying and told him exactly what had happened. His friend told him not to worry and to go again the next day and this time address the rare carpet he would find in the glass room.

So the next day Ilyas went to the palace again and this time, when he was taken to the glass room he looked around for the carpet. On seeing the beautiful carpet he greeted it in the same manner he had greeted the *chiragh* and asked it to relate it's story. Again, everyone was astonished when the carpet spoke and said it would ask all present to answer a riddle it would narrate.

Then the carpet related it's riddle, 'Three friends were travelling together. One was a carpenter, the second, a tailor and the third an alchemist. After journeying for long, they stopped to rest and since the territory was unsafe, they decided they would take turns standing guard. The carpenter took the first watch. To pass the time he cut a branch from a tree and proceeded to carve the figure of a beautiful maiden from it. When it was the tailors turn to keep watch, he saw the figure carved by the carpenter and he took some cloth he had brought and stitched a lovely dress for the figure. Then it was the alchemist's turn. When he saw the statue of the lovely maiden, he decided to use alchemy and breathed life into it. The figure came to life and was transformed into a most alluring woman.

Came morning all three friends were smitten by the maiden and began to lay claims on her. The carpenter said, 'If I had not carved her she would not even exist.' The tailor argued, 'Since I stitched clothes for her and ensured her modesty, she belongs to me.' Likewise the alchemist insisted, '...but if I had not put life into her she would be a piece of wood. So she belongs to me.'

'Now the riddle is complete,' said the carpet, 'Who does the maiden belong to?'

The King obviously spoke first. 'She rightfully belongs to whomsoever she might fancy.'

The minister then gave his opinion, 'She very obviously should be given to the carpenter, who created her in the first place.'

'But you are both wrong,' Zulekha spoke once again, 'This riddle is entirely different from the first. Then, we were talking about a human being with a mind of her own. This time the woman has been carved and modelled by men. The tailor and the carpenter can be compensated for their labour; but the alchemist, who brought her to life and endowed her through his divine skill cannot be compensated, for it was by the power of his mind that he did this. Thus, he rightfully deserves her.'

Everyone was impressed with her logic. The King thought, 'My daughter is as intelligent as she is beautiful. Why should I give her to a nobody like Ilyas, when I can marry her off to a rich prince.' Aloud he said, 'I wish her to talk for a third time and if you succeed, then I will give you everything I own.'

Ilyas once again returned to his friend. This time the boy told him, 'Go back in the morning, and this time speak to the exquisite necklace you will see in the glass room. Afterward, to satisfy himself that the princess is really cured, the King will want the princess to speak to him alone. At this point introduce yourself as a prince and tell the King you will take the princess with you, and when she is able to talk fluently you will return with her.'

So it was, that the beauteous necklace related the third riddle, 'Once upon a time, there was a King who had three sons. He loved them all dearly. However, all three were in love with the same girl, who happened to be their uncle's daughter. The King was aware of this dilemma and knew that if a solution was not found, soon there might be discord among his three sons. Wanting to avoid a clash at all costs, the King told his brother, who was one of his vazirs, that if he did not find a solution to the problem he would be banished.

The uncle went home sadly and told his daughter about the King's threat. The daughter was very intelligent. She told her father not to worry, as she would find a way to avoid any conflict between the brothers. She then invited her cousins and addressed them, 'I am equally fond of all three of you, as you are of me. But I can marry only one of you and I do not want to hurt anyone of you. So I have decided that I will give each one of you an equal sum of money and you are to go out in the world and seek your fortunes. I will marry the one who returns after three years with the most money.'

So, the three princes set off in different directions, each one set upon making more money than the others. They decided they would meet again at a specific rendezvous after the allotted period and compare their fortunes.

The eldest became an assistant to a famous *hakim;* the second to the royal *ramal,* or astrologer. The third, however, could not find a suitable profession and wandered around, until the three years were almost over.

One day, when there were just a few days left of the allotted time, the youngest brother was lying under a tree bemoaning his fate, when suddenly he heard a great commotion in the distance. It seemed as if the mountains were moving and the ground would split open. The prince climbed up on a ridge to see what was causing the cataclysm and beheld three huge giants fighting and bashing each other. They were grappling with one another and what a loud noise they made!

Suddenly they stopped fighting and one of them roared, 'What is this I smell? A human being!'

The prince was scared out of his wits.

Then another giant spoke, 'Maybe this human being can solve our problem.' The prince felt relieved.

Then the giants called to him in a booming voice, 'Look, our father left us three gifts—a tablecloth, a carpet and a crown. Each one has magical properties. The tablecloth when laid out immediately becomes covered with all you could wish to eat; the carpet when rolled open and mounted can fly you to wherever you want to go; and the crown, when you wear it renders you invisible. Now, which one of us should get what? Decide for us.'

The prince at once thought of a plan. He said to the giants, 'Leave the three objects here and each one of you give me your caps.' He then took the three caps and threw them down the mountain and turning back to the giants, told them, 'Now run and fetch your caps. Whoever comes back first gets the tablecloth, the second gets the carpet and the third the crown.'

So the three giants ran off to retrieve their caps. As soon as they were out of sight, the prince put on the crown and became invisible. Then he quickly tucked the tablecloth under his arms and unrolled the carpet. While the giants were still looking for their caps, he mounted the carpet and took off. He did not stop till he reached the spot where he and his brothers were to meet after the allotted time.

After exchanging pleasantries, the three brothers began to wonder who their cousin would choose to marry. Then they began to doubt whether she had waited for them these three, long years. What if she had married someone else? At this the brother, who was a *ramal,* waved his hands and looked into his crystal ball and became very upset at what he saw. He had seen a vision of their cousin, lying mortally ill and she had very little time left to live. They were extremely perturbed and all of them got on the magic carpet and in no time they arrived at the side of their beloved. The second brother, who was a *hakim,* treated her with herbs and potions and soon she recovered.

Now came the crux of the problem: 'If I had not seen her in my crystal ball, she would not be alive today,' said the *ramal.* 'But if I had not treated her, she would have surely died,' said the *hakim.* The youngest one said, 'If I had not brought all of you here in time on my magic carpet, all your skills would have been in vain.'

'So,' asked the necklace, 'Whom should the girl marry?'

The King stated that she should marry the *hakim*; the minister opined she should marry the *ramal*.

Once again, it was Zulekha who spoke the most wisely.

'Don't forget the original bargain,' she said, 'The condition was that she should marry the one who made the most wealth. Well, according to that she should marry the youngest prince, because he had more wealth then the other two. Remember, he can have all the food in the world; travel wherever he desires and become invisible whenever he wants. He is undoubtedly the wealthiest.'

Ilyas then asked the King if he was satisfied that Zulekha was cured. But the crafty king wanted to speak to his daughter alone. At this Ilyas revealed to the King that he was a prince, and told him he would take Zulekha with him and when he had taught her how to talk fluently, he would bring her back.

'Right now she can only speak when she strongly feels the urge to say something.'

Then the princess spoke to the King, 'Father I have been waiting for such a person all my life and I will go with him.'

Thus the King had no option but to agree.

Ilyas and Zulekha reached the tree where his friend was to meet them. When they met, the boy said, 'Now it is time to redeem your pledge with me to divide everything equally.'

'Of course', replied Ilyas. 'I have not forgotten. You can take all the wealth. I only want the princess.'

'No!' said the boy, 'We decided everything is to be divided equally.'

'Then divide everything as you think best and take whichever half you want,' said Ilyas.

'This is not what we agreed upon. *Everything* is to be divided in half,' the boy insisted.

Then it dawned on Ilyas what his friend meant and he was aghast, 'But surely you cannot divide a human being into two. Take everything, because some things can't be divided. I do not want anything. You have been such a good friend and I owe all this to you.'

But again the boy shook his head seriously.

Ilyas became angry and taking out his sword, cried, 'All right! You want to split a human being in half. Here take my sword and *do* it.'

The boy raised the sword above the girl's head and she began to scream in terror at what looked like certain death. When she opened her mouth wide, a huge snake slithered out of her throat and the boy instantly struck the serpent.

'My friend,' he said happily, 'This was the reason the princess was unable to speak all these years. This evil serpent had lodged itself in her throat. I had to trick it into emerging and now that I have killed it, she is completely cured. My friend,' he continued, 'I do not want this wealth nor this beautiful princess that you have fallen in love with. I am the sea prince you once saved from being killed and cooked by your father. Now I have repaid you for saving my life. You see, *I* was the lantern, the carpet and the necklace.'

He then gave him a potion and told him, 'Take this to your father. This will cure his illness and he will forgive you for letting me go many years ago.' With this the young man disappeared.

Ilyas took Zulekha back to her father, as he had promised. There, they were married with much pomp and splendour. Then the newly married couple took leave and travelled back to Ilyas' own kingdom. By now the King was on his deathbed. However, Ilyas gave him a drink of the potion the sea prince had given him. The King recovered instantly. He was overjoyed and forgave Ilyas and made him King. The kingdom celebrated this event for days, and everyone was happy that now the kindhearted Ilyas was on the throne. He and his bride lived happily ever after.

ADAMIZAD—THE LEOPARD AND THE HUMAN BEING

Here is a simple story that I enjoyed narrating to my children, many years ago.

In a very large jungle, lived a leopard who was very proud of his good looks and mighty strength. He felt that he was lord of all he surveyed and that the very earth trembled under his feet when he passed. His conceit was understandable, because in his life he had never encountered a human, or for that matter any other animal except those of his own species.

One day the leopard came out of its den, stretching and admiring itself, 'Look at what a strong and handsome creature God has created. I really have no equal in the entire world.'

He then sauntered into the jungle and his eyes fell on a miserable scrawny cat, which was crouching and whimpering under a bush. He recognized it as a distant cousin and stopped to ask why it was in such a sorry state.

'My dear cousin,' the cat replied, 'If only you knew what is happening to the animals in this world. How all the animals are weak and helpless in front of a certain very powerful creature.'

The leopard didn't like to hear of anything that seemed stronger than himself.

'Show me this creature which claims to be so mighty. I will show him what real strength is. I cannot allow a member of my family to be treated in this manner,' he growled.

The cat then told the leopard of her master, who was cruel and nasty and beat her mercilessly if she stole so much as a small piece of meat, '...I feel so miserable. I have to obey him and do whatever he tells me.'

This made the leopard really furious and he roared, 'Take me to where this animal lives and I will teach him a lesson.'

'Its no use. You are no match for him. For this creature is a human being, an Adamizad. He does not live in the jungle or a den.'

'Well, if he doesn't live in a den, then he could hardly be as big and mighty as he pretends.'

'He's not big. But you better be careful. These creatures may seem weak, but they're invincible and can defeat animals even bigger than yourself. Don't pick a fight with them.'

The leopard smiled knowingly and thought, 'Foolish cat. How can you be related to me and still be such a sissy? Who is this Adamizad anyway? How can he possibly be a match for my unparalleled strength and fighting ability?'

So he sprinted along, in leaps and bounds, imagining how he would free the cat from oppression, and make her happy and she would admire him for the valiant deed.

Suddenly he spied an unfamiliar creature coming towards him from a distance. 'This must be the Adamizad,' he thought.

He stalked it and pounced upon it, pinning it to the ground.

'Hey! You Adamizad,' he growled, 'You dare to oppress animals. At last you have met your fate. Prepare to meet your doom.'

But it was not a human being he had attacked, but a donkey, with a saddle on its back. The poor beast, on hearing himself referred to as a human realized there was some mistake and got over its initial fright.

'Your Highness seems to be mistaken. I am but a poor donkey, and I too, am a victim of this dreaded Adamizad. I am made to carry burdens heavier than I can bear. I do so much work for them, yet they call me 'long ears' and consider me to be the stupidest creature in the world.'

The leopard realized his mistake and let the donkey go.

'I have never seen anything like you before. Since you are not the Adamizad I am letting you go. However, maybe you can tell me where I can find this creature that is going around making the lives of so many animals miserable.'

The sad, little donkey pointed in the direction whence he came.

'You will probably find the Adamizad, if you follow this path. But I warn you. The creature you are looking for is no ordinary one. Don't let its size fool you. It possesses great strength, and no one can defeat it.'

The leopard, however, thought, 'This creature might be superior to this poor donkey, but it can't possibly be a match for me in any way. What does this poor donkey know of strength.'

With a toss of his head the leopard continued on its way to find the Adamizad.

Before long he saw another creature coming towards him. It had long legs, a very long neck and was extremely tall.

'Aha! Now I have him,' thought the leopard, 'It looks very big, but it is so thin, it can't be all that strong. I'll surprise it before it can come up with any of its tricks.'

Crouching low, he leapt in front of the creature and let out a ferocious roar.

'Hey! You Adamizad, do you think just because you have such a big body you can go around bullying everybody. Look I am not afraid of you. You can't do me any harm,' the leopard challenged.

The creature the leopard had mistaken for a human this time, was actually a camel. The bactrian was taken aback by the sudden appearance of the feline, but thought that probably he was addressing someone behind him. He certainly had not made anyone's life miserable. But there was nobody behind him.

'Oho! This fellow thinks I'm an Adamizad. What a foolish creature,' thought the camel, but aloud he said. 'My dear sir, you are under the wrong impression. I am a camel not an Adamizad.'

'You can't fool me,' replied the leopard, 'I've heard enough about you to know who you are.'

'But sir, I am a camel. A beast of burden, who too, is a victim of this Adamizad.'

'What! You are a camel,' the leopard said disappointed.

'Yes. I am but a lowly worker for this creature you seek. I bear his heavy burden from morning till night, never complaining. Sometimes he even forgets to feed me, but I have conditioned myself to go for days without food or water. They even slaughter us sometimes, when they are celebrating, and feast on our meat. These creatures have turned a magnificent animal like me into a domesticated pet. I am no better then a mouse. Alas! Alas!'

This made the leopard really furious, 'Why is it that you continue to suffer this cruel creature? Why can't all of you get together and get rid of him?'

'Perish the thought! Not even fifty camels together can do it any harm,' the camel exclaimed, 'Brother leopard, I would advise you not to seek the Adamizad. Before you know what has happened, he will imprison you and turn you into a slave. Please do not go any further.'

But by now the leopard was quite sick of the advice he was getting from all quarters to leave this Adamizad alone.

'I'll show them,' he thought and bounded along in the direction the camel had come from.

The leopard was really raring for a confrontation. After a while he saw a cow with a thresher tied behind it. Of course, the leopard didn't know this was only a cow. To him this creature fitted the description of the

Adamizad. When the bovine saw the leopard it naturally took fright and started running in circles with the thresher trailing behind. The leopard roared at the top of his voice.

'You Adamizad! You oppressor of animals. I have come to take revenge.'

He approached the cow cautiously but by now the poor animal really thought it's time had come, 'Look here Adamizad, I am an honourable creature called a leopard. Your bullying ways do not frighten me in the least. Let us face each other as equals. I am not going to show you any mercy until I have given you the thrashing you deserve.'

On hearing this, the cow was relieved and couldn't help laughing, 'Do you really think I am the Adamizad?'

'Of course you are,' asserted the leopard, 'I have travelled through the jungle and the desert searching for you. Now I have found you at last.'

The cow let out another hearty laugh, 'If you are looking for the Adamizad you have certainly come to the right place, but you have not found him yet! I am just a humble cow. I have to plough his fields all day long and when I become old and am no longer of any use to him, then he slaughters me and eats me up. I am but his slave and he is my master.'

The leopard's blood boiled and he shouted belligerently, 'Tell me where this strange creature is. How dare he treat you so cruelly? Show me this Adamizad so I can give him the beating he so richly deserves.'

The cow pointed to a peasant, working in a field nearby with a spade, 'That is the Adamizad you are looking for, but be very careful.'

The leopard was delighted, but not being one to take advice, he sprinted towards the man and let out a blood-curdling roar, 'So you are the Adamizad! Finally we meet.'

The peasant was thin and weak and frightened by the sudden appearance of the leopard. But he kept his composure.

'Yes I am. What do you want?'

The leopard sensed the man's fear and let out another roar, 'At last I have managed to find you. At least you have admitted you are an Adamizad—you are not a donkey, a camel or a cow. You don't even look like an animal.'

At this point the peasant began to realize that he might be able to get out of this situation by using his wits.

'All right. So you have never seen a human being before. So take a good look and I will answer any question you want,' he said.

The leopard told him that he had heard that the Adamizad was supposed to be more powerful than any animal and could enslave whichever one he chose, '...but now I have come to challenge your supremacy!' He roared again.

The peasant tried not to show any sign of weakness. 'Yes. You have heard correctly. I am more powerful than all the animals and can conquer anyone who tries to challenge me.'

At this, the leopard's pride was hurt, and he replied, 'You are only pretending to be unafraid. You are nothing but a weakling and I can kill you with one swipe of my powerful paw.'

'Ho! Ho! Ho!' The man laughed as if he found this amusing, 'I have heard that many times before. Many leopards have come claiming to be great warriors and champions and have tried to conquer the great Adamizad. But where are they now? When it came to the crunch, they ran away with their tails between their legs.' He thus taunted the feline.

The beast was now really bristling with anger.

'That is impossible. No leopard would run away from a scrawny creature like you. One blow and you will become history.'

The peasant quickly thought up a plan to get rid of this menace.

'Of course, you are a leopard and full of pride and arrogance,' he said, 'Just yesterday, one of your kind, much more ferocious than you, came to me and challenged me. I told him I do not fight with my hands, instead I have devised tools for this purpose. We call them weapons. I asked him to wait a moment while I got my weapon, however, when I got back he had run away. Now what do you have to say to that?'

'That is a lie! No leopard would do such a dishonourable thing. Go ahead. Get your weapon, or whatever you use to fight with. I will not run away.'

The peasant turned to go, then as if some thought had occurred to him, he stopped and came back.

'I don't trust you,' he said to the leopard, 'How do I know you will not run away also, like your brother did yesterday.'

The leopard assured him that he would never run away from a challenge. However, the peasant refused to be convinced.

'Let me get some rope and tie you up. Then I can be certain you will be here when I return,' he suggested.

This really infuriated the leopard and he snarled, 'You have no idea how quickly I can finish you off right now. Why should I be afraid of you and run away? You don't have to tie me up, I will be waiting right here for you when you return. Now hurry up and get whatever you want to fight with.'

But before the leopard realized what was happening, the peasant brought a strong rope and tied him securely to the tree. The leopard could hardly move. The peasant then picked up his spade and waved it at the animal.

'This is the only weapon I need. This is what I will fight with,' he said.

He started to beat the leopard with his spade. The beast was stunned by the heavy blows. It seemed impossible that this weak creature could administer such a dreadful beating. The leopard cried out in pain, 'You have deceived me. Is this the way your kind fights? With lies and no honour.'

'Yes,' replied the peasant, 'How else can we match your superior muscle power, except by using our higher intelligence. You think that with your greater strength you can overcome the Adamizad. Well, you are sadly mistaken.'

The leopard was suitably humbled and begged the peasant to let him go. The peasant kept him tied up for three days and when he saw that he was sufficiently weakened from hunger, he freed him. At once the leopard ran away, his tail no longer waving proudly behind him, but tucked between his legs.

And this goes to show that it is better to be intelligent than to be only physically strong.

In the days of my childhood, we heard stories of how foreigners kept cats and dogs as pets and how nicely they treated them, allowing them inside the house and caring for them like members of the family. We found this fascinating because for us, keeping pets, especially dogs, inside the house was unheard of. Dogs were considered 'najis', which means unclean, and were kept at a distance. Nevertheless, we also heard many stories about how loyal dogs are to their masters; how they are used as guide dogs to help the blind and that they are considered man's best friend. But here is a story, told by a close friend, which reveals a dog's capacity to seek revenge. Unbelievable, but true. I will narrate it to you as it was related to me.

We lived in a nice friendly neighbourhood. Adjacent to our house resided a very respectable Colonel with his family. Everyone referred to him as Janab Sarhang (respected Colonel). He would involve himself in all community activities and took upon himself the responsibility to make sure the municipality did their job. He had a dog named, Kocholoo, which means 'tiny' in persian. The size of the dog belied its name. He was a huge German shepherd and anyone who did not know how gentle he was, could not help being afraid of him. Kocholoo would play with the children of the neighbourhood and was especially attached to our family. The Colonel loved the dog and indulged it like a child.

One day there was a knock on our door and one of the servants came running in and announced, 'Janab Sarhang is at the door and he wants to see the master.'

We thought it strange, as the Colonel was not the 'visiting type' and usually confined his social calls to Eid. My father went to the door and saw the Colonel standing there with Kocholoo. Father was a bit surprised at this, but invited them in.

After the preliminary small talk the Colonel said, '...my dear friend I am being sent far away from here on training, and shall return after a few months. I am taking my family with me. But there is a slight problem. I will not be allowed to keep Kocholoo with me in the training center. I was hoping that you could keep him till I return. Your children are quite fond of him and he is well trained and will not give you any trouble.'

My father readily agreed. The Colonel tried to offer us some money for the dog's food, but of course, my father refused.

'Please keep the money. The dog will eat whatever we eat.'

'No, no,' the Colonel explained, 'Kocholoo eats only special meat. The neighbourhood butcher knows and will give it to you.'

'Do not worry about Kocholoo. We will look after him in the best possible way,' father assured him.

Then the Colonel handed over the special brushes and shampoos that were used to keep the dog clean.

They bid each other goodbye and that is how Kocholoo came to live with us.

From the day he entered our household Kocholoo became the center of attention for all of us. We took care of him and made sure he never went hungry or got bored. In fact we could ill afford the special food that Kocholoo was used to, but father insisted that we give him the best, as he had promised the Colonel that we would look after him well. In any case, Kocholoo refused to eat any other kind of food put before him. But despite all our efforts, Kocholoo always looked sad. He would wail and whine for hours, apparently missing his master. It was heart rending to see the dog cry. However, with time he began to get used to our household and seemed to settle in.

We all grew very fond of him. But having a big dog had its disadvantages. Many of our friends stopped coming to our house, as they were mortally scared of him; children were terrified of him and also, many conservative minded people we knew felt he had rendered our house impure and did not like to come in contact with us. But we paid no attention to all that and continued to look after Kocholoo and in fact we had begun to truly love the dog.

But, there was one person in our household, Nanna, who did not share our feelings. She had brought us up and we respected her a great deal. She was old, afflicted with rheumatism and moved around the house with the aid of a stick. She hated the dog because she considered it *najis*. She would often complain and

grumble, 'When will Jenab Sarhang return and take this creature back. I can't stand him.'

The feelings between her and Kocholoo were mutual.

'Make sure Kocholoo does not go into Nanna's room,' I would have to keep cautioning the younger children.

But just as frequently, I would hear one of them shout, 'Mama! Mama! Kocholoo has gone into Nanna's room.'

Chaos would ensue. Nanna would scream, 'Get this creature out of my room!' Then she would run after the dog, waving her stick trying to beat him with all her strength. Nevertheless, the dog would repeat the act again and again. It almost seemed as if he was deliberately teasing the old lady.

We tried to explain to Nanna that there was nothing impure about dogs. They too were God's creatures, and in any case, we kept him so clean that he couldn't possibly dirty the place. But Nanna was not one to be moved from her convictions.

One day this problem reached crisis proportions. Kocholoo had entered Nanna's room and this time she was more furious than ever.

'Either this dog goes, or I leave the house!' she screamed and shouted at the top of her voice, 'I refuse to live under the same roof as this horrid creature!'

'Why Nanna what has happened,' I said running to her side. Being the eldest I had to intervene to maintain peace and calm.

'This creature went and sat on my bedding. Look, I usually put it away in this wooden box. Today I left it lying on top, and he went and made himself comfortable on my mattress. I cannot possibly sleep on it now. It will have to be thrown away This miserable creature has polluted it,' Nanna was almost hysterical.

We calmed her down with great difficulty and arranged for some new bedding.

Several months passed by. All this time there was no news from the Colonel. After six months a letter arrived from him, addressed to my father. He wrote, 'I apologize for not having written earlier. I have been very busy and now, have been posted abroad. I do not want to burden you with Kocholoo for too long and have spoken to some friends in the CID, who will come and fetch him. They are going to train him to sniff out narcotics from baggage. He will be well taken care of. Thank you once again for looking after my dear dog.'

In those days, the practice of using dogs for detecting smuggled narcotics had not yet been adopted in the Gulf countries. The government was keen to introduce a team of trained and intelligent dogs to aid the custom officials as smuggling had increased tremendously in recent years. Thus, Kocholoo was going to be a pioneer.

I informed Nanna who was delighted.

'Al-Hamdolillah, my prayers have at last been answered. When is this wretched creature to leave my house?'

'Soon, very soon,' I answered.

Sure enough, within a few days some CID-type men came to the front door and wanted to see Kocholoo. The children were excited for Kocholoo was to be involved in high adventure, although they did not want to part with him.

'So this is the dog we have heard so much about?' said one of the men.

'Yes, yes,' cried the children excitedly, 'He can even fetch a ball.'

'He certainly looks very clever. Soon, we will be able to detect contraband,' said the man who was obviously their superior officer.

With this, they led Kocholoo away on a leash. All of us bid the dog a tearful goodbye. We were unhappy to see him go.

'We will never see Kocholoo again,' cried the children.

'Thank God for that. I hope I never see that miserable creature for as long as I live,' said Nanna loudly.

Kocholoo turned to look back at Nanna, almost as if he had understood her, with a strange expression in his eyes, which seemed to say, 'We will see about that.'

Several months passed by and we got used to not having Kocholoo around. We heard he had been taken to Europe to be trained. Then we began to hear some incredible stories of a dog, which was said to be so highly skilled and sensitive, that he could sniff out even the tiniest quantity of narcotics no matter how ingenuously the smuggler had tried to hide it. We had no doubt in our mind that this must be our very own Kocholoo and felt proud of his achievements.

One day there was a harsh knock on the door. One of the children opened the door and there stood some soldiers and Kocholoo.

'Mummy! Mummy! Come and see. It is Kocholoo. He has come to pay us a visit,' the child shouted excitedly.

Everyone eagerly came to the door to greet Kocholoo. Nanna, however, locked herself in the room. We were so happy to see Kocholoo, that at first we did not notice that now he looked different. There was a severe expression in his eyes and when the children hugged him, he did not wag his tail in delight. He seemed almost arrogant.

All of a sudden, he started to walk towards Nanna's room. We thought he was up to his old tricks. On reaching the door he began to paw it determinedly. We could not understand why the officers, who had accompanied Kocholoo, came inside with him. They started to bang on Nanna's door.

'What does the damn dog want?' shouted Nanna from inside.

'Open the door immediately, or we will break it down,' ordered the soldiers sternly.

We were shocked at their tone, and also by the look of purposefulness in Kocholoo's eyes.

'What is going on? Why are you being rude to Nanna?' I asked the soldiers.

'Just tell the old woman to open the door. We want to search the room,' answered one of the soldiers very gruffly.

'What has she done? What are you looking for?' I insisted.

'We have been ordered to search every place that the dog points out. Those are our orders and we have to obey,' explained the soldiers. 'Now tell the old lady to open the door, or we will break it.'

'It's all right Nanna. Open the door. These soldiers only want to see your room,' I reasoned with her.

Slowly Nanna opened the door. Kocholoo bounded in and started smelling underneath the bed. The soldiers dragged out the box in which Nanna kept her bedding and lifted the top. There was another wooden box inside. They opened this. Kocholoo was getting excited, as if sensing some kind of victory. Inside the wooden box was a snuffbox and when the soldiers opened this, they found a small quantity of opium. Kocholoo began to bark in frenzy.

'Oho! Mr Kocholoo is right as usual. Where did you get this opium old woman? Don't you know it is a crime to possess it?' said one of the soldiers.

'But, but I never smoke opium. I only crush it in small quantities, to put in a child's ear if he has an earache,' cried Nanna.

'It's true. Nanna never smokes opium. She only uses it as medicine for the children,' I corroborated Nanna's statement.

'We are not interested in all this. We have orders to arrest anyone with even the minutest quantity of opium. The old lady will have to come with us. She is under arrest.'

Needless to say, all our pleadings fell on deaf ears and the soldiers led poor Nanna outside like a prisoner.

'Will we ever see Nanna again?' cried one of the children.

'Never again,' Kocholoo's eyes seemed to reply.

Kocholoo had had his revenge.

However just as Nanna was on the verge of being taken away by the police, a senior police officer who happened to be a friend of my father's came visiting. When he saw Nanna's plight he intervened and managed to convince the officers to release the old woman. We were all immensely relieved and for a while it had been touch and go. However, Nanna was saved from what might have been, incredible as it may sound, vengeance master-minded by a dog.

THE HALF BLIND KING

This is a tale from a faraway land. As the story progresses, it is interwoven with many other tales, until in the end there is a surprise.

In days gone by, there lived a cruel, half-blind King. One of his eyes was permanently shut and the vision of the other was badly impaired. Obviously this affliction distressed him very much and he was scared that one day he would lose whatever remained of his sight. So he called all the astrologers and the wise men of the court and asked them to find a cure for his disability. All these learned men put their heads together and after a great deal of deliberation, arrived at a solution to the problem.

'Your Majesty, the treatment for your eyes is very simple,' they advised the King, 'All you have to do is eat the red fish which is found in our own seas and, not only will your eyesight improve but you would also feel better.'

So the King ordered the royal fisherman to set sail at once and catch the red fish, as quickly as possible. The fisherman got his gear together and was about to set sail, when the King's son, the young Ibrahim, came to the shore and asked the fisherman to take him along, as he loved the sea and fishing. They sailed out into the sea and cast their nets and waited for the red fish to be ensnared. Several days went by and all they did was wait. Finally, one fine day they caught the red fish or at least it certainly looked like the fish they were supposed to catch. It was so beautiful that Ibrahim did not have the heart to take it out of the water to be cooked, so he threw it back into the sea. The next day, once again they caught the same fish and once again the boy threw it back into the sea. This happened three times, until the fisherman, fearing for his life, began to object. Ibrahim assured him that as long as he was with him, he need not worry. Thus, many days passed. In fact, months passed and the two decided to return to the kingdom empty-handed.

The King was not happy about this. He asked the fisherman why they had failed? Of course the fisherman could not tell the truth, so he mumbled something incoherent. This infuriated the King, who was now really worried about his eyesight. He ordered the poor fisherman to be thrashed and put into prison. He was beaten so severely, that he was compelled to tell the King that thrice they had caught the fish and each time the prince had thrown it back into the sea, because he felt sorry for it. The King was shocked at the news. How could his son prefer to save the life of a fish to the health of his father? He ordered the prince to be brought before him and had him lashed several times and banished him from the palace forever, with nothing but his faithful horse.

Ibrahim was crestfallen and slowly rode out of the kingdom. He kept going for several days without laying eyes on any human being. Tired and dejected he came upon a small cottage.

'Is anyone there?' he called out, 'Please help me for I am truly worn out.'

After calling out many times, an old woman came out of the cottage and invited him in.

'Guests are the chosen ones of God. My eyes lie at your feet (as is said in Iran and in Arabia). Come in my son.'

Ibrahim went in and the old woman brought out whatever she had for him to eat and drink. She said to herself, 'This young man is so tired and dirty, yet he seems to have the bearings of noble birth.'

Ibrahim inquired from her if she had any one living with her.

'I have no one to call my own. I am all alone in the world,' the old woman replied.

The kind-hearted Ibrahim was saddened by this and said to her, 'Don't be sad. I too am alone. Why don't you adopt me as your son and I will look after you?'

The old woman happily agreed to this. Ibrahim had no money, so the next day he took his faithful horse to the marketplace and sold it. He used the money to buy meat, oil, rice, and other things that they needed. Ibrahim knew that the money would not last long, and thus everyday he went to the marketplace and tried to look for work. But who would hire him? He had no skills nor had he ever worked before. Days went by, and Ibrahim started to get desperate as the money was running out. One day while wandering around the bazaar, he saw a man sitting with a big box in front of him.

'This box is for a 100 tumans only. Anyone who buys this box will be sorry, so will anyone who sells it,' the man was shouting.

Intrigued by the man's strange spiel, Ibrahim asked if he could see what was in the box. The man refused.

'You will have to buy it as it is. I cannot allow you to see what lies within,' the man retorted.

All this mystery aroused Ibrahim's curiosity. So he bought the box with the last bit of money he had.

He carried the box home with great difficulty. There his adopted mother opened the box. To their utter amazement, out jumped a young boy. He seemed to know Ibrahim and addressed him by his name.

'How do you know my name?' asked Ibrahim in surprise.

'Ah!' said the boy, 'I know you very well. Very well indeed.'

'What is your name?' asked Ibrahim.

'My name is Abr (meaning cloud.) Now that I have been sold to you, I suppose you are my master.'

'All right, you can live with us and we will look after you. However, you are no slave and I am no master,' Ibrahim assured the boy.

'Okay, but we will see who will look after whom,' said the boy in an all-knowing tone and laughed heartily.

Abr had a small body, but seemed to have surprisingly strong muscles. It was all very, very, intriguing.

One day Ibrahim sent Abr to the bazaar with six shahies and asked him to get a kilo of rice. Off the boy went to the grocers shop and asked for a kilo of rice. The grocer looked at the six shahies.

'Do you think I'm stupid or something? How can you get a kilo of rice for so little money?' he said angrily.

Apparently Abr was not one to accept such behavior. He gave the grocer a tight slap who fell flat on the ground. Then Abr picked up a big bag of rice, put it on his head and walked away. Ibrahim was surprised to get so much rice for only six shahies. Abr proudly related what he had done to the grocer. Ibrahim realized he was heading for trouble.

Anyway, the next day Ibrahim gave Abr three shahies and asked him to get half a kilo of oil. Abr went to another grocer and asked for half a kilo of oil for three shahies. The shopkeeper pushed him away.

'Are you mad. Who will give you that much oil for so little money? Go away.'

This infuriated Abr and he turned and gave the grocer a tight cuff on his ears, and the man fainted. He then took a whole tin of oil and marched off home. When Ibrahim was told of what had happened, he became very apprehensive.

'Surely this boy is going to land me in a lot of trouble,' he thought, 'If he continues like this, I will have the whole town raring for my head.'

Several days went by. One morning Ibrahim again gave Abr three shahies, and asked him to go to the bazaar and get some wheat and some corn for the horse. You see, Ibrahim had by now managed to earn some money, with which he had bought a horse. So

Abr went to a third grocer and asked for corn and wheat, much in excess of what he could pay for. As you can guess, the boy reacted just as he had earlier. By now everyone in the bazaar had heard of this terrible boy, who was very strong and going around beating up grocers. He had created quite a stir. Each time Abr was sent on an errand, he would end up causing more and more trouble. By now, Ibrahim was afraid that the townspeople would not stand for this much longer and throw them out.

One day Abr went to the local blacksmith and asked him to make a *gorz*, (an iron pole) which was to be four metres long and weigh four maunds (a maund is forty kilos). By now everyone was thoroughly scared of him, so the blacksmith agreed to make the *gorz* for the meager sum of money that Abr offered him. With great difficulty the blacksmith moulded the large pole. Abr slung the heavy pole across his shoulders and carried it home. Ibrahim was surprised that such a small boy could carry the heavy pole so easily, but he did not say anything.

In the evening Abr said to Ibrahim, 'Come with me. Together we will go into the wide world to seek our fortune.'

When Ibrahim wanted to know where exactly they were supposed to go, Abr said, 'Don't ask questions. Just follow me.'

So the two set off, with Abr carrying the heavy *gorz* on his shoulders. He seemed to have some definite destination in mind and by nightfall they arrived at a beautiful mansion. Abr told Ibrahim, that this mansion belonged to a rich and powerful princess called Sitara Bano.

'She is beautiful,' added Abr, 'And is sleeping at the moment.'

Abr seemed to have some mysterious knowledge about all this and Ibrahim listened out of curiousity to what he had to say.

'I will tell you the location of the room. You go in, kiss her on the cheek and come right back.'

Ibrahim protested vehemently, but Abr said, 'Do what I say or you will have this gorz on your back.'

Ibrahim knew better than to disobey so he entered the mansion and passed through a maze of corridors and doors, till he reached the room that Abr had told him about. Sure enough, there was Sitara Bano, lying in all her beauty, dressed in shimmering white chiffon sleeping peacefully. With great trepidation Ibrahim went up to her and gently kissed her on the cheek and raced out of the room. He did not stop till he was outside.

The next morning Sitara Bano woke and when she looked in the mirror she saw a small stain on her cheek. She rubbed it, but it would not come off. She wondered what had causcd the stain.

The following night, Abr once again took Ibrahim to the mansion and told him to go inside and kiss the maiden, this time on the other cheek. Again he threatened Ibrahim, 'You cannot lift this gorz but I can make it spin like a top and drop it on anything or anyone. So do what I tell you to do.'

This time Sitara Bano looked even more beautiful than the night before. She was dressed in pure green silk. Her beauty overwhelmed Ibrahim. Quickly he kissed her on the other cheek and again made a hasty exit.

In the morning, Sitara Bano discovered that both her cheeks had tiny stains and she realized that something must have happened in the night. So the following night she decided she would only pretend to sleep and see if she could find out what was causing the stains. By now, Ibrahim was deeply in love with Sitara Bano. He could not get her out of his mind.

'This is a fine web I have woven myself into,' he thought.

That night, Abr gave him different instructions.

'Tonight you will go to the princess again, but whatever she does or tells you to do, you will first come and tell me. I warn you. Do not make any decisions on your own.'

Ibrahim trembling with love, agreed to all of Abr's conditions. It was strange, Abr seemed to know something was going to happen that night.

Once more Ibrahim went into Sitara Bano's room. She lay there, watching with half closed eyes. She saw a handsome young man dressed in ordinary clothes, but of noble bearing enter the room. She thought that perhaps he was someone important and fell in love with him. When Ibrahim bent down to kiss her she sat up and startled him .

'Who are you?' she asked.

'I am Ibrahim, the son of the half-blind King.'

On hearing that he was a prince, Sitara Bano implored with him, 'Ibrahim take me away from here. I am suffocating in this golden cage.'

Ibrahim was surprised, but he remembered the instructions that Abr had given him.

'Wait here,' he said to the princess, ' I have a friend outside whom I have to consult. He will find a way to get us out of here.'

Abr gave his consent and Ibrahim re-entered the mansion and brought Sitara Bano back with him. The three then went into the stables and got two horses. Abr told the young couple that they could ride and he would follow on foot.

In the morning when Sitara Bano did not emerge from her room, all the servants and courtiers of the mansion went looking for her. She was nowhere to be found. The King was immediately informed. He concluded that she had been kidnapped, and ordered his soldiers to go and find her. Soon they caught up with the trio and surrounded them. When the soldiers began to close in, Abr told Ibrahim, 'Take the princess and slowly, very slowly go on while I fight the soldiers.'

Ibrahim, however, was afraid that Abr would not be able to withstand the army on his own, so he galloped off at a fast pace with the princess. As the two were riding, they were confronted by another King, who happened to be passing by that way with his entourage on a hunting trip. This King captured them and took them back with him to his palace. He threw Ibrahim into a deep well and made the beautiful Sitara Bano a prisoner in his palace.

Meanwhile, Abr armed with the gorz faced the army. He lifted it high and spun it around and threw it on the ground. As it hit the earth, water came gushing out with great force. It turned into a whirlpool and stopped the soldiers dead in their tracks.

Then Abr quickly went to the place where Ibrahim and Sitara Bano should have been, had they walked slowly as he had instructed them. But he did not find them there and at once he knew that some misfortune must have befallen them. He set out to look for them.

After walking a considerable distance, he met a small bald-headed boy standing alone, away from all the other children.

'Hey! Kuchali (meaning bald little boy)!Why are you not playing with all the other boys?'

'They don't like me, as I have a bad temper,' replied the boy.

'You seem to be a gutsy young fellow,' said Abr, 'Here take this money and tell me, have you seen a man and a woman pass by this way? They must have been captured! If they have, tell me where they have been taken?'

Kuchali happily took the money and said, 'All right, lets do it this way. I will snatch the hat from your head and run with it. Wherever I hang it, that is where the woman is and where I jump and fall down, that is where the man is. Okay, lets go.'

So kuchali snatched the hat and ran with it. Abr ran after him, a bit doubtful whether the boy was a rogue or a simpleton. After running for some distance, they passed a large palace. Kuchali put the hat on the gate of the palace. Then a few yards further, he fell on the ground. He then got up and quickly went and handed Abr his hat back and ran away. Abr began to look around. In front of him he saw a huge boulder, which looked as though it was put there to cover a hole in the ground. Using the gorz and exerting all his strength, he managed to remove the boulder from the mouth of the hole. Sure enough, it was a dry well and inside he found Ibrahim. Abr helped him out with a rope.

'Didn't I tell you not to go far. This is what happens when you disobey me,' he admonished him.

Ibrahim was sorry for what he had done. But they had no time for explanations, now the important thing was to find the princess. The kuchali had already indicated that she was in the palace.

Abr strode into the palace with his gorz swung across his shoulders. Everyone inside had seen how he had removed the huge boulder and pulled Ibrahim out single-handedly. They thought that surely he must be a famous *Pahlavan* (champion). He certainly looked the part, with the gorz, that looked so heavy that not even five men could lift it. All of them respectfully kept their distance and when he asked to be taken to see the ruler they immediately did his bidding. The King's ministers advised him to ask this *pahlavan* to marry his beautiful daughter. Then they could ask him to remain in the kingdom and take charge of the army. With such a champion, they would have the strongest army in the land and become very powerful. The King thought this was a very good idea and asked Abr if he would marry his daughter.

Abr refused, 'I have not come here to marry your daughter,' he said in an authoritative voice, which caused the king to tremble, 'I have come to take back the woman you kidnapped. She is my friend's wife. Release her at once and we will be on our way. Or else...'

He did not have to complete his sentence, as the King not only freed Sitara Bano, but also ordered a great feast in their honour. When they started on their way the next day, they were properly equipped with two fine horses. Abr had once again decided to walk.

Everything was going well, until they reached a thick dense jungle. Suddenly in front of them, blocking their way, were two ferocious giants.

Abr whispered to Ibrahim, 'Take the princess and walk along very slowly. Do not run. I will quickly deal with these giants and join you.'

But as soon as they got behind the cover of the trees, Ibrahim decided to make a run for it. He wasn't sure that this time Abr would be able to survive these dangerous looking behemoths. Needless to say, they hadn't gone far when, once again they were captured by another King. Ibrahim was pushed into a well and Sitara Bano was locked up in the castle.

Abr quickly overcame the giants. He simply picked them up and threw one towards the east and the other towards the west. That was the end of those two. Then Abr tried to find Ibrahim and Sitara Bano in the place where they should have been and when he realized they were missing, he was very upset. He was very fond of Ibrahim and it saddened him to see that his friend did not have confidence in him and didn't listen to him.

Abr once again went looking for him and Sitara Bano. He came across a farmer ploughing a field with a cow. The curious thing was that the man was dressed in black from head to toe and the cow was also painted completely black. Abr came up to the farmer and after greeting him inquired why everything was black.

'You see we have a very cruel King and he has committed many misdeeds. But this time he has gone too far,' the farmer replied, 'He has captured a beautiful princess and keeps her imprisoned in the castle and has pushed the poor woman's husband, a fine young man, into a well. This is our way of protesting. The entire town has joined in and everything has been blackened.'

Abr knew at once that the farmer must be talking about Ibrahim and Sitara Bano. True enough everyone in the town was wearing black. They told him that they had all tried to move the big boulder, which covers the mouth of the well but try as they might, they could not budge it. When Abr saw the stone, he moved it away easily with his super human strength— which, by now, we know he possessed. A sheepish Ibrahim was pulled out of the well. He apologized to Abr, for disobeying him once again and begged him to rescue the princess. It did not take much doing. When word reached the King that there was a man with super human strength, who had moved the heavy boulder single-handedly, he was very scared and at once released Sitara Bano. Of course he too tried to entice Abr into joining the court by offering him his daughter's hand in marriage. But Abr spurned the offer, saying he was not the marrying kind.

Off they went. They rode a long distance, until at last they returned to Ibrahim's father's palace.

Abr took Ibrahim aside and said to him, 'This is where I will leave you.'

'No, no, you cannot do this,' implored Ibrahim 'After all you have done for me, now is the time I shall be able to repay you. My father is the King and I have come to know that the people of the kingdom were very unhappy when I was banished and they have prevailed upon my father to take me back. You can't leave now.'

But Abr cautioned him, 'I know your father only pretends he wants you back. Actually he hates you for not bringing back the red fish which would have cured his eyes. He plans to kill you.'

'That can't be true. My father truly loves me,' insisted Ibrahim.

'Be that as it may. Still I am warning you. Do not eat anything without offering it to a cat first. If the cat lives you know you are safe.' With this Abr bade them goodbye, but before he left he told them to come and meet him after one week, by the seashore at sunset. Then he was gone.

Ibrahim and his beautiful princess were received with great pomp and show by the now, totally blind

King. Ibrahim was convinced that his father had forgiven him. But when they sat down to eat, Ibrahim tested the food as Abr had advised him and saw that the cat died on tasting the food. Ibrahim thanked God that for once he had heeded the words of his friend. Actually the King had never forgiven Ibrahim and blamed him for his blindness. He had only pretended to be happy when he took him back, because the people of his kingdom loved Ibrahim and had rebelled when he had exiled the prince. Afterwards the old, blind King had to abdicate and give the crown to his son Ibrahim.

A week later, Ibrahim and Queen Sitara Bano went to the seashore to meet Abr as they had promised. He was waiting there for them. As they came nearer, without saying a word Abr waved goodbye and dived into the sea. Then, to their surprise they saw that as he swam away he slowly transformed into the red fish— the same that Ibrahim had caught thrice and thrown back into the water each time, thus saving it from being eaten by the King.

In case you are wondering, the truth of the matter was that the King's cure did not lie in the eating of this fish. The astrologers and the wise men had just made up the story to escape the wrath of the cruel King.

THE GREEDY JACKAL

Once upon a time, in the woods on the edge of a village, lived a sly and cunning jackal. Everyday he would enter the village and steal chickens and fruit. The villagers were utterly sick of this creature, but the jackal somehow managed to elude all their attempts to catch him and continued his thieving ways. With each passing day he became more and more daring in his escapades.

One day, a frail old man came to live in a small cottage, on the edge of the village. The house had a beautiful garden, with a small vineyard that the old man tended most lovingly. One day, when he returned home from an errand he found that his succulent grapes had been eaten up; two of his chickens were missing and the garden was in a mess. The old man had heard of the jackal and knew at once that this must be its handiwork. He resolved to teach the thieving animal a lesson.

Although the house and the garden were surrounded by high walls, there were a number of inlets for streams, which brought in water for drinking as well as for irrigating the vineyard. The old man concluded that the animal must have gained entrance into his property through one of these, and had them blocked up temporarily. He then opened the front gate and hid behind it with a heavy stick ready to ambush the jackal. As soon as the sun went down, the jackal appeared and finding all the inlets blocked went up to the gate which was open.

'This is strange,' said the jackal to himself, 'The old man usually locks and barricades the gate securely. This must be a trap.'

Being extremely cunning, he thought he would give the old man a few hours in which he would surely tire and go to sleep. This is exactly what happened. Several hours later the old man got tired of waiting and dozed off. The jackal now saw the way was clear and went in and helped himself to the succulent grapes.

Early the next morning, the old man woke at the sound of the cockerel. For a moment he was confused, then slowly he took in the scene of havoc in front of him. The jackal had outsmarted him. He was furious. He knew that he could not keep the inlets of the stream blocked up for very long. Without water his garden would wither away. So he thought up another plan to get the jackal, once and for all. He mounted his donkey and rode off to the butcher's shop that was a few miles away. There he bought a big piece of beef. Back home, he placed the beef on the gate, to tempt the jackal, and tied the meat to a metal trap, that would be activated by a slight pull and its clamp would close suddenly on the jackal's paw. It would thus be unable to run away and he would give it the thrashing of its life—or so he thought.

As usual the jackal arrived at night and finding the holes still blocked, went up to the gate. There he saw the big piece of meat hanging on the open gate, just waiting for him to sink his teeth into. How tempted he was. But once again, he sensed that this must be a trap.

'No one would leave such a large piece of meat just like that,' he said to himself, 'This meat must be poisoned or there must be a trap somewhere.'

So the cunning jackal resisted the temptation to take a bite from the meat and instead, strolled into the garden and feasted on the grapes. The next morning the old man came out, expecting to see the jackal trapped. But alas! The trap was empty and his garden was a mess with almost all his grapes eaten up by now. He was absolutely livid and vowed to kill the jackal.

For a long time the old man plotted and planned. At last he hit upon a plan which could not fail. He went to the town and bought wooden planks to make a big chicken coop. Inside the coop he dug a large hole and placed a trap at the bottom, then camouflaged the pit with leaves and branches. After that he put many nice fat chickens and roosters into the coop. That night he hid in the shed nearby, with one hand holding a long string, which would spring the trap as soon as the jackal fell into the hole. This time the old man was absolutely sure he would get the sneaky animal. He chuckled to himself at the thought of how the villagers would proclaim him a hero for getting rid of the marauder.

As darkness approached, the jackal came out to commit his vile deeds. But he did not feel too well.

'I must have eaten too many grapes last night. Maybe I better go back to my den and rest tonight,' he

thought. So he padded off home, to sleep off his stomach cramps.

It so happened that another fox, new to the area, was passing by the old man's garden. He entered through the open gate, saw the coop and cautiously took a peek inside. The sight of all those juicy chickens made his mouth water and he bounded in to catch a few. No sooner had he entered, he fell straight into the hole and the trap was activated.

The old man entered, all excited shouting, 'I've got you at last, you miserable jackal,' and began to thrash the poor fox, who literally did not know what hit him.

Mercifully, for the fox, the old man soon realized that it was not the jackal that he was beating up, but a fox, so he let it go. The fox ran as fast as it could, leaving the old man raving and ranting and shouting at the top of his voice what a phantom creature this jackal was, that it was able to get away each time.

Now the poor fox was limping along the forest path, cursing his bad luck at having fallen into a trap. But he remembered what the old man had shouted about the jackal, and being a clever animal, he realized that the beating he had got was actually meant for the jackal. Suddenly he spotted the jackal in front of him.

'Whatever happened to you?' asked the jackal.

The fox decided to get even with the jackal for the beating he had got on his behalf.

'Well,' said the fox, 'No one has done anything to me. I happened to be walking along and fell into a ditch. But let me tell you of the lovely garden I was in with the juicy grapes and even juicier chickens,' he continued. 'I even killed a few and ate my fill. I am telling you this because I am not a selfish animal. I want to share my good luck with you and others.' The fox then described the exact location of the garden.

The jackal realized it was the same garden that he used to plunder and thought, 'Why, the old man now has a chicken coop. How mortifying that this puny fox has been there before me. I will show the old man who really owns the territory.'

So the following evening, as soon as it became dark, the jackal headed towards the old man's cottage. He saw the streams were flowing once more and the gate was wide open.

'Has the old man died or has he become so rich that he does not care?' thought the jackal. The vision of the fox feasting on the chickens before him disturbed the jackal. Carefully he entered the coop, cautiously he looked around and saw the small pile of dried leaves.

'Oho! So this is what the old man is up to. He has this hole covered with leaves and he thinks I am foolish enough to fall into it. So that's why the fox was all beaten up.'

So he started to circumvent it when CLANGG! the trap clamped on to his paws. You see, the old man had realized that the jackal was too clever for conventional methods and had tricked him into going towards the side where the trap was actually set.

The jackal was finally trapped and what a beating the villagers gave him. They did not want to kill him, but only teach him a lesson not to steal their fruits and their chickens. After a sound thrashing the villagers released him and he limped away, cured of his thieving ways and suitably chastised.

THE ONE-SIDED WEDDING

The following is a story based on an old custom in China. Its poignancy moves listeners and sometimes even brings tears to their eyes.

It was late in the afternoon on an autumn's day. Some clouds floated across the sky and the sun shone through the gaps. A strong wind was blowing. All the inhabitants of the locality were standing outside in the street, waiting for a procession to pass by. An air of expectancy hung over the bystanders. A bridal procession was to pass but, why was there so much sadness all around? Weddings are supposed to be a time for celebrations and festivities. Where were the trumpeters, the drummers and the dancers in their colourful clothes? Everyone seemed to be looking sorrowful. Instead of rejoicing, they seemed to be in mourning. What was wrong?

Suddenly a lone trumpet sounded. Everyone stopped talking and looked in the direction of the sound.

'Is this a funeral procession?' asked a small boy, perched on his mother's shoulders to get a good view.

'Shush!' said his mother, 'Keep quiet! It's not a funeral. It's a wedding procession.'

The little boy was perplexed. Never had he seen such a mournful assembly of people passing by.

All the regalia of the wedding procession came in full view. There were banners and streamers and men carrying two sedan chairs. On one of the chairs sat a young girl, no more than eighteen years of age. She was bedecked from head to toe in black silk, the colour of mourning. She was beautiful but looked pale and frightened, like a small deer caught in a snare. The only bit of colour about her was her red lips, otherwise she looked as though she was a marble statuette. The other chair was empty—there was no bridegroom. On this chair there was only a wooden tablet.

'Who is she?' asked the curious little boy, 'She's so beautiful. Just like a princess. Why is there no bridegroom? How can there be a bride and no groom?'

'She is the Zhiang family's daughter-in-law,' the mother replied, 'The rich family that lives in the big mansion on the hill.'

'But where is the bridegroom?' the little boy persisted.

'He died a few months after they were betrothed,' his mother told him.

In those days, it was the custom among the upper classes in China, that if a couple were betrothed and the man died before the wedding, the girl would have to go through the entire ceremony as if he were alive. Thereafter, she would live in the home of her in-laws for the rest of her life, as a widow. It was a cruel custom, and this was the reason for the mournful procession that was passing through the streets that autumn afternoon.

The procession passed by slowly, with the musicians playing tunes that sounded like dirges, until it came to a halt in front of the gate of a large mansion. A large

retinue of servants was in attendance. Two women, 'dressed in white, helped the bride to alight from the chair. Then two men, wearing long gowns and short jackets, took the wooden tablet that had been lying on the bridegroom's chair. Together they marched slowly into the house. The tablet represented the dead bridegroom. When they reached the big hall of the house they stopped, and the tablet was tied to the bride with a sash of black silk, about ten yards long. The band continued playing a hauntingly sad melody. The bride stood alone on the blue carpet, with the plaque to her right, where her husband should have stood. She bowed to the heaven and earth and then to the ancestral shrine.

After the ceremony, they— the bride and the tablet, entered the hall of the mansion and here she bowed in front of the groom's parents. Then she was escorted to the bridal chambers. The tablet was placed upon an altar on which an oil lamp was burning with a flickering, blue flame. A plain, white cloth was draped over the bronze bedstead by the window. The pillowslip was decorated with the traditional embroidered ducks and drakes, to signify a long and happy marriage. The bride was to live here with the tablet, just as she would have with her husband.

When everyone left, the bride sat down all alone on a chair next to the memorial tablet and stared at it. A gust of wind caused the lamp to flicker and cast eerie shadows on the wall. The leaves of the bamboo trees outside her window rustled and seemed to be humming a mournful song. Thus, the bride passed her wedding night.

Time passed by very, very slowly. The young bride did not know what to do with her life. She would go through the motions of living, while her heart cried out in loneliness and despair. The only goal was to pass each day. The weeks turned into months and soon spring was in the air.

One afternoon the bride went out into the garden for a walk. The air was fresh and laden with the heavy fragrance of flowers. Butterflies, startled by her presence, rose from among the blossoms and fluttered all around her. She bent down to pick up a willow branch and sat down to do some weaving. She was very skilled and loved to make beautiful handicrafts with her hands. She gazed at the peonies that lined the garden path. Her eyes alighted on two sparrows, chirping merrily and busy looking for twigs among the flowers for their nest. Everywhere there were birds flying and all of them were in pairs. The bride was sad. Every living thing seemed to have a companion on this lovely spring day, except her. Why had fate dealt her such a heavy blow? She searched her soul for an answer and none was forthcoming. The delicate willow tendrils now lay crushed on the ground. Slowly the bride got up and walked into her room.

She went to the altar on which the wooden tablet was placed and wondered if this was what she would have to spend her entire life with? She happened to glance at herself in the mirror. Her cheeks were glowing and were bright crimson in color. Her eyes were unnaturally bright. She was overcome with an emotion she had never experienced before.

'Am I going out of my mind?' she asked the wooden tablet. Like other times when the bride had spoken to it, there was no answer.

The following morning sunshine streamed into her room lighting it up. The maid brought water for her ablutions, but the door was locked from the inside. The maid knocked on the door and called out, 'get up mistress, it is quite late. Open the door.'

There was no sound from inside. The maid then went outside and looked in through the window and let out a terrified scream. She ran to the mother-in-law trembling and crying.

'Madame, the mistress is no more. She has gone to meet her master. The mistress has hung herself.'

THE YOUTH AND THE STRANGER

Once upon a time, in the deserts of Egypt, there lived a successful and hard working merchant, who was renowned for his honesty. His family consisted of his wife and a son, Mustapha, whom he dearly loved.

One day he called his family and told them, 'My dears, I have become very old and might die very soon. I wish to say a few words to you. I have worked very hard in my lifetime to earn a good name for the family. I hope this will never be tarnished.' Then he turned to his son and said, 'So far, you have had no responsibilities, but after I'm gone I am entrusting you to carry on my work and to look after your mother's welfare. Also, since you have been betrothed to my brother's daughter, your cousin, since childhood, I want you to marry her, and try to build a warm and happy family life with her.'

'Don't worry father, I will happily carry out your every wish and do the best I can,' Mustapha assured him.

Shortly thereafter, the merchant died peacefully in his sleep. Unfortunately, after his death his son fell into bad company. He began to gamble and indulge in all sorts of vices. These so-called friends took advantage of the wealth he had inherited. He did not even marry his cousin. In fact he broke every promise he had made to his father.

His mother was very worried about the change in her beloved son. There was now, not even enough money to buy food for the house and moreover, she heard terrible rumours that he was badly in debt and owed huge sums of money to various people. However, the youth paid no heed to his mother's warnings and kept gambling and soon lost everything, even the house they lived in. They had to sell all their belongings and move to a one-room house, which they took on rent.

When all his friends deserted him, Mustapha realized that they had taken advantage of him and now he had lost everything. One day, overcome with despondency, he sat down near a ditch on the roadside and started weeping. He then went home to his mother and poured out his heart to her, telling her about his addiction to gambling and the fact that all his so-called friends had discarded him after his money was all spent. His mother, being a very kind-hearted soul, said to him, 'I am glad you have realized your mistake and now you can endeavour to change your life.'

'Mother you must give me some money so I can travel to another town and try to find myself a job.'

But she did not have any money. All she had was a straw mattress on which she would sit.

'I am sorry to ask you for this mattress. This is the only thing left to sell,' said Mustapha in desperation. His mother gladly gave it to her son. He had been reduced to selling the last article of comfort she had.

However, he received very little money for the straw mattress. No one would hire him in this town because of his bad reputation. Dejected, Mustapha headed for another.

On the way, he heard someone call out to him, 'Hey you! Son of Mehmood the merchant, where are you headed?'

Mustapha turned around to face a distinguished looking gentleman, whose face was hidden behind a mask.

'Whoever you are don't waste my time, I am headed for another town,' replied the youth.

'The whole town knows how you disgraced your family and wasted away all your family's wealth,' the stranger admonished him, 'You sank so low you sold your mother's straw mattress. You didn't even marry your cousin, as you had promised, and now you are running away.'

'You seem to know everything about me. Just leave me alone,' said Mustapha, 'It is not your concern anyway.'

'I have a proposition for you,' insisted the stranger, 'I am willing to help you. I am going to give you 1000 dinars, out of which you should use 500 dinars to start a business and buy a decent house, and 500 dinars you must give to your cousin to prepare for your wedding. However, you must not take your cousin to your house till you have my permission.'

Mustapha was speechless for a few minutes, a perfect stranger had made such an offer to him. In his situation he had no option but to accept. So he thanked him profusely and promised, 'I will carry out all your bidding. You have helped me in my darkest hour, for this I shall remain eternally grateful.'

Mustapha then bought some food and other necessities for his mother and hurried back home. He told her about the stranger.

'Who could it be?' his mother wondered, 'Maybe it is one of your late father's friends.'

'Whoever he was, I am going to do exactly as I promised him. I broke the promises I made to my father and had to face such bitter consequences. I will not repeat the same mistake.' He then told her about the stranger's condition about bringing his bride home.

'Maybe he wants to marry your cousin. She is very beautiful and talented, you know.'

'I will never allow that to happen. I promised father I would marry her and I shall,' said Mustapha with new-found confidence.

He then went to his Uncle's house to beg his forgiveness.

'So now you have come to me. You have been indulging in all kinds of disreputable activities. You have sullied the good name of our family. You have also hurt my daughter's feelings very deeply. I do not want to have anything to do with you,' his uncle scolded him.

'Please uncle! I know I have hurt all of you very much. But now I have mended my ways. I will never again give you or Fatima, any cause for concern. Please find it in your heart to forgive me,' pleaded Mustapha.

'All right,' said his uncle, 'But I will have to ask Fatima if she can accept you as her husband?'

The uncle called his daughter and asked for her opinion.

'Well if he has seen the folly of his ways I am willing to forgive him,' she answered.

Mustapha was relieved and handed over the 500 dinars for the wedding preparations, just as the stranger had instructed.

Thereafter, Mustapha worked hard to set up his new business and regain the lost prestige of his family among the townspeople. Slowly his confidence grew and he prospered in his business. He admitted to his mother that there really was no other way except honesty and hard work to succeed. His mother would thank the stranger daily in her prayers, for having set her son on the right path.

Mustapha slowly built up his fortune. He also bought a house for his mother. It was not as big as the one they had lived in when his father was alive, but it was well furnished and comfortable. He now felt he was ready to get married. So he went with his mother to his uncle's house and set a date for the wedding, which was fixed for a week later.

His mother reminded him of his promise to the stranger about seeking his permission before bringing his bride home. Mustapha had not forgotten. He set out to find the stranger. He looked all over the town for days without any luck. The wedding day was approaching and all the festivities had been planned. His uncle had wanted a lavish wedding for his beloved

Fatima. Mustapha was getting very anxious. He had to keep his promise to the stranger; he would not be able to get married without first taking his permission.

On the day of the wedding, Mustapha set out early in the morning desperate to find the stranger. He looked in every street and lane, but there was no sign of him. Dejected he went and sat in the same place where he had first met his mysterious benefactor. By now it was close to the time the wedding festivities were to begin. Mustapha was at his wits end. There seemed to be nothing he could do, he gave up all hope of being able to marry his cousin and was very sad. Suddenly he heard the neighing of a horse. He looked up and his face brightened with happiness. There was the stranger in the mask.

'I have been looking all over for you,' said Mustapha, 'Today is the day of my wedding. I have kept every promise I made to you. I run an honest business. I had promised you that I would not wed until you gave me permission. I have come to ask you for it.'

The stranger did not look very impressed. 'I'm not so sure about your wedding. Has your cousin forgiven you for the way you neglected her?'

'She has and she is marrying me today,' Mustapha was almost pleading.

'I have to see this for myself. Take me to the house of your betrothed, so that I can ascertain the truth personally.'

Mustapha readily agreed.

But when they reached the cousin's house, it was locked and deserted. There were no signs of festivity, nor were there any guests around.

'Are you sure this is a house where a marriage is to take place?' asked the stranger, 'I don't see any sign of any such activity here.'

Mustapha was extremely perplexed. 'Where are the ladies singing and dancing? Where are the streamers and the lights? Today is the day of the wedding. Why is everything so quiet?' he said to himself.

Aloud he said, 'I swear to you that today is the day I wed my cousin. I don't know where everyone is?'

'Are you absolutely sure you are telling the truth? Did you give them the 500 dinars I gave you for the wedding preparations?'

'I did. Fatima will vouch for it. Where in the name of God is she?' Mustapha called to her, but there was no answer. He started to lose his nerve and could not understand what was happening. 'Fatima! Fatima! Please come out and tell this gentleman that you have agreed to marry me and that today is our wedding day,' he shouted.

Still there was no answer.

'Where are you, Fatima?' he called out desperately.

Then a voice answered from behind him, 'Here I am.'

Mustapha swung around and saw the stranger remove the mask. It was Fatima standing before him. *She was the stranger.* Mustapha was awestruck.

'Please sit down and let me explain,' said his cousin, 'I love you a lot and when I saw you on the path of ruin, I felt I had to do something to help you. But I knew there was nothing I could do. So I had to wait until you were at the lowest ebb of your life. I did not want you to feel humiliated by accepting money from me. That is why I disguised myself. I knew in my heart that you were a good person, led astray only by bad company. I was right. See how well you have done for yourself.'

Then she clapped her hand and the doors opened. The entire wedding preparations had been in all readiness. All the guests and relatives greeted them and the festivities began. An old aunt brought in *bakhur* and rose water and sprinkled it on everyone. There was a great deal of clapping, ululating and singing. As per tradition, all the guests were given sweets and money and *nuql* was showered on the couple. The two were wed and the singing and merriment continued till late in the night.

When they were alone at last, Mustapha thanked his dear wife for showing him that true love can conquer all and he vowed never to give her any reason to be unhappy. He asked her to give him the mask, which he wanted to keep, to remind him forever of the understanding and love that she had given him in his darkest hour.

▓ A DEAD MAN COMES BACK ▓ TO LIFE

This story is about the days when there was strict segregation between men and women, and it was unheard of for a man to lay eyes on a woman, other than those he was related to. Many tales are told of men who have been enamoured by the mere glimpse of a woman. This tale, however, has an intriguing twist and we will begin it with a newspaper vendor shouting the headlines in the street.

A dead man comes back to life! Read the story of a dead man who has come back to life!'

Haji Agha's wife heard the cry from her house and it roused her curiosity, so she sent her son to buy a copy.

'How can a dead man come back to life?' she wondered.

Apparently a rich merchant of the town, Qassim Agha, who was supposed to have died and buried ten days ago, had returned to his house alive and well. The newspaper went on to describe the event in great detail.

When her husband, Haji Agha, came home, she showed him the paper, 'Come and read about the dead man who has come back to life,' she told him.

Haji Agha was a pious and well-respected man in the community. He was known to be a caring and devoted father and husband. Of course he had no time for such an irreverent task.

'What nonsense these newspapers print. Why do you waste your time on such rubbish. Now come and give me something to eat,' he admonished his wife.

'But look, they are writing about Qassim Agha. Remember he is the same person who fell into a deep well and survived, some years ago. Everyone says he has nine lives like a cat,' his wife persisted.

'What did you say? Qassim Agha!' the Haji said, extremely surprised, in a voice high pitched with astonishment.

'But I buried him myself.' He grabbed the paper from his wife's hand and read it. A shiver ran down his spine. It was true. It *was* Qassim Agha whom the newspaper was referring to as the dead man who had come back to life. This is where our story ends, but we will have to go back to the beginning, to understand why Haji was so upset by this news.

Haji Agha lived in one of the small towns that dot the beautiful Iranian countryside. Life in this small community was friendly and intimate and most people knew each other. Haji Agha was not an old man as the title Haji would seem to suggest. While most people perform Hajj in their forties or fifties, he was still quite young and had already made the pilgrimage to Mecca. In those days the journey entailed great hardship, as no mechanized transport was available. Anyone who managed to perform Hajj was revered and greatly respected. Thus, it was that Haji Agha was both wise, as well as still young and healthy. The townspeople greatly admired him and sought his counsel in personal as well as public matters.

Each morning, neatly dressed in *aba* and *qaba*, with his well-kept beard and dignified posture, Haji's familiar figure could be seen walking through the lanes to his shop in the *souq*. As he would pass the houses bordering the lane, he would often look up to observe the facade of one house or another, which caught his fancy. However, most of the time he would walk with his eyes cast downwards, as befits a gentleman. Occasionally he would see children playing outside a gate or catch a glimpse of some woman, completely wrapped in a *chaddar*, buying vegetables or fruits from one of the vendors. Sometimes, Haji would feel that he was being watched from behind the shuttered windows of the houses he passed. Maybe, from a partly open window or a crack in the door, the ladies within these cloistered homes would be peeking out into the world to watch the people passing by.

One day, Haji happened to be looking at a particularly interesting green shuttered window, when he saw 'her' looking down shyly from behind the casement. He didn't even see her face, all he saw was her eyes above a veil. But the sight caused his heart to skip a beat. The next day he passed that way again and looked up at the same window, and saw her once more. Haji was smitten.

'Those eyes, so sparkling and piercing,' Haji would keep thinking to himself. Everyday now he would take the same route, and when passing that particular house he would look up and there she would be, with her face all covered, except for the eyes. 'If the eyes are so beautiful what will the face be like?' Haji kept imagining her beauty. He was by now completely infatuated and could think of nothing else but the few, brief moments when he could look upon those eyes. 'Surely she too waits for me to pass by as impatiently as I do,' Haji would wonder. At other times he would be imagining what exotic messages of love and passion those eyes must be sending him. His imagination had really run riot. He could not concentrate on his work or on anything else.

Haji made discreet inquiries, not directly—that would have been improper—but about the house and its owner. He found that a rich man called Qassim Agha lived in the house with his family. Qassim was an old man, but he was reputed to be shrewd and clever. Also, it seemed he must have some guardian angel, as Haji heard that once he had fallen into a deep well and had come out totally unscathed.

One day, Haji was passing by the house and as usual, looked up. To his utter disappointment, his beloved—for now he had begun to think of her as such—was not at the window. He was distressed, but then, concluding that maybe she had gone out somewhere, he took heart and continued on his way. However, on the following day she was not at the window, and he was devastated. He was so upset his legs refused to carry him any further, and he sat down on the stone *sakoo* outside the house. These stone platforms are built outside every house, and are used by the men to sit and talk, drink tea and smoke *qalyoon* in the evenings. While he was sitting there crestfallen, the gate opened and Qassim Agha came out.

'Haji Agha, why are you sitting all by yourself outside? Are you feeling all right,' he asked, recognizing his compatriot and feeling concerned when he saw how upset he looked. 'Come and sit inside. A cup of tea will do you good.'

Haji entered the house, and secretly in his heart he was hoping that maybe he would be able to catch a glimpse of his mesmerizing beloved. The house was very tastefully decorated. Qassim took Haji to the courtyard where there was a *houz* (artificial pond) and around it were wooden benches covered with richly woven carpets. There were trees and vines and flowers. There were glittering samovars and trays full of sweetmeat and assorted fruits. To Haji this was like paradise, especially because this was where his beloved lived.

'Shabnam, we have visitors. Bring us some tea,' Qassim Agha shouted out to someone inside.

Shabnam came out with a tray. Haji could not believe his eyes. It was the same woman he had been charmed with for so long. Those eyes were just right for the beautiful face. He could now see clearly through the gossamer viel. 'Shabnam, what a lovely name. She looks as soft and fragile as the dewdrop on a rose petal,' thought Haji, lost in those eyes.

'Please meet my wife, Shabnam,' Qassim said. Haji was jolted back to his senses. 'Shabnam this is Haji Agha , he is a very respected elder of our community.' Actually she had been allowed to come in his presence only because Haji Agha was considered such a respectable and pious man, who had performed the pilgrimage at a young age. As he sat, Haji caught glimpse of a sign from her that seemed to convey that she too reciprocated the attention he had been giving her from afar, and she was also glad to appear in his presence. All the time she was serving tea, they kept stealing sidelong glances at each other.

'This was delightful. Do come again Haji Agha,' Qassim said politely at the end of the visit.

'I wonder if he suspects? Why would he invite me again to his house if he does,' thought Haji, as he bade goodbye.

After that Haji became a regular visitor to Qassim Agha's house. Each time he met Shabnam he was in seventh heaven, although all that happened was that they exchanged a few furtive glances. Qassim seemed to enjoy his company. Needless to say, Haji went to great pains to cultivate his relationship with him. Qassim was frail and plagued with chronic asthma, which kept him indoors most of the time. Haji was always on hand to tend to him. One evening, however, Qassim took a turn for the worse and died a few days later. Shabnam was devastated. According to custom, after Qassim was buried she had to observe the compulsory four months and ten days of *Edda*. During this period she had to remain segregated. She was not allowed to meet any men, even relatives.

Haji would stop by every day and solicitously inquire if the household required anything. Of course he was not able to see Shabnam, but she managed to get a couple of notes across to him. Haji now started dreaming of marrying his Shabnam. 'There is nothing wrong with marrying a second time. Many men have two wives,' he would reason with himself. That was why it came as such a great shock to him when he heard the story of the dead man come back to life in the papers. 'Did Qassim Agha know what was going on and fake his death to trick Shabnam?' The possibility that he knew terrified him. The more he thought about it the more it tormented him. But now there was nothing he could do. Never again was he going to look at another woman.

As for Shabnam, it was said that she kept mumbling over and over again to whoever was willing to listen, 'I cannot live with a dead man, I cannot live with a...'

THE STORY OF GOUMUZ AND THE GARBAGE MAN

The story is set in Turkey. I heard it almost sixty years ago.

In a small town in Turkey, there lived a frail old man by the name of Helo. He was the local garbage man. He would go from house to house, collecting garbage, loading it onto his cart and disposing it off in the outskirts of town. His cart was pulled by his beloved horse, Goumuz. The horse had literally been born in Helo's arms and the bond between the two was very strong. He treated Goumuz like a son.

You see, Helo was alone in this world. His wife had died when his three sons were very small. He did his best to provide a good life for them, but he never had enough money to feed or clothe them properly. One by one his sons left him to seek a better life for themselves. Helo did not resent this, in fact he was happy for them, knowing that now they were better off. All he had was his faithful Goumuz, who would listen to every command he gave and tirelessly make the rounds with him everyday.

One cold winter's day the municipal authorities of the town confiscated his horse and cart. He was informed very brusquely that someone from the district of Balough, a younger man, would be taking his place

and that his services were no longer required. Helo was heartbroken. Not only was his beloved horse no longer with him, but his meager livelihood had been taken away as well. He was distraught and there was nothing he could do. All his life he had been a garbage collector and he did not know any other line of work. But he worried most about Goumuz.

'Goumuz is not used to taking orders from anyone. He only knows me,' thought Helo, 'What if the young man from Balough does not understand this and beats him. My poor Goumuz! What is to become of him.'

He thought of all the love he had lavished on the horse and about the time it had hurt it's ankle. Helo had tended to him just as he would his own son.

Helo decided he was not going to sit by and let his horse and cart be handed over to some young man from Balough. The townspeople knew him well. He would go and tell them what had happened and surely, they would intercede on his behalf with the municipal authorities and get his horse and cart back.

'They will tell the officers that I am a more experienced man and that I should be allowed to go on collecting the garbage,' he thought,

'Besides the man from Balough doesn't know a thing about my Goumuz. When I am reinstated I will once again walk with my head held high with my beloved Goumuz beside me.'

Helo was thus sitting in a corner, all huddled up against the cold, thinking of how he would get back his horse, when a road sweeper who knew him happened to pass by. Seeing Helo sitting all alone in the cold he stopped to inquire as to what the matter was. When he heard that Helo had lost his horse and cart to a younger man from Balough the sweeper was grieved for him. He sat down with him and sympathized. Helo told him he intended to ask the townspeople for help and the sweeper agreed that it was a good idea to do so. While they were sitting and talking, the door of the house in front of them opened, and a well-dressed man stepped out.

'He is a famous lawyer, everyone in town respects him,' Helo informed the sweeper, 'He gave me the most *eidiya* last Eid. He is very kind and even gave me a coat.'

'Come on, he is coming this way. Let's ask him to help me,' Helo suggested. They both stood up and greeted him respectfully. But much to their surprise, the lawyer merely shook his head and quickly walked past as if they were invisible.

Then the door of another house down the street opened and another well-dressed man emerged.

'Ah! Now that is the great doctor,' said Helo, remembering how kindly he had bandaged Goumuz's ankle when it was hurt. 'If there is any man that the municipal officers would listen to, it would be the doctor. Let us ask him to help.'

Once again they stood up expectantly and greeted the doctor. But he just gave them a cursory glance and walked away. They were crestfallen. The sweeper had to get back to work, so he wished Helo good luck and left.

Helo once again sat down on the side of the road, dejected and sad. His earlier optimism was beginning to fade. After a while a lady passed by. Helo recognized her. Everyone in town referred to her as 'aunty'. When she saw Helo, she stopped and asked him what was the matter and why he was sitting all alone. At this time he was usually up and about collecting garbage.

'What can I say Aunty? I have been replaced by a young man from Balough,' Helo told her. 'After all my years of faithful service I have been kicked aside.'

'Well, that is the way things happen,' sympathized Aunty, 'Remember my grandson, Sigdi? He worked hard all his life. Even rose to become the Head Clerk. How do you think his company rewarded him for all his loyalty and hard work? They gave his job to the boss' son.'

Helo was shocked that such things could happen. He told her how they had deprived him of his horse also and how worried he was about the animal.

'Life is not fair and anyone who thinks otherwise is a fool,' Aunty admonished Helo, 'It is no use crying over Goumuz. No one is going to help you. Don't behave like a fool. Start thinking of how you are going to spend the long harsh winter. There is a storm predicted for tonight. Do you remember how cold it gets after that?'

'How could I forget. It was on just such a night that my Goumuz was born in a warm stable,' said Helo sadly.

The Aunty went off in a huff. All her advice had been in vain. Helo would never learn.

Brooding thus over his fate, Helo returned to the stable where he lived and once had shared with his horse. The stench from the manure was unbearable, but it did not seem to bother Helo.

'If only I could see Goumuz once,' he thought, 'I would die a happy man.'

Every day, he would walk through the town hoping to catch a glimpse of his beloved horse. He asked the townspeople if they had seen him, but no one was able to tell him where his horse was. One day he managed to find out where the young man from Balough lived. Helo walked many miles to his house, in the hope of seeing Goumuz there. When he came near the house, he saw a horse lying on the ground and a large man beating it with a big stick. He knew it was Goumuz. He ran forward and grabbed the man's hand to stop him beating the poor beast.

'You cruel man. Why are you beating my Goumuz so mercilessly?' he shouted.

'This nag is good for nothing. He is the most miserable excuse for a horse that I have ever seen,' the man with the stick shouted back angrily, 'He does no work and does not listen to my commands. He refuses to eat and refuses to pull the cart. Because of this creature I have lost my job. This miserable horse deserves to die.' With that the man gave Goumuz a couple of hard blows.

Helo threw himself in front of the horse and put his arms around it's neck.

'Goumuz, my child! What has this man done to you?' he cried.

On hearing his beloved master's voice Goumuz opened his eyes and looked at him adoringly. Tears streamed down Helo's face as he sat next to the animal. He stroked and kissed it as if it were his child and implored the heavens to make it better. Goumuz opened his eyes and they looked at each other for a long time. Then the horse breathed his last.

'Get out of my sight. Take this useless corpse with you,' shouted the man from Balough.

Helo lifted Goumuz on his shoulders and despite the heavy load, walked away with it.

'My dear, dear Goumuz, what irony! Once I rode you and now you are riding me. What a twist of fate!'

The story that you are about to read comes from Persian mythology. The name of the story has been forgotten with time, so I have decided to call it Samad, after the name of the hero of the tale.

This was the time when the cruel and greedy King, Ghafar Shah, ruled over a vast empire. He was rich beyond imagination and owned vast quantities of precious jewels. Yet he was never satisfied and would never miss an opportunity to increase his wealth, even if it meant resorting to unjust and unfair means.

He had two daughters, both of whom were unmarried. The elder daughter, Nargis, was plain looking and not very clever. The younger daughter, whose name was Farangis, on the other hand, was very beautiful and intelligent. All the eligible men in the kingdom dreamt of marrying her. But as per tradition, the elder sister had to get married first, only then could any proposal be entertained for the younger one. Since there were no suitors for Nargis, all these young men had to defer their aspirations and wait patiently. This situation did not make the King happy. He had no son to succeed him and had hoped that one of his daughters would marry a mature and intelligent young man, whom he could nominate as his heir.

Now the King had a wazir, who was just as greedy and scheming as his master. He had a young son who he wished some day would be able to marry Farangis and be declared the heir to the throne. He would spend long hours scheming of ways to get Nargis married to some unintelligent lazy man, so that his own son would seem more suitable in comparison and become the obvious choice of the King to succeed him. So far all his schemes had failed. One day he was strolling with the King in the garden. It was evident that the King was troubled.

'What's bothering you, My Lord?' asked the Wazir, in a concerned voice.

'My friend, I need your help. I do not have an heir and I am getting on in years. If my daughters were married at least I could nominate one of their husbands or maybe even a grandson, as my successor. Help me find suitable husbands for my daughters,' replied the King. He then added, 'Remember, Nargis is to be wed first.'

The Wazir was delighted that the King had taken him into confidence.

The following morning he went to the King and declared, 'Your Majesty, I have a brilliant plan. Let us announce throughout the kingdom that you will give your older daughter's hand in marriage to the person who will stand up before the court and tell the most outrageous lie.'

The King, who by now was really desperate, agreed to this proposal, 'Why, that is an excellent idea. Let the announcement be made in the entire kingdom and beyond, that I will give my older daughter's hand in

marriage to the person who proves himself to be the biggest liar in the kingdom.'

The news of the challenge spread far and wide. But unfortunately for the King, his reputation of being cruel and unfair made the people think that this was perhaps some sort of trap. They were afraid of what the King might do to them if they failed. There was no response from anyone in the kingdom.

However, in a small town, in a remote part of the kingdom, lived a man called Ahmed-the-dyer. He was so named because he was an expert dyer. People would come from far and wide, to have their silk and cotton cloth dyed by him. His jars of dye were precious to him. But in spite of his skill, Ahmed remained very poor. He had a wife and a son, Samad, to support and had to work hard to earn his meager income. Soon his health began to fail and because he had no money for proper treatment, Ahmed soon died.

The King had decreed that whenever a husband or a wife died, the spouse of the dead person was to be incarcerated in the burial caves, along with the body of the deceased. This was a cruel custom and many unfortunate people had lost their lives, because none could escape from those dreadful caves. Ahmed's wife was 'buried' with him and Samad was left all alone in the world. He was a young lad of eighteen and was determined to change his life.

Samad heard of the King's announcement and decided that since he had nothing to lose, he might as well try his luck in the court. He thought, 'My father used to often reprimand me for fabricating stories and my friends tell me I am quite good at it. Why not put this skill to some use!' So he went to the royal court and announced his intentions before the King,

'My Lord, I will weave a fascinating tale for you and you be the judge if it is the biggest lie you have heard or not.'

The King was relieved that someone had responded to his proclamation and asked Samad to proceed.

Samad began his 'lie' with words of compliments for the King and then commenced his narrative. 'Sire, my father was the wealthiest man in this kingdom. Every summer we would leave our mansion in the plains and go far away to our grand house on the highest mountain to escape the heat. One summer we made our usual journey and when we reached our house we discovered that we had forgotten to bring our chickens with us. You see, my father always made sure that we were well provided for by way of food. By chance we happened to look down into the plains below and to our amazement, we saw that it had turned white under what appeared to be a blanket of snow. Now we all know that it cannot possibly snow in summer, so we climbed down the mountain to see what it was that had made the plains white. When we reached the bottom we saw that one of the chickens we had left behind had laid so many eggs, that the entire village was covered with them. I tell you, your Majesty, it was a sight to behold.'

The courtiers were fascinated with the 'lie' and were very impressed at Samad's obvious ability to spin a tall tale. But the King was skeptical. He was still uncertain and said to Samad, 'You have made up an interesting story, but I would like to hear more. So come back tomorrow and we will see.'

Samad had no choice but to do as he had been told. The next day he again presented himself in the royal court. The King once again ordered Samad to proceed, and so he continued his tale.

'Sire, do you remember that yesterday I told you that one of our chickens had covered the entire plains with her eggs. Well my father collected all these eggs and had them transported on the backs of hundreds of bullocks, camels and donkeys to the mill where wheat is ground into flour. Do you know what happened when the miller started to grind these eggs? Out popped millions of roosters and hens. It really was a sight to see. Hundreds of thousands of roosters and hens clucking around.'

The entire court was very amused and said to the King, 'Your Majesty, he certainly is a very talented liar. You must accept him as your son-in-law.'

The King, however, was still not impressed.

'Why are all of you so quick to take his side? Do you want me to give up my daughter to the first liar that comes along?'

He seemed to overlook the fact that nobody else had turned up and this contender was the only one who met the condition he himself had laid down.

'Come back tomorrow and we will test you again,' the King told Samad.

Secretly the king hatched a plan, 'I will order him to tell us an even more spectacular story and whatever he says I will insist that it is true. This will disqualify him.' He also ordered his courtiers to proclaim that Samad's story was true, no matter what he said.

So Samad returned the next morning to the court. This time, however, he did not come empty-handed. He had brought one of his father's jars of dye on the back of a horse.

The King was perplexed. 'Why have you brought this monstrosity into the palace?' he asked Samad.

'Sire, this humble jar is very essential to the story I am about to relate,' explained Samad.

'All right get on with it,' ordered the King.

Samad began his story from where he had left off. 'Your Lordship surely remembers the millions of eggs that turned into hens and roosters? Well my father then sent word all around that he had hundreds and thousands of fowl to sell and he was going to offer them at very cheap rates. All the merchants came from far and wide, with carts laden with gold, silver and precious jewels, to buy the roosters and hens. Soon, my father had managed to sell all his stock. He made enough gold and silver to fill forty jars, each like the one you see on this horse's back. After he filled the jars, he brought them to the court of your father, 'Your Majesty,' he said addressing your father, 'This is a loan which I am honoured to offer to you' My father was the richest man in the kingdom, so he was the first one your father approached for help at that time, when the treasury was empty and the country on the brink of disaster. Your father graciously accepted the loan and the country was saved. Now all I ask you, My Lord, is to return the loan your father took.'

The story ended. All the courtiers nodded their heads in agreement, 'The story is true. The King must return the loan.'

Needless to say, the King lost his royal temper. Samad had outwitted him. If he agreed that the story was true he would have to give Samad forty jars filled with gold, silver and jewels. The thought really upset him.

'Shut up all of you. Can't you see that this is the biggest lie ever told? I do not owe him any money.'

Samad interjected, 'Your Honour, if this is a lie then you must give me your daughter's hand in marriage, according to your own proclamation.'

The King thought, 'Well, no one wants to marry Nargis anyway. So I might as well give her away, rather than my wealth.' Aloud he declared, 'Let the young man be wed to my beloved daughter Nargis.'

The Wazir was delighted that his plan to marry off Nargis had worked and now the field was clear to get his son wedded to the lovely Farangis. So Samad and the King's elder daughter were married, and the couple went back to Samad's dwelling far away in the remote town. Nargis was not used to any hardship. All her life she had been waited on by an army of servants. She was unable to cope with life as a commoner and soon fell ill and died. According to the custom of the land, Samad was escorted to the burial cave along with his dead wife. There he was left with some food, water and candles, as the tradition demanded.

Although genuinely grieving for Nargis, whom he had grown to love, Samad was determined not to die. So he braced himself to somehow survive the days ahead in this terrible place. The smell of corpses was overwhelming and the sight of so many dead bodies horrified him. But Samad gritted his teeth, 'I am going to endure and survive. I am going to prove to the king that this custom is cruel and meaningless.' He walked as far into the caves as he could and found a niche where the smell was not so powerful and there he made himself a small shelter. Every few days he would walk to the entrance of the cave to collect the food left there by the villagers. He made sure he kept out of the way of the living brought in with the dead. He secretly watched them die within days, having lost all hope. Every burial brought fresh offerings, which Samad would collect for himself.

A few weeks after Nargis' death, the Wazir found an opportune moment to approach the King. 'Your Majesty, I am devastated by the death of your beloved daughter. I fully share your sorrow.' The King was moved by the Wazir's words who continued, 'I want to lighten some of your burden. Please consider my son as your own. Please give him the honour of marrying your beloved Farangis.'

The King was overjoyed, 'I am grateful to you, dear friend. You have taken a load off my mind. Order the festivities to begin immediately.'

There was a great deal of activity throughout the kingdom in preparation for the grand wedding. Rice was imported from Damascus, cooking oil from

Kurdistan, and sheep and goats from Afghanistan for the feast. Exotic dishes were prepared for the wedding celebrations, which were to last for forty days. Many contests were organized; swordsmen and acrobats demonstrated their skills. On the final day there was an archery contest. The important guests were watching from a pavilion. Unfortunately, an arrow missed its target and hit the bridegroom right through his heart and he died instantly. The wedding celebrations turned into chaos. Everywhere there were people crying and mourning. People bemoaned the fate of poor Farangis, who would have to be buried in the caves with her husband. But none could stop this as it was the custom of the land, decreed by the King himself. The mourners took the dead body of the bridegroom along with the beautiful, newly-wed Farangis, and shut her in those fearful caves. They also left behind her wedding robe, which was encrusted with jewels, as well as the traditional food and candles. Samad watched the entire spectacle from the darkness. He recognized Farangis at once.

When the funeral party left after sealing the mouth of the cave, Samad softly called out to the princess, 'Farangis don't be afraid. I am Samad, your dead sister's husband. I have been living here among the dead for several months. Please do not be afraid.'

After overcoming her initial shock, Farangis realized that she was not alone. 'No! No I am not afraid. But please come closer so I can see you,' she answered, though still fearful.

'Grab hold of this stick and I will guide you to a place where I have some light,' Samad said extending a pole to her. Farangis held the pole and walked slowly, terrified at the dead bodies all around her.

'Don't be afraid. I am here to protect you,' Samad reassured her. He led her to the corner he had cleared for himself. You too have become a victim of the unjust system of our country.'

'But you have survived. Are there any more of us here?' asked the princess.

Sadly Samad shook his head, 'It is not easy to live among the dead. Do you think you can manage?'

'Yes, I can,' answered the brave Farangis. Samad was pleased to have found a companion.

The two continued to live in the cave, hidden away from the sight of the living. There was no way they could leave, as the entrance was always sealed after a fresh burial. The only time they would venture to the mouth of the cave was when they needed fresh supplies. One day while searching through the catacombs, Samad spotted a small dog sniffing around. 'How did a dog get into the cave? There must be another opening,' he said to himself, 'I will follow the dog. It will surely lead me to it.' Samad followed the dog and sure enough, he discovered a small fissure in the roof of one corner of a tunnel.

'Fresh air,' he cried and was exultant. Quickly he ran to get Farangis, who was also overjoyed at the discovery. For a long time they breathed the fresh air. Farangis then said, 'Samad, maybe if we crawled up

we might be able to get out through this opening.
Let's try.'

Samad went first, sliding on his belly and managed
to squeeze himself through. Farangis followed. Once
they were outside, they hugged each other in delight.
Then the reality of their situation dawned on them.
They could not afford to let anyone see them, because
to escape from the caves of death was a violation of
the law of the land, and they would be put to death
immediately. Reluctantly, they returned to the cave to
think up of some plan, which would enable them to
leave this Godforsaken place forever.

Remember the jewel encrusted gown, which had
been left in the cave with Farangis. With the gems
from this gown, Samad and Farangis knew that they
would have enough money to change their identities
and start a new life. However, they would have to
look for the right opportunity to do this, as they did
not want to spend the rest of their lives looking over
their shoulders to make sure nobody recognized them.
They continued to stay in the cave, venturing out only
at night to breathe in the fresh air and to look at the
stars, twinkling brightly above. They spent many
evenings looking at the sea, which was near the caves.
Many times they would see ships sailing by and
wished that somehow they could sail away in one of
them.

One evening when they went out they found a ship
had run aground and was wedged between some rocks.
There was no sign of life aboard. Samad and Farangis
watched the ship swaying with the waves for a long

time. No one appeared on its decks. There seemed to be absolutely no sign of life. So they decided to have a closer look. With the driftwood strewn along the beach they made a small raft, and tested it to see if it was seaworthy. When they were satisfied it could take their weight, they rowed over to the ship and boarded it cautiously. They looked in every nook and corner of the ship. It seemed there were no survivors on board. In the hold they stumbled across some dead bodies and there they saw some large trunks. On opening these they saw great quantities of gold, silver and gems stashed in them.

In the captain's cabin they found a log book. This gave them a clue to what had happened. Apparently the ship had sailed from Cairo, and either the crew had lost all their supplies in a storm and died of starvation or they had killed each other over the treasure. Whatever tragedy had befallen the ship, Samad and Farangis realized that this was the kind of opportunity they had been waiting for.

They meticulously recorded every detail of the treasure and sent this list to the King. In the letter they wrote, 'Your Majesty, my wife and I are merchants from Egypt. We have been shipwrecked on your shores and have lost all our crew. We were on our way to do business in your country. We will request you to kindly assist us in towing our ship to port. For your help we will repay you with the treasure on board.'

When the king received this letter mentioning gold and silver, his eyes lit up, and at once he despatched a contingent to help the 'merchants'. Soon all the treasure was transferred to the royal palace. After a few days Samad and Farangis again wrote to the King, 'Sire, we are about to leave your fair country. If you may be so kind as to grant us an audience, we will be highly obliged.' The King readily agreed.

When they were presented before the King, Farangis placed a large chest in front of the king as a gesture of respect, 'This is a humble gift for you, My Lord.'

The King was delighted at the thought of more gifts. But when he opened the chest his face fell. Inside were the jewels from the royal wedding robe, as well as the jewels left with the bridegroom. The King was furious.

'What is the meaning of this? Who are you?' he screamed.

Farangis lifted the veil from her face, 'It is me, your daughter Farangis, whom you left in the cave to die according to your cruel custom.'

The King was too stunned to speak.

Then Samad spoke, 'You are a cruel King. You have caused so many needless deaths in the name of custom and tradition, so that you could keep your hold over the people of this country. You do not deserve to be a ruler.'

The King recognized Samad at once. 'This can't be happening! It's a nightmare!' he shrieked in a loud voice, 'There is no way in which people can come back from the dead.' His heart was pounding and he was going red in the face. Suddenly he slumped forward and died. The shock had been too much for him.

Farangis did not feel any sorrow at the death of her father. Samad was at once proclaimed the King, as the late ruler had always declared that one of his sons-in-law was to be the heir to the throne. Farangis and Samad were officially wed. Together they ruled the kingdom justly and fairly. Needless to say, one of their first acts was to repeal the cruel law of burying the living, bereaved spouse with the dead. Also the wazir was summarily dismissed. There was great rejoicing in the kingdom. The people now had a benevolent King and Queen, who reigned in peace and happiness.

THE NAGGING HUSBAND

This is an amusing story, which I heard many years ago. It is about a time when modern conveniences were not available and everything had to be done manually. In those days there was strict division of labour between men and women and it was inconceivable to even think of exchanging roles. Also work such as cooking, stitching or embroidery had not yet begun to be done on a commercial level, where men were involved. Surprisingly though, the theme of the story remains as true today as it was in those days.

There was a man who worked all day in the fields. Every evening when he returned home from a hard day's work he would nag his wife.

'You lazy woman, all day I toil in the field while you sit at home and relax, and have a good time. I really envy you!'

This would happen every single day and the wife would bear it with great patience. One day, however, she decided to teach him a lesson. She told him, 'Today I will go and work in the fields, while you do the housework.'

The husband was delighted at the suggestion. 'Oho! I'm going to do all the easy tasks and relax at home, while she finds out how hard I work,' he thought.

So the next morning the wife went off to the fields. Before leaving she said to him, 'I will be back at

sunset. In the meantime please do two things. I need food when I get back, make sure you have a meal ready. Since today is Saturday I usually cook groats. So prepare that dish and churn some butter to go with it. Also, the cow has been locked up in the shed for a long time, make sure it is let out to graze on the fresh grass.'

'How difficult can all this be?' thought the husband and sat down with his pipe to relax. After resting a while he went to the well and drew up some water to cook the groats in. He lit the fire and placed the pot with the groats over it to boil, stirring it continuously so that it did not stick to the bottom of the pot. Unfortunately for him he had completely forgotten about the cow, who started bellowing loudly as it wanted to be let out. The husband thought that if he left the pot to attend to the cow, the groats would stick to the bottom. So he put in more water. The water overflowed and put out the fire. When he tried to re-ignite the wood it would not burn, as it had become wet. So he went to look for some dry sticks to re-kindle the fire.

In the meantime, the cow was getting more and more impatient and was creating enough noise to bring the house down.

'By the time I take the cow outside to graze and bring it back, the groats will be burnt to cinders,' he thought. 'Why don't I take the cow to the basement and tie it up there. There is plenty of hay and straw for it to eat down there.'

So he took the cow to the basement, tied it there with a piece of rope, and returned to the kitchen. Then he remembered that he had not yet churned the butter. He took out the butter-beater, put in some fresh milk and started churning to separate the butter from the cream. This was hard work, and by now he was beginning to feel thirsty. He went into the storeroom to help himself to a jug full of the delicious sherbet that his wife made from vinegar, rose water, lemon and syrup, and stored in a drum.

But when he went into the storeroom he forgot to close the kitchen door, and a goat and her kids entered the kitchen, and ran over the butter-beater causing it to spill. When the man returned to the kitchen he found it in a mess with butter and cream spilled all over. Then it occurred to the husband that after taking the sherbet from the big drum, he might have forgotten to close the tap. So he hit the goats to get rid of them and hurt one of them badly. He had to drag the injured goat outside, and then quickly rush to the storeroom to check on the syrup. Sure enough, he had left the tap open and all the tasty syrup that his wife had made for winter was drained to the ground. What a waste!

Then an awful smell started coming from the kitchen. The groats had started to burn.

'Never mind,' thought the husband, 'I will mix it with some water and butter and it should taste all right.'

So he took the butter-beater and went to the well to clean it as well as draw some water for the groats. As luck would have it, he placed the beater on the edge of the well and accidentally knocked it over. The beater, which had been in his family for generations, was lost forever in the deep well.

The groats had burnt up, there was no butter and all the syrup had been spilt. There was nothing to eat and the place was in a terrible mess.

'There must be some butter in one of the big drums in the storeroom. Let me look,' said the husband to himself, by now thoroughly frazzled.

In the storeroom he bent over a large drum to see if there was any butter inside, and slipped and fell in. The indignity of it all! Whatever was he to do now? He would probably suffocate in here and no one would ever rescue him!

Thus, the day passed and evening set over the house. The wife returned from the field after a hard day's work, to find everything in her neat home turned upside down. The floor was covered with butter and cream, and everywhere, there was the strong smell of burnt groats. She was taken aback, but quickly recovered.

'Where in the world is my husband? I hope he's all right,' she worried.

She called out to him, but there was no answer. Meanwhile, the cow, realizing that its mistress was home, started mooing as loudly as it could. The wife rushed down to the basement, from where the sound seemed to be coming. The husband had tied the rope around the cow's neck so tight, that its eyes were popping out and if she had been any later, it would surely have departed for a heavenly abode. She quickly untied the cow.

'Where are you, husband?' she called out. Still there was no answer.

The wife then noticed that the door of the storeroom was ajar. She went in and saw her husband's legs sticking out from the drum. So this was where her quixotic husband had ended up.

'Get me out of here, or I'll suffocate. Please hurry,' whimpered the husband.

The wife hurriedly pulled him out. She did not say a word to him about the mess he had made, rather, she helped him get cleaned up. Then she handed him his pipe and told him to relax, while she cooked some food for them. Together they ate freshly-made, delicious groats with butter.

Never again did the husband nag his wife. He had learnt a valuable lesson in humility at least.

This story will acquaint you with the social, moral and family values that existed in Dubai in the 1950s. Mona is the protagonist of this tale, and it was through her that I realized the importance of the role of Bibia, who herself was just a young seventeen-year old housewife, and the contribution she made in making the lives of the young girls and women around her, rich and meaningful. She extended her hand in friendship to all and indeed made a lasting contribution to the society and culture of Dubai. Even today there is hardly any family from those early days in Dubai, whose lives were not touched in some way by Bibia.

'**G**et ready, Mona, and go at once. Bibia can't wait all day for you lazy girls to get together. As it is, she generously gives so much of her time. If you don't benefit from this you have only yourselves to blame, ordered her mother, anxious to get Mona on her way.

Bibia was a newly married bride, living with her in-laws' extended family in one of the Bastaki houses in Dubai, in the early fifties. Unlike women in those days, she had been educated abroad and wanted the women of the local community to benefit from her knowledge. In those days, women required as much help as they could get and were very keen to learn all kinds of skills. The girls and young mothers of the

locality had only received rudimentary education, learning to read the Holy Quran, as well as reading and writing in Arabic. They often felt the need to study a second language like English, which was an important language and in fact it was a necessity to know it.

Bibia also taught knitting, crochet and the traditional craft of *khoos-doozi*, in which she excelled. In *khoos-doozi* strands of gold, silver and a coloured wire are interwoven and embroidered on plain or decorated net material. Normally no needle is used in creating these beautiful and intricate designs. Ladies wear such embellished fabrics as headscarves, or *shelas* as we called them. Black and white were the usual colours. Young girls, especially those who were of marriageable age, had to learn hand and machine embroidery, as well as other arts and crafts. Thus Bibia's tuition was a great boon. Apart from this, she offered free classes in English, which were in great demand. She conducted separate classes for teenage girls and this was a blessing in those days of more strict segregation.

Mona was a young daughter of one of the neighbouring households. She was to be married in a year's time. She had been betrothed for two years and now both the families were in the final stages of completing the preparations for the marriage. Her mother Fatima, who had never been able to improve her own education or skills, was keen that her daughters should have every opportunity to develop their talents.

'Mona, what excitement! This evening we are all going on a picnic to *Konar-e-Agha*. You better go to Bibia and come back soon to help make the arrangement for the trip.'

'*Hader,* Mama,' she replied as she ran happily to Sheikh Muhammed Sharif's house, which was an impressive double-storied Bastaki house with several wind towers. Bibia lived in one wing of the top floor.

Most of the ancient houses in the Bastakia area looked the same except for their varied sizes and were built according to the traditional design of Lingah and Bastak. The first such houses were those of Haji Abdul Qadir Abbas, Farooq, Haji Ahmed Arshi, Bookhash and several others. All these were located near the sea, on the Dubai creek side from where the loading and unloading of boats and barges were visible. Sheikh Muhammed Sharif's house is one of the few of these old, imposing residences still standing proudly. It bears testimony to the simple and sincere values of those bygone days. Sheikh Muhammed Sharif was a rare personality, well known and respected by the community. In addition he was a legal adviser and close compatriot of the late ruler, Sheikh Rashid Bin Saeed Al Maktoum.

Unfortunately, many of the old houses have been demolished over a period of time and modern buildings have come up. However, some old houses have been preserved and major restoration work is now underway. This is a source of delight to the old-timers, who have been born and bred under the majestic 'Lingah style wind towers of Dubai' and regard them with nostalgia.

Mona returned home from her classes at Bibia's and found the entire household in a state of great excitement. Women had few opportunities to go out in those days, so the idea of a picnic filled them with delight. *Konar-e-Agha*, was a sacred tree in Bur Dubai, near the old fort that now houses the Dubai museum. The story goes that a devout, elderly man, by the name of Sayyed Muhammed Omar, had traveled from Ras Al Khaimah, and being quite exhausted, sat on a stone to rest and pray. He poured water for his '*vodhoo*' (ablutions) and soon thereafter, a huge tree grew on the spot. This was indeed a miracle, as in those days nothing much grew in the Emirates, with the exception of some date palms and *loor*, which is a huge tree with small edible fig-like red fruit, that grows wild in the desert. People from far and wide, Sharjah, Ajman, Fujairah and even as distant as Abu Dhabi, used to come and pray and seek divine benedictions under this imposing tree. If their wishes were fulfilled, goats were sacrificed and there were great celebrations. Young girls often tied green handkerchiefs to the branches and wished for good husbands, and untied them after they were wed.

Since they were going there, Mona decided to wish quietly and tie something on the tree, and keep it hidden from sight. Her wish was somehow to meet her fiancé.

Abdullah, her betrothed, was studying in Bombay and had been gone for a long time. Boys were usually sent abroad for higher education for several years. Sometimes, in their absence and without consulting them, the elders of the family would decide to betroth them with one of their cousins, and they would be informed of the decision later. Out of respect for their elders, the grooms-to-be seldom raised any objections. Moreover, girls never had anything to say in the matter whatsoever, nor did they dare to. They would just remain at home and wait for their fiance to return. When the boy's education was complete, then the betrothed were wed in an elaborate ceremony. Thus, the boy would have had the opportunity to see more of the world, get properly educated and return intellectually enriched with a sense of accomplishment; while nothing much changed in the girls' lives. He was the breadwinner, the master, the all-knowing, while she was the submissive, passive partner with no ambition and no entity. 'What need has she to broaden her horizon?' 'In any case what can we see of the world in one lifetime?' were the oft-repeated phrases whenever the question of education for girls were raised. In those days, very few girls managed to get a proper education. Thus, Bibia was a beacon of light in this environment.

Another source of excitement for the ladies of that period, was to go to the beach. Usually they were allowed to go on this outing only three times in a year. In summer, during the full moon, on the thirteenth, fourteenth, and fifteenth of the month, women would get together for this excursion. What a thrill it used to be for them. They would go in a large

group, carrying their mats, teapots and flasks. *Tokhma,*
borki, the dried up roasted seeds of watermelon and
other nuts were eaten with great relish and formed an
integral part of the picnic menu, as was *kondrok,* a
kind of local chewing gum. They would dip in the
water fully dressed and come out drenched. Then they
would sit together on the mats, singing, joking and
gossiping. When it was time to return, they would put
on their *abayas* and come home elated and refreshed.
Such was the simple and segregated life of the women.

A few days later it seemed as though the wish Mona
made under the *Konar-e-Agha* was granted. Her
younger sister, Fauty, came in all excited.

'Guess what Mona! Abdullah was in the *Majlis* with
the men today,' she announced.

Mona's heart soared with joy. At last she would be
able to communicate with her betrothed.

'Fauty are you sure you saw him?' She wanted to
be certain.

'Yes, yes,' replied her sister, 'I spoke to him myself.'

'Fauty, my good sister, I will place a letter for him
in the vegetable basket. Please, please give it to him,'
Mona pleaded with her.

The vegetable basket was the safest place for such a
note. People would think it was just a shopping list.
As most families lived on the upper floors, these
baskets were lowered with the list and the vendor
would accordingly put the vegetables in the basket,
which would then be hauled up. So it was, that Mona
lowered the basket with her letter addressed to
Abdullah, and Fauty collected it from the ground floor

and delivered it to him. Thanks to Bibia, Mona knew how to write both in English as well as Arabic. This was no ordinary accomplishment for a girl in those times, and Abdullah was most impressed by his bride-to-be. The reply was also put in the basket and Mona hauled it up.

The couple continued to communicate with each other in this clandestine manner for a couple of months. No one suspected that it was not only vegetables going up and down in the basket. There was no other means of communication in those days of strict segregation and this was a source of great happiness and comfort to the couple.

'I must remember to untie the handkerchief. I have been blessed beyond expectations,' she vowed.

Her heart sang with joy. Soon they would be married.

So began the most important activity of women in those days—preparation for a wedding. These began with several women, known as a *zan-gardoon*, getting together to deliver the invitations to the wedding. Groups of women, sometimes as many as twenty or thirty, would go on foot, or use the *abra* if they were going to Diera, in hot or cold weather. The group would carry parcels of cardamoms and *noql* (a kind of sweet) in green, embroidered handkerchiefs and a spokeswoman would deliver these, alongwith the invitation. There were no lists or cards. It seems there was so much grace and sincerity in this more personalized method and it constituted an integral part of the marriage customs. The community tried to make sure that no two weddings would occur on the same date. Each tried to accommodate the other in every way they could and tried to make both celebrations a success. Even today, some families do not send cards, but personally go in cars or buses to invite the guests.

Rice cleaning was another ritual when all the women of the family and neighborhood would gather in the bride's house. Many kilos of rice would be picked and cleaned, accompanied with a great deal of singing and dancing. Henna cleaning and soaking was also a part of the preparations, that all would join in. The wedding rituals lasted for more than a month, in both the bride's and the groom's house.

Then there was the all-important task of the bride's makeup on the day of the wedding. The *mashatas* did the makeup and this was a lengthy process. It usually took several hours and included sequins, fruit, and glue. Every step in the makeup was traditional and had to be followed meticulously.

The bride would wear a large number of traditional gold jewellery. Some of this would be new and some would be handed down from generations as heirlooms. The gold embroidered bridal dress was completely hand crafted and took months to prepare. Nothing was available ready-made. In fact the trousseau could take as much as two years to complete.

However, in the period that Mona was married, a few somewhat contemporary customs had been adopted, and one day was reserved for the bride to be dressed in modern clothes. The influence of the subcontinent could be discerned in this variation, as many brides would opt to wear *saris*. This was the occasion when Bibia's services were utilized. All the brides expected that Bibia would do their hair and makeup. There were no salons in those days. In any case, it was unheard of for the bride to go out of the house during the wedding festivities. Mona, like so many other brides of Dubai, was grateful to have an accomplished woman like Bibia in their midst, who would come to their house and make them look very modern and beautiful. They would accept everything Bibia did as the last word in fashion. Bibia cut Mona's hair and curled it up. She expertly applied makeup and Mona had never looked as beautiful as she did for the *fashti* or 'the day when the bride could keep her eyes open and look at people around her.' Of course, there would only be women present and she was still not expected to talk or laugh.

Then there was the Henna ceremony. The bride was completely covered, except for her hands and feet, where Henna was applied. On *dozi* night, the bride was fully covered but one could catch a glimpse of her face. Close friends and relatives stayed with the bride and sang and danced through the night. They breakfasted on *halwa*, homemade mava bread, beans, honey and several other delicacies and then went home to sleep. Refreshed after sleeping all day, they would resume the singing and dancing at night. Whereas nowadays, a large part of the festivities have been curtailed and wedding receptions normally take place in hotels, still the expenses now are many times more than in those days. Then, everything was done at home.

The groom does not receive the attention the bride gets. His dress on that all-important day is a *dishdash* and *aba*. The focus is entirely on the bride and most of the functions and rituals centre around her. Mona too, went through the entire gamut of tradition when she was married to Abdullah.

Afterwards, Mona did not stop attending Bibia's classes. Abdullah was a progressive person and wanted her to have a good command over English. Soon, however, she needed Bibia's help again, to help her through her pregnancy. In those days there was no concept of 'pre' or post-natal care. There were only one or two hospitals and they were located quite some distance away. Bibia was often seen accompanying women, sometimes even in a serious condition, to the hospital, in an *abra* across to Diera. From there they would usually take a truck to go to Kuwait Hospital, where there were some good doctors. The most common practice was that midwives delivered the babies at home. Even here Bibia was often called, to supervise the birth and make sure that everything was done under hygienic conditions.

Under such conditions of almost primitive healthcare for women, the UAE Women's Society was formed. Doreen Chapman was one of the founding members. She has remained active till today. She recalls that in 1955, there was only one cemented building at the site of Al Maktoum Hospital, which catered to the medical needs of the entire area. There was only one doctor, Dermond McCaully. Dr McCaully would often seek Bibia's help. Together with Khadija Abbas they arranged for sheets, nappies, blankets, and clothes for the hospital. They even provided assistance in childcare. Today Bibia and Khadija continue to be the President and Treasurer of the Society respectively. In those days the Society's weekly meeting would be held either at Bibia's house, or the British embassy. The ruler of Dubai H.H. Sheikh Rashid Bin Saeed Al Maktoum, and the ladies of the royal family, supported the Society and helped build the premises, where it is now housed. It is the centre for all social and cultural activities of the members of the Society.

Today's Dubai is a modern city, which can easily boast of being at par with any city of the western world. The rapid growth of its infrastructure has been phenomenal. Yet the inhabitants have not forgotten their traditional Islamic values. They continue to abide by them, while simultaneously reaping the benefits of technological advancements. The museums and heritage centres, with their artifacts, keep the past alive. The people, as indeed the rulers, keep the spiritual richness of their heritage intact as a part of their daily lives.

SHANKAR THE FORTUNE-TELLER

The story of Shankar was particularly amusing for me, as I too, dabble in fortune-telling, particularly palmistry. I have read extensively on the subject and in following this vocation I have met a wide number of people, from all walks of life. Thus, not only have I increased my knowledge in this field, but also have gained some insight into the human psyche. I use this skill to entertain my friends and many actually believe that I have powers to look into the future. Often I have been the fortune-teller at garden parties held to raise funds for charity and have enjoyed myself thoroughly on these occasions. I think I even succeeded in making some people very happy, just like Shankar.

Shankar was a peasant who lived in a village with his wife. He tilled the land and made a fairly decent earning from it. However, unlike the other peasants in his village, Shankar was literate. He was completely self-taught. In fact, he was so interested in reading and improving himself, that he would often spend his free time reading words from the dictionary. He also possessed the gift of the gab, and was able to easily convince the simple villagers of his point of view in any dispute that arose among them. People trusted him and came to him to discuss their problems. They would also consult him for selecting auspicious dates for weddings and laying foundations of new

houses. Looking at him one couldn't imagine that he was so intelligent and educated. He had beady eyes, flaring nostrils, a big mouth and an even bigger stomach. In fact he so resembled a frog, that his friends lovingly called him 'froggy'.

Shankar's wife, whom he loved dearly, had an arthritic leg, which gave her a lot of trouble. Shankar looked after her with great care and tenderness. However, in the course of time he noticed that sometimes when it was going to rain, the pain in her leg would become unbearable. At other times when the weather turned out to be dry, she felt more comfortable. Thus Shankar found he could predict whether it would rain or not by the degree of pain his wife was feeling in her arthritic leg. If the pain was slight, Shankar knew it would be overcast and if the pain was bad, he knew it would rain. The system never failed.

One day, the sun was shining brightly and the sky was a deep blue with no clouds in sight. But his wife's leg had been giving her a lot of trouble, so Shankar put on his raincoat and went off to the fields to work. When the other villagers saw him they taunted him.

'Old man! Have you gone out of your mind. There is no sign of rain and you are wearing a raincoat. Are you all right?'

'No. Nothing is wrong with me. But it is going to rain and I for one do not want to get wet,' Shankar retorted.

Sure enough, after a little while the sky became overcast and it started to pour. Needless to say everyone was drenched and Shankar had the last laugh.

Another morning, Shankar looked up at the sky and it was overcast. However, when he asked his wife if her leg hurt, she replied, 'No, it is better than yesterday.' Shankar knew it would be a fine day. So he laid aside his raincoat and umbrella and walked to the fields. When his neighbors saw him, they wondered why he was dressed for a sunny day when the sky was so cloudy.

'It's not going to rain today,' Shankar announced with supreme confidence; and it remained dry all day.

Now the neighbors really began to believe that he was able to predict the weather and their admiration for him increased. They began consulting him in this regard. Soon, they even started consulting him about the weather before embarking on a journey. Of course, they did not know that before making his prediction, he would go inside and ask his wife how she felt.

One day, his daughter-in-law came in very agitated and said, 'Father, I have lost my gold earring and cannot find it anywhere. Please use your powers to help me.'

Shankar thought for a while then said to her, 'Go and look by the side of the well. You will find your earring wedged between the stones.'

The daughter-in-law took his advice and sure enough, she found her earring beside the well. Actually Shankar had simply used his logic to determine the most likely place the piece of jewellery may have fallen. He had noticed his daughter-in-law had been wearing it when she had gone to draw water from the well and when she returned she didn't have it on. However, the woman was amazed at his powers and thought he had some divine gift.

One of Shankar's friends had left the village to look for work in the city. His family, however, still lived in the village and they had not heard from him in a long time and were extremely worried. One day the friend's father came to Shankar.

'Can you tell me if my son is all right? When is he going to visit us? It's been such a long time,' he inquired.

Shankar knew that his friend's wife was due to have her baby any day now and his friend would never miss the celebrations that follow the birth of a child. He told the father that his son would be home soon. Sure enough the friend turned up a week later to celebrate the birth of his child.

By now everyone was convinced that Shankar was gifted with the ability to look into the future. He helped all those who came to him for advice, using his intelligence and logic. He never took any money for this service, and was willing to oblige all the villagers who came to him. Thus he became very popular and his fame began to spread far and wide.

Shankar was destined for bigger things. One day the Emperor lost a valuable pearl which was as big as an almond. He was very upset. He gathered all the officials of the palace, together with the grand wazir, and ordered them to find the pearl within three days.

'You know that I pay all of you handsomely and you all live lives of luxury and comfort. But if you cannot find my pearl *within three days*, all of you are going to end up living the rest of your lives in penury.'

He specifically addressed the Grand Wazir and made him responsible for the search. The wazir was the greatest beneficiary of the Emperor's largesse and stood to lose the most. Also, he felt particularly frightened because it was *he* who had stolen the pearl.

The grand wazir pretended to investigate the theft thoroughly. He conducted raids on the houses of citizens and questioned many people. All the time he knew perfectly well that they were innocent. He even consulted astrologers and diviners, whom he knew to be fakes. He happened to hear of Shankar. People described him as a gifted fellow who could unravel the mysteries of the unknown. The wazir did not want the Emperor to think that he had left any stone unturned in looking for the pearl. Personally, he scoffed at the idea of a poor villager being a diviner, but he went to Shankar's humble house in the village and summoned him outside.

'I have heard you have great powers and can help us find the precious gem that has been stolen from the Emperor's treasury.'

Shankar became very frightened and stammered, 'No! No Sire. I am but a poor illiterate peasant and know nothing about finding lost treasures. I have only been playing the fool with my friends.'

The wazir smiled, 'Well, you suit my purpose perfectly. If you were a true diviner I would not have bothered you. Just make sure you say something to the Emperor to convince him that you will be able to locate the gem.'

You see, the three days were almost over and the wazir wanted to find some pretext to prolong the search, in the hope that eventually the Emperor would give up and consider it a lost cause. He certainly had no intentions of returning the beautiful pearl which he had coveted for so long.

'If you are sure you can protect me from the wrath of the Emperor when I talk rubbish, then I will come with you,' said Shankar, knowing he had no other option but to obey the wazir. But why is he not interested in finding the pearl, I wonder?'

Shankar went inside to tell his wife that he was going away for a few days and she should not worry. Then he gave her very strange instructions.

'If I am not back in seven days, set fire to the haystack near the back of the house.'

He then bid her goodbye and consoled her as her legs hurt terribly. He then set off with the wazir. As they travelled he casually announced, 'Sire, its going to pour today.'

The wazir was not impressed. 'How can this fool think it's going to rain when it is a perfectly fine day. Well, it shows how silly he is. Fits into my scheme perfectly,' he thought. Outwardly he smiled indulgently at Shankar.

They had hardly gone a few furlongs when clouds gathered in the sky, there was a loud clap of thunder and it began to rain heavily. The wazir was taken aback and thought, 'If this man could predict the weather so perfectly, then maybe he *will* be able to divine where I have hidden the pearl?' However, he quickly regained his composure, '*All* these peasants know about the weather and such things. It doesn't prove that he can see into the unknown.'

When they reached the palace night had fallen and the wazir put him up in a room close to his house. He went home to rest. By this time Shankar's intuition was working overtime. He did not like the looks of the wazir. Also the remark that he had made about him suiting his purpose, especially if he did *not* have any genuine powers, convinced him the wazir had something to hide. It did not take long for an intelligent man like Shankar to deduce what it was.

Meanwhile, the wazir was beset with doubts. What if Shankar knew? He had after all predicted the rain accurately. If Shankar told the Emperor who the thief was, then surely he would find himself in the deepest dungeon for the rest of his life. The wazir was terrified as he thought of such a fate. His guilt made him feel more restless. He could not sleep.

Finally, he could not take it anymore and he ran to the room where Shankar was staying. He found him sitting in a trance-like state. Actually, Shankar knew that the wazir would come back to check on him and was deliberately performing this charade.

In a loud, almost delirious tone, he kept intoning, 'I must do my duty, God is the all-knowing. I must do my duty.'

The wazir was terror-stricken and went down on his knees. He begged Shankar's forgiveness and pleaded with him to save him from the wrath of the Emperor.

'Please Sire, have mercy on me. You already know that I have stolen the pearl and buried it beneath the palm tree in the royal garden. Save me, somehow,' he begged, 'I will make you rich beyond your dreams.'

So the cat was out of the bag. The grand wazir was nothing more than a petty thief and a coward to boot.

Shankar, still in a trance-like state, said to the wazir, 'I will ask God to forgive you. Now go, for I must meditate.'

The next day, the master took Shankar to the Emperor's court where he bowed and knelt. 'So,' the Emperor finally asked Shankar, 'Do you know anything at all about what has happened to this most valuable treasure which I have lost?' Shankar kept his head down, occasionally gazed up at the Emperor with mysterious expressions and counted on his fingers for mystical effect. 'Your majesty, do you have a palm tree in the garden?' 'Yes, yes we do,' was the excited reply. 'Well, I see a silver lining in the sky above that particular palm tree, your majesty.'

The Emperor's officials rushed out to the garden and began digging furiously. When they uncovered the pearl, the master was the first one to exclaim, 'Thank God!' The Emperor stood up, livid with anger and shouted, 'Who stole this pearl and buried it here?' Shankar went into a state of divination, shaking his head, 'The luminous pearl is a state treasure, your majesty. Year after year it had received the essence of the sun and moon and naturally this resulted in the pearl possessing the power to move itself. It was not necessary for anyone to bury it—it moves by itself'. 'Phew,' the culprit heaved a heavy sigh of relief as somehow, everybody agreed with this logic. The Emperor's vanity about his pearl made him gullible enough to imagine that it actually had such powers and he believed Shankar's story. Thus the wazir was saved from the fate he feared.

The Emperor was impressed by Shankar's powers and decided that from then on he was to live in the palace close to him. He was given a magnificent room and servants to do his bidding. But he was homesick and pined for his wife. His pleas to the Emperor were in vain.

When a week passed by, he told the Emperor, 'Your Majesty, my house in the village has been destroyed by fire and I must go and console my wife.'

The Emperor refused to let him go. Instead he sent his officers to see if the house had really caught fire. They returned and reported that this had indeed happened. This reinforced the Emperor's belief in his powers and further convinced him to keep Shankar in the palace. He even bestowed him with the title 'Guardian of the State.'

Shankar was distraught. He longed for his family and friends. He missed the clear blue sky and the rain and all the people who came to him for advice. One day, the Emperor had enough of his constant pleading and thought of a plan whereby Shankar would have to stay forever in the palace.

'I will let you go on one condition,' he said to him. 'You must tell me what lies inside this box. You have until this candle burns out to guess.'

The box was made of gold and encrusted with diamonds and rubies.

'What treasure has the emperor hidden inside this beautiful box?' thought Shankar, 'How in the world am I going to tell him what lies inside?' He was faced with a real dilemma. He pondered for long until the candle had burnt nearly to the end.

Finally, in exasperation, he exclaimed, 'I never expected Froggy to be trapped inside the box.'

The Emperor was amazed, because there was a frog in the box, which he had put in to trick him, although Shankar had merely been referring to himself by his nickname when he said that 'froggy was trapped'. He had somehow come through.

The Emperor had no alternative but to let Shankar return to his village. He did give him enough gold and silver to last him a lifetime. So it was that Shankar the 'fortune-teller' became a rich man due to his intelligence, wit and, of course, a lot of good luck.

Muhammad Ali, the blind storyteller of Ajman, narrated this story. He used to come once a month to Dubai with his son, travelling all day on his donkey. His visits were always a treat, as his stories would always weave a magical spell around the listeners, young or old. This story of friendship, is one of the many fascinating tales he told us, and I still remember it even after so many years.

In a small village, an old woman lived all alone in her hut. She had no one to take care of her in the whole wide world. She did not have any children and her husband had passed away some years back. Thus, she led a solitary existence, with no one to keep her company except her goat. She looked after the animal as best as she could. Every day she would milk the goat and keeping some for herself, sell the rest of the milk in the village, and thereby eke out a meager existence. It wasn't her frugal circumstances that bothered her so much, as that she had nobody to talk to. She yearned for someone to call her 'nanoo jan' (meaning mother).

One day, while returning from her daily trip to the village bazaar, she saw a little mischievous looking black and white cat. The cat came up to her and rubbed itself across her feet, meowing softly. But each time the old woman would stretch out her hand to pat it, it would run away. Of course the old woman was too slow to catch it, but she really wanted to take the cat home and keep it as a pet. The old woman gave up after several attempts and walked on home. Much to her delight, when she reached her hut she found the cat sitting on her doorstep, as if waiting to be let in.

So the cat became a much-loved member of her house. Both the cat and the goat got along very well and every morning the two would go out in search of food. When they had found enough to eat they would return and sit by the old woman and she would give the cat some milk, which she had saved from her own share. Then she would sing to them and talk to them. Together they were very happy in their own way.

One day, the old woman went off to the market after milking the goat and setting aside some for herself in a bowl, which she placed on a tray. When she returned she found all the milk gone and on the tray were faint marks of a cat's paw. The old woman was very distressed, not only because she would have to go hungry, but that the cat had betrayed her trust. She admonished the cat and explained to it that if they were to live like friends, then they must never deceive each other. The cat promised never to repeat the act. But after a few days, the cat was unable to resist temptation and once again drank the milk. This time the old woman did not want to scold the cat, lest it run away and never come back. But if the cat continued to devour all the milk, then the old woman would go hungry. So she had to be taught a lesson.

The old woman got some tar from the bazaar and spread it on the tray. She then left the milk in the bowl as usual and went out. When the cat stepped on the tray to lap up the milk, it's tail got stuck and try as it might, it remained firmly glued to the tar. Now the cat had a beautiful, thick, furry tail and was very proud of it. When the old woman came back, the cat implored her.

'Please help, my tail is stuck.'

'All right,' said the old woman and ran out, got a pair of scissors and cut off its tail.

After this, whenever the cat went out, the other cats would jeer and taunt, 'What a sight. Did you try to steal something and get your tail lopped off?'— ' What is a cat without a tail to swing around?'— ' What an ugly sight.'

The cat was very upset. It also knew that it deserved the punishment. So it went to the old woman and begged her forgiveness.

'Nanoo Jan, I know what you did was right. I betrayed your trust. But I will never do such a thing again. Please stitch my tail back on.'

The old woman was delighted at being addressed as Nanoo, and said to the cat, 'All right I will stitch your tail back, but before I do that you must bring me some milk, as punishment for the milk you stole.'

The cat ran to the goat and told him about the promise it had made to the old woman.

'Please give me some milk, which I will give to Nanoo and she will give me back my tail,' begged the cat.

'But I am so hungry. I do not have any milk,' the goat replied, 'However, if you bring me some fresh leaves from that tree by the river then I will be able to help you.'

The cat ran to the tree and said, ' Tree, Tree, please give me some leaves so I can give it to the goat, she will then give me some milk. This milk I will give to Nanoo and she will give me back my tail.'

The tree had no fresh leaves and it looked all dried up.

'I would like to help,' replied the tree, 'But as you can see the river which used to flow by my side has dried up. Without it's nourishing water my leaves have all dried up. If you can persuade the river to flow alongside me once more, I will give you all the fresh leaves you want.'

The cat then hurried along to the mouth of the river and pleaded with it, 'River, River, please start flowing by the tree again, so that it begins to blossom and gives me some green leaves, which I can give to the goat. The goat will then give me fresh milk that I will give to Nanoo, who will then give my tail back.'

After hearing the cat, the river sympathized with her and said, 'I do want to help you get your beautiful tail back. But as you can see I am tired and can barely move. A gypsy used to sit by my bank everyday and sing lovely songs. There was so much melody in her voice that I would be inspired to sing and dance and flow with the music. Now that she does not come, I really do not feel like flowing anymore. If you can ask the gypsy to come back, then I promise to flow by the tree and you can get your tail back.'

The cat, by now almost in tears, went to look for the gypsy. After a long search she found the gypsy sitting forlorn and lost on a rock.

The cat went up to her and in a pitiable voice narrated her tale. 'Gypsy, Gypsy, If you come and sit by the river and sing, then the river will happily flow by the tree. The tree will then blossom with fresh leaves, which I will give to the goat who will then give me some milk for my Nanoo. She will then give me back my tail.'

The gypsy was moved by the cat's plea but said, 'Go away. I am hungry. I haven't eaten all day. How can I sing on an empty stomach? Get me some bread first then I will sing by the riverside.'

The cat then thought that she would go and ask the *nanwa* for help. She ran to the *tandoor* as fast as she could and begged him.

'Please sir help me. The gypsy is hungry and cannot sing. Please give me some bread, so I can give it to the gypsy, who will eat it and sing by the river. The river will then flow by the tree, which will blossom and give me fresh leaves. I will give the leaves to the goat who will give me some milk to give to my Nanoo who will then give me back my tail.'

The *nanwa* replied, 'I have seen you with your beautiful furry tail. You really looked nice. But how can I give you bread, when I have no flour to bake the bread with. If you can bring me some flour then I will bake the bread for you.'

Now the cat was really distressed, but nevertheless persisted in her endeavour to get her tail back. She ran to the miller.

'Mr Miller, please help me. I need some flour to give to the *nanwa*, who will then bake me some bread for the gypsy. When the gypsy has eaten she will sing to the river, which will flow by the tree. The tree will blossom and give me fresh leaves to give to the goat, who will give me some milk for my Nanoo. When I give Nanoo the milk, she will give me back my tail.'

When the cat had finished her story the miller said to her, 'I wish I had the flour to give you. But alas, my fields are lying fallow. There is no way I can plough the field to get some wheat to grind into flour. However if you get me a cow, then I can plough the field and grind the wheat into flour for you.'

The cat, who by now had almost given up hope of ever getting her tail back, ran to the cow. In a sad voice she pleaded, 'Cow, Cow, please help me. Please come and plough the field, so that the miller will have wheat for his mill. With the flour the *nanwa* will bake some bread, which I will give to the hungry gypsy. The gypsy will sing by the river, which will flow by the tree. The tree will blossom with fresh leaves, then I can give those to the goat. The goat will give milk, which I will give to Nanoo and then she will give me back my tail.'

The cow listened patiently and then sighed, 'Can't you see how tired and thin I am. I have not had green grass to eat for a long time. I do not have the strength to pull the plough. If you can get me some green grass, then I will come with you to the field.'

Now the cat was truly dejected. It seemed there was no way she could get her lovely, furry tail back. Slowly she started to walk back to the house, when all at once she saw a field with lush green grass. She bounded into the field and with her claws began to scrape off the grass. With great difficulty she carried the grass, bit by bit, to the cow. The cow relished the grass and happily went to plough the field. Soon the wheat was planted and bundles of wheat were taken to the mill. The miller gave the flour to the cat, that she took to the *nanwa,* who baked some delicious bread with it. The gypsy ate the bread and sang a melodious song by the riverside. The water flowed merrily past the tree and it's leaves blossomed. The cat took the fresh leaves to the goat. The goat devoured the juicy green leaves and gave milk by the bowlfull. Then the cat took the milk to her Nanoo.

Nanoo was delighted to have her precious cat back. She had really missed her. When she heard of the cat's adventure in getting the milk she exclaimed, 'Why did you not simply bring the grass and feed the goat?'

'But how could I not keep my promise to all my friends? They all really wanted to help me and would have gone lacking, without my help. I would not have been happy with my tail, if I had betrayed them,' the cat replied.

The old woman was very happy that her dear cat had learnt to keep promises and thought it a lesson well learnt. She sewed back the tail and all of them lived like true friends for a long, long time.

BABA AND THE LAMB

The setting for this story is the Bastaki sector in Dubai and takes place in the early 1940s.

One day Ali saw his father entering the courtyard, with two big, beautiful, white-coated lambs. The lambs had red patches of colour from henna on them. Ali ran out excitedly to his father.

'Baba! Baba! Are these lambs for me and Bilal to play with? They are so lovely,' he exclaimed.

'Have you forgotten that a couple of weeks from now is *Eid*,' said the father.

'I know it is *Eid*. How can I forget. But what does this have to do with the lambs? Are they Eid gifts for Bilal and me? Thank you Baba. This is the best *Eid* gift ever,' Ali had both his arms around the gentle lambs and was cuddling them.

'No these are not *Eid* gifts for you. Don't you remember this *Eid* is *Eid-ul-Haj* (the day of pilgrimage), the *Eid-ul-Qorban*. We will be sacrificing these lambs on that day. In the meantime you and Bilal look after them.'

Ali was so excited that he did not pay attention to what his father had said, and went off to play in the outer courtyard with the two lambs in tow. The houses in those days had several courtyards. One was attached to the women's quarters, where only *mahrams* i.e. close family members like father, brothers, husbands, grandparents etc. were allowed to enter. The men's section had a courtyard of its own, with a separate entrance to the *majlis*. There was another section where the domestic staff lived, a kitchen area, and another where livestock was kept.

Ali ran and informed his elder brother Bilal of their new playmates. Together they made arrangements for their food and water in special clay pots. Baba went out leaving instructions with the household to let the two little boys be in charge of taking care of the lambs.

Ali was totally involved with the lambs. Bilal, however, had other interests as well. The next day, the younger boy brought his friends home from the *maktab,* to show off his pets. Seeing how attached he had become to the lambs, Ali's mother began to feel apprehensive about the effect the sacrifice would have on her son. She tried to divert his interest, but to no avail.

'Mother, please let me be with my friends. They are so trusting and follow me around. I love them,' the boy said blissfully.

She just didn't have the heart to warn him or try to explain to him, that the lambs would not be his pets for very long, and that in a few days they would be slaughtered and their meat distributed among the neighbours. This was their religious duty and there was no foregoing the custom.

As the days passed, Ali became more and more fond of his pets. He had named them, Aloo and Maloo. Even their bleating at night was like music to his ears. Baba would often inspect them to see how they were getting on. He would praise his son, 'Bravo, young

man, you are looking after the lambs well. See how fat they have grown.' Ali would feel very proud of his achievement.

Only one week remained for *Eid*. Preparations were in full swing for the occasion. Material was bought from the bazaar to make new clothes for everyone. Sewing machines were constantly whirring. Gunny bags full of rice were brought into the house, and all the women were busy cleaning it. Rice cleaning was a task in which even the neighbours participated. Everything was in abundance. Huge quantities of delicious food would be cooked on that day, and everyone in the household would eat their fill. It was all very exciting. But Ali was oblivious to all the hustle bustle around him. All he had time for were his beloved Aloo and Maloo.

Some members of the family had left for *Haj* that year. In those days the pilgrimage to Mecca was fraught with hazards. The journey across the mountains was very risky and the roads were rough and dangerous. Many were injured on the way and some did not return. But such is the importance of *Haj*, that even disabilities resulting from the journey were considered a blessing. Ali's family was proud that almost every year some members of their family performed Haj. There would be a big send-off party for them and the whole town celebrated when the *Hajis* returned.

The big day finally arrived. Ali had gone to sleep the previous night full of joy at the thought that tomorrow was *Eid* and he would accompany his Baba to the mosque for the *Eid* congregation. When they returned from the mosque there would be a sumptuous breakfast of *halwas*, the special *regag nan* and the *muttabak*, a delicious concoction of egg and sugar. He would wear his new *dishdash*, with his new boots. The thought of all the *eidee* he would collect from the elders was especially pleasant, as he planned on buying a tricycle with the money. Most of all, he looked forward to taking his Aloo and Maloo for their daily run in the outer court-yard.

Ali fell asleep with the sound of their bleating, which for some reason seemed louder than usual. He woke up several times in the night wondering what was wrong with them, but each time he would go back to sleep, as he was tired from playing with them all day.

When Ali woke the next morning, it seemed to him as though the sound of bleating had changed. Aloo and Maloo seemed to be in pain. They were moaning and gasping. He quickly jumped out of bed and ran to the outer courtyard to see what was troubling his pets. There he found two ferocious looking men, bending over his friends. They held shiny knives in their hands that were dripping with blood. His beloved Aloo was lying still, with his neck slit open. Maloo was still gasping. Ali went and threw himself on his lambs.

'What have you done with my friends?' he cried out loudly.

Baba, who was standing at some distance to avoid being splattered with blood, quickly came forward and grabbed Ali and pulled him up.

'You silly boy. Get away from here.'

'But Baba these men have killed my Aloo and Maloo,' Ali cried, sobbing uncontrollably.

'Get up Ali. Is this the way you wish your father *Eid Mubarak*. It is *Eid* and these lambs had been nourished for today's sacrifice,' Baba was getting annoyed at his son for not observing the importance of this custom and carrying on like this.

'But Baba, they were my friends,' Ali kept repeating.

'Someone please take this silly boy away, and keep him under control until he comes to his senses and learns how to talk to his father,' Baba was very annoyed at being interrupted in the ritual of *Eid-ul-Qorban*.

Ali left and sought out Bilal. Together they hugged each other and wept. Their mother tried to comfort them and explained to them the significance of sacrifice, but Ali was inconsolable. Everybody around him were wishing each other *Eid Mubarak* and looking happy and celebrating. But for Ali there was no joy on this occasion. He just couldn't contain his sorrow.

In the years that followed, whenever there was lamb served at the table, Ali would feel the pang of grief. Even after he had grown into a young man and was a student at Oxford, his friends noticed that he would leave the table if lamb was served. They could not understand the deep impact that that childhood experience—the memory of his Aloo and Maloo, with their trusting eyes and henna dotted coats— had left on him.

THE VEGETABLE SEEDS

This story is not a fairy-tale. The characters in it could have existed and the events may have occurred. It relates to the China of the forties.

It was lunchtime in the commune in the Minglian village. The cooks were busy laying out the midday meal for the hungry workers. Today they were serving hot spring rolls. These were everyone's favourite, including Ming's. Even so she seemed very distracted and not her usual cheerful self. Everyone in the commune loved the tall, slender, nineteen-year-old girl. Her large, expressive eyes and long swinging plait tied with a red scarf, made her look very attractive. She was their vegetable team leader and took her duties very seriously. But today she was very restless and everyone wondered why.

Ming's mother was sitting and chatting with a group of ladies, when she ran up to her, 'Mamma! Mamma! Is there any mail for me today?'

The ladies of the group began to tease her, 'Whose letter are you so desperately waiting for? Is he handsome? Are we to hear wedding bells soon?'

'Please don't tease. Mamma, the postman is usually here by this time. Is there a letter for me?' Ming was becoming increasingly agitated.

'No, there is no letter for you. Now stop being so nervous and get me some food from the canteen. Get some food for yourself as well. You haven't eaten all day,' said her mother.

When Ming had gone the ladies started to ask her mother about this mysterious letter, 'Has Ming finally fallen in love? Is she waiting for a letter from him? Do tell us.'

'It is my fondest wish to see Ming married and settled down,' her mother told them, 'But she is always so busy with her duties. I wish it was what you are thinking. But alas! That is unlikely, as Ming is too involved in her work to think of getting married.'

Ming's mind was in a turmoil. 'There is a real crisis brewing and if what I fear happens, then I would be solely responsible for it.' The thought was really upsetting her.

You see the planting season was upon them and she was in charge of procuring the seeds for sowing. That year, all the communes across the country were increasing their production of vegetables and the demand for seeds was much greater. Everyone was finding it difficult to obtain seeds and Ming was worried that she would not have enough when sowing was to commence, and her commune would be faced with a shortage of vegetables. Some days ago she had decided to write to all the neighbouring communes for help. The notice read:

'Attention all Production Brigade Leaders!

As per the directive of the Central Committee, production must expand in our village. Our problem is that we do not have enough seeds to implement this. All our attempts at obtaining seeds have failed. If

you have any surplus seeds, or know of anyone who has, please inform us. We will immediately come and buy them from you.

Thanking you, Ming,
Leader of the Vegetable Team,
Mingalian Production Brigade.'

It was the reply to these letters that Ming was anxiously waiting for. The aroma of spring rolls being served in the canteen added to her worries.

'Next year when there are no vegetables for the rolls, the commune will blame me. What am I to do?'

Five days had passed since she had sent off the notices and so far, there had not been a single reply. Ming's father, who was Brigade Leader, had already reprimanded her for not being prepared.

'You will make us the laughing stock of the commune.'

'I promise to have everything under control in seven days,' she had told him.

But it looked as though she would not be able to keep her promise. Ming was really miserable. She lost her appetite and was unable to sleep at night. The thought of letting her commune down weighed heavily on her mind.

Finally, she could not wait any longer for the postman to come. She rushed over to the Brigade Office to check for herself. The office was closed when she got there. She peered through the windows and saw four parcels lying on the table and her heart jumped with joy. These must be for her. She could not wait for the staff to return from lunch. There was a broken window, so she climbed in through it, scraping her knees as she went. She winced slightly, but she was so excited that she was oblivious to the pain. The parcels *were* addressed to her. She picked them up and ran back to the vegetable plot to open them.

Inside were small gifts of seeds from communes scattered over the country. The letters accompanying them were warm and encouraging. People had even sent seeds that they had saved for their own gardens. Ming was touched by the response and tears welléd up in her large eyes. But the amount of seeds was not enough. She still needed more, much more.

She was sitting in the patch wondering how she could overcome the shortage, when through the tears in her eyes she saw a man walking towards the village. He seemed to be weighed down with two heavy packages. He had to cross a small bridge to come to the village. As he was doing so his foot slipped and he fell into the water. Ming ran to help him. He was thoroughly wet and the packages were dripping.

'Thank you Comrade,' said the young man, 'Could you tell me if this is the Mingalian village?'

'Yes, this is,' replied Ming, 'Are you visiting relatives here?'

She saw that he was tall and slim, with a broad forehead, square jaw and lively sparkling eyes.

'Where have you come from? You look like you have travelled a long distance,' asked Ming.

'No, I do not have any relatives here,' the young man replied, 'I am looking for a comrade Ming. Do you know where I might find her? I have some important parcels to deliver to her.'

'Ah! You are looking for me. I am comrade Ming.'

The young man seemed pleased at this and extended his hand to shake hers, 'My name is Wang. I have come from the Leap Forward Commune in the South. I have brought you vegetable seeds.'

Ming was delighted. The commune from which he had come was the most prosperous in the country and was held as a role model for the others. It was at least thirty lis away. He must have walked all this way to bring them the seeds.

Ming thanked him profusely and picked up one of the heavy parcels to assist him. All this time she was aware of how handsome and muscular he looked.

'How did you find out that we needed the seed? You live so far off,' Ming asked.

'I came last week to this part of the country to learn about chemical fertilizers. I saw one of your notices and thought you must really need help. So when I went back, I asked our Brigade leader if we had any seeds to spare. Unfortunately there was none to spare. So I went around the neighbouring communes and collected whatever seeds I could and brought them here myself,' Wang explained.

Ming was very impressed by his concern. 'You could have mailed it to us, or we would have come and collected it ourselves,' she said.

However, she was very glad he had come. Wang by now was convinced of how sincere Ming was and also how beautiful she was. He began to feel attracted to her. He too, was pleased that he had come.

'Initially, I had thought of mailing the seeds to you, but my commune leader thought that maybe you needed some help in the planting as well. So I have come to offer whatever assistance I can,' Wang replied.

Ming was overjoyed, 'He will be staying for sometime,' she thought and her heart danced with joy.

She clapped her hand and exclaimed, 'You seem to have thought of everything. Our vegetable team has only just been formed and we have much to learn. I'm sure you are an expert and we will be honoured to learn from you.'

Wang was embarrassed by such praise and blushed slightly,

'But first you must rest,' Ming continued, 'You have walked such a long distance and must be tired.'

'No, no, I don't need rest. Let us go to the vegetable plot and start work right away. I have to leave early tomorrow morning,' Wang told her.

'Okay, even if you don't need rest, I am certain you need something to eat. Please accept our hospitality,' Ming insisted.

The young man could not refuse, 'Well, I cannot turn down a meal. But let's look at the plot before we eat.'

The two walked to the village. Wang kept stealing sidelong glances at Ming. He forgot his fatigue and seemed to be walking on clouds. While they were inspecting the plot, Ming's mother saw them. She was bringing a basket full of hot food to give her daughter lunch and was pleasantly surprised to see her Ming with such a handsome and impressive looking young man. She quickly ran to the canteen and collected some more food. Then she went to where her husband was working and asked him to come home quickly.

'Come on, go back to the house and get washed and changed. Hurry.'

'But why, woman, are we expecting some important guest?'

'Don't ask questions, just get changed fast. Our Ming is bringing home a boy.'

'What boy? Who is he and what is Ming doing with him?' the father asked a bit irritably.

'Remember the letter that Ming was anxiously waiting for. It seems that the letter has arrived in person,' replied the mother excitedly.

The accountant sitting with Ming's father heard this and clapped his hand, 'Ah, it looks like there will be a wedding soon.'

'Keep quiet, has everyone gone mad. I have not heard Ming talk of any young man. What's going on?' Ming's father was getting more annoyed.

'Just do as I say. Ming will soon be home with her boyfriend. You can't meet him looking so untidy'

In the face of such earnestness, he had no alternative but to do as his wife bid him to do.

After some time Ming and Wang came to the house. Ming introduced Wang to her parents.

'Father, Mother, this is Wang from the south. Wang, this is my father. He is the head of our production brigade and this is my dear mother.'

Wang shook.hands with them. Ming's mother could barely conceal her excitement and began to ask him all kinds of personal questions, '...how old are you? Do you live with your family? How many brothers and sisters do you have?'

'I live with my mother,' Wang told her.

'Your mother is lucky to have such a strong and handsome son,' she exclaimed.

Ming guessed what her mother was up to and explained, 'Comrade Wang has brought us seeds from the communes in the south and he is going to advise us in regard to sowing these seeds. Hc will be going back tomorrow.'

Ming's parents were disappointed. Her father glared at his wife, 'This is what happens when you presume too much. Why do women look on every young man as a prospective son-in-law?' he seemed to be thinking.

In spite of their disappointment they extended full hospitality to the visitor.

After lunch the two young people walked to the field. Ming had sent word for the whole team to gather there. Everyone was keen to learn as much as possible from this young man. They listened intently as he showed them new techniques of planting systematically to obtain optimum utilization of space. He taught them strategy and demonstrated planting methods. The villagers were very impressed with the depth of his knowledge.

Wang stayed with them all day and through the night. The next morning he prepared to depart. The Brigade leader and members of the commune thanked him and bid him a safe journey. Ming walked silently beside him, up to the river where they had met.

She then took his hand and said, 'How can we ever thank you for all you have done for us.'

Wang looked at Ming and felt his heartbeat quicken and a warm glow spread through his body. But he was too shy to express his feelings. Instead he said, 'There is no need to thank me. I just hope you have a good crop.'

'You must return in the autumn to see for yourself what a good crop we have,' Ming replied.

Wang nodded, looked at her warmly and began his trek back to his commune.

Ming watched him for a long time. She knew that this gentle and intelligent man had stolen her heart and that the feeling was mutual. Life would never be the same again for her.

Suddenly Ming's mother came rushing up to her, 'Stop him he has forgotten his bag.'

Ming took the bag from her mother and calmly told her, 'Don't worry, mother. He will be back in the autumn. We will return his bag then. If for some reason he does not come, I'll take it to him myself!'

THE LAST FRIDAY OF RAMADAN

In the olden days, the square around the mosque used to be the centre of activity in the city. It used to be a very lively place, and people would spend more time in the mosque than anywhere else, especially during Ramadan. On the last Friday of the month of fasting, there would be great pomp and gaiety here, as the King would come to the mosque. A little boy, the protagonist of our tale, lived near the mosque and studied in the maktab attached to it. He always dreamt of the day he would see the King. He idealized the monarch. To him the King was capable of the bravest of deeds. He imagined him to be big and strong and believed he could even put his bare hands in the fire without any fear. Why he could even fly in the air, such was his power. In those days tales of flying carpets fired people's imaginations.

The little boy longed to see the King. But each time the King was to come to the mosque on the last Friday of *Ramadan*, all the children were shooed away from the square. It was feared that they would create a disturbance when the King passed by, although to be quite honest, each year it was the grownups who created a greater disturbance, trying to break through the cordon and get as near to the King as possible. Every year the little boy would come home in tears and stand on the balcony, hoping to catch a glimpse of the Royal entourage. He would feel angry at the grownups who, in his opinion, were allowed to get away with everything. They considered children to be pests. So he would just mope around the house all day. Sometimes he would amuse himself by taking a stick and ride on it, imagining he was one of those splendid horsemen who escorted the King.

Although the little boy could not see the ceremony himself, in his mind's eye he could picture all the pomp and show. There would be music, and paper streamers of all the bright colours of the rainbow, fluttering in the air. He could imagine the soldiers marching to the rhythm of the band, the guard of honour being presented and people lining the roads, cheering at the top of their voices, as the King passed by. In the evening when his father would return, he would tell them all about the parade. Yes! thought the little boy, the King was a very special person. He must be a superman.

So the boy was eagerly awaiting the last Friday of the month of Ramadan. Maybe this time he would be lucky enough to catch a glimpse of the King. Oh, how wonderful that would be! The little boy could think of nothing else. But two days before the special day, he heard unusual news. The King had been ousted in a revolution and had barely escaped with his life. He had fled the country with his wife and children to Italy, on board a big modern ship. This ship had huge rooms and even modern toilets.

'The King had a wife and children?' thought the little boy, 'A person like the King has children like us

ordinary human beings?' The little boy was extremely perplexed. He ran to his mother, who was busy in the kitchen.

'Mother is it true that the King has children just like us? Do they dirty themselves and go to the toilet?'

'Of course they do,' said his mother a trifle impatiently, 'Whatever made you think otherwise?'

The little boy was disappointed. He waited impatiently for his father to come home, so he could find out about the astonishing things that he had heard about the revolution and the ouster of the King. Did this mean that he would not be coming to the mosque on the last Friday of *Ramadan*?

As soon as his father entered the house, the little boy began pestering him with all the questions in his little mind. The father was very tired, but tried to answer his son's questions as best as he could.

'You see son, there has been a revolution.'

'What is a revolution and what does this have to do with the King?' asked the little boy.

'A revolution, my child, is like a train,' the father explained, 'It sweeps through the entire country and can bring devastation. The aftermath *could* be a stable and better government, but the revolution itself always brings death and destruction. Many people are killed and many more put in prison. There is always violence.'

His father would not say anymore, 'Go to bed. I want to rest.'

The little boy was not deterred, 'What does it really mean father? I do not understand.'

'Son, a revolution actually means a change of government. Now go away.'

The boy did not know what a government was, so this explanation was no help. He did not understand what 'change' meant either, but he didn't like it one bit.

'Father, please tell me, does this mean that on the last Friday of *Ramadan* there will be no ceremony and the King is not going to pray for us?' asked the little boy again later.

'Prayer is for God alone,' his father replied seriously, 'Muslims perform their prayers and it makes no difference whether the King comes or not. Nobody needs Kings for their prayers. The only King that you pray to and believe in is Allah. So boy, put this into your head, that a person does not need the King to come to the mosque to pray for him.'

'But, father, you used to be proud to pray close to the King. You told me so yourself.'

'Now enough of this 'king' nonsense. Go and let me rest,' his father admonished, getting somewhat irritated by now.

The boy could not believe that a revolution could oust a big strong man like the King. He remembered that every last Friday of *Ramadan,* when the King would pass by, everyone would shout at the top of their voices, 'Long live the King! Long live the King!' Why had all that changed, just because there was a revolution? In the square today everyone had been cursing the ruler. How could that be possible?

He ran to his mother, 'Mama, what are they saying?' 'They say that the King was a thief, and the people did not like him and they are glad that he has gone.' How can he be a thief? Don't you remember all the cheering, the flags and the music?' His mother simply gathered him to her bosom. These were bad times. Everyone kept their opinions to themselves.

The next day early in the morning, he got up and ran into the square. It was filled with soldiers, but they did not look friendly like the ones in the Royal entourage. Some people had begun to gather in the compound. Then the boy heard cheering and slogans. But what were they saying?

'Long live the Revolution!!'

But just two days ago, these same people were shouting, 'Long live the King!' The little boy could not take this any more. He jumped up on the raised mound in the square and began to shout.

'Long live the King! Long live the King! Two days ago this is what you were saying. I hate your revolution.'

On hearing this, the soldiers came and held him roughly by the shoulders, 'Tell us boy, which house do you come from. There is no way a young boy could say this on his own. Surely his parents have taught him this.'

The boy was really frightened, but he continued shouting his slogan. The soldiers began to drag him away. Someone rushed to his house to inform his father what was happening. His parents came running out and begged the soldiers to release their little son.

'He is just a little child. He does not understand that the King was a thief and a scoundrel and we are glad to be rid of him. Please let our son go. We will make sure he understands that the revolution was the best thing that could happen to us,' they pleaded.

'Everyone is joyfully accepting the change and are glad that the corrupt man is gone. This chit of a boy still says 'long live the King'. He has to be taught a lesson,' said the leader among the soldiers. Fortunately for the boy, the Imam of the mosque intervened and undertook the responsibility of converting the boy to the new way of thinking. On the assurance of the Imam, the little boy was released.

Time passed by and the child grew into a young man. He went to a good school in the city and learnt a lot about revolutions and history. He forgot all about the celebrations, but he never forgot what happened that day in the square. He still could not understand why his father, now old and gray, would sit in the local tea-house and boast of the part he had taken in the great revolution. He would boast about the processions and the meetings he had attended. All the little boy remembered was the eagerness of his father to pray as near as possible to the King on the last Friday of *Ramadan* only two days before the revolution. This is the way it is. The grownups change with the wind; only a child's heart remains constant.

*I heard this story many years ago and have enjoyed
narrating it to children and even adults. It can be
described as the story of Cinderella, in an eastern
setting.*

Once upon a time, there lived a wealthy merchant
called Abu Ameen. He married a beautiful,
fragile woman who bore him three daughters.
Unfortunately she contracted pneumonia, and died
when the youngest daughter was only four years old.
Abu Ameen was devastated, for he loved his wife
very much. He never remarried and devoted himself
entirely to bringing up his children, and tried to be
both a mother and a father to them. The best tutors in
the land took care of their education and the girls
grew up lacking nothing.

Abu Ameen had an easy and affable relation with
his daughters. However, there was something in the
personality of his youngest daughter, Bilquis, which
he could not fathom. She possessed an inquiring mind
and was headstrong and even stubborn. She loved to
dance in front of the mirror and had a lovely voice.
She could sing very sweetly and had a natural talent
for playing the *ude*. Bilquis also loved animals and
birds and seemed to live in a world all her own. Her
father found it difficult to understand her; on the one
hand she spent most of her time in seemingly frivolous

pursuits, such as decorating her hands with henna patterns, while on the other hand she liked to study serious subjects like philosophy, literature and classical music.

Bilquis was now eighteen years old and had grown to be a beautiful girl. She had a soft, glowing, complexion with slender arms and legs. However, her most striking features werE her eyes, which were so light that they appeared almost transparent. The color would change with her mood, just like her mother's did.

Abu Ameen, despite his high status and success, was really quite insecure. He was in the habit of constantly asking his daughters to prove their love for him. One day he called his daughters to him, one by one.

'How much do you love me?' he asked his eldest daughter.

The eldest one smiled and replied, 'As much as life itself father. You have been both a father and a mother to us. May Allah preserve you.'

'I am pleased with your answer, my daughter,' said Abu Ameen beaming with joy.

He then asked the second daughter, 'Have I been a good father to you? How much do you love me?'

'My love is as big as the universe. You are everything to me. I live for your well being and pray to Allah to grant you a long and healthy life.'

The father was delighted with this show of devotion by his second daughter.

Then he called his youngest daughter, whom he considered an enigma.

'Well! How much do you love your father?' he asked her.

'I love you father, as much as fresh meat loves salt,' Bilquis replied.

Abu Ameen was furious, 'What! Am I to be compared to a piece of meat and salt? How ungrateful you are.'

On seeing their father become so angry, the two older daughters rushed to him and tried to soothe him.

'Bilquis is only a fanciful child. She doesn't know what she is saying. Forgive her father.'

But he refused to be placated. 'I have always suspected that this chit of a girl does not love me,' he shouted angrily, 'I do not want ungrateful children around me. She must leave my house immediately. I cannot bear the sight of her.'

Bilquis was flabbergasted. She had not expected her father to react in this manner. But she knew that once her father had made up his mind about something, nothing could change him. If he'd decided to throw her out of the house, it was hopeless to try to convince him to alter his decision. So she packed a few dresses, took some gunnysacks with her and she left the house. Her mind was in a daze and she did not have a clue as to what she would do. However, soon she realized that she could not wander about in her fine dress and her jewellery. Quickly she covered herself with a sack, took off her gold ornaments and hid them deep in her pocket. She then smudged her face with some coal dust thus obscuring her beautiful face.

She kept on walking, wondering what she would do, when in the distance she saw a huge mansion. Bilquis hoped that she might be able to find some work there, and thus be able to earn a livelihood. She was not afraid of hard work.

Bilquis went up to the mansion and knocked on the back door. A servant opened the door.

'Please help me. I am an orphan with nowhere to go. I am looking for some work, please,' she pleaded in a soft voice, 'I can take care of the children or work in the kitchen. I do not require any wages. Just some food and a place to sleep would do.'

The servant felt sorry for her and took her to the mistress of the house. The mistress took one look at the grubby girl in front and exclaimed in irritation, 'Why have you brought her into the house? She is so dirty. What is her name?'

'She has no name,' the servant replied nervously, 'But she has asked to be called Kees, after the sacks she is wearing.'

'Well, whatever her name, I don't want her inside the house. Give her some work in the grease kitchen. It's always so dirty and all of you are constantly complaining of being shorthanded there,' said the mistress, as she dismissed them.

While they were leaving she said, 'Under no circumstances is this dirty creature to be seen in the house.'

So it was that Bilquis was set to work scrubbing pots and pans. At first Kees was very sad and missed her old life. She had never seen a grease kitchen, let alone cleaned a pot or pan. She did the best she could. Slowly her cheerful disposition reasserted itself and she began humming and singing sweet songs as she toiled.

All the other servants were drawn to this young girl, with the lovely voice and comical looks. Whilst she worked, her quick mind observed the details of the life-style of the people in the mansion. She saw that the custom of the veil was not observed in this house, and men and women mixed freely with each other. It was like the stories she had loved to read about and quite a contrast to the secluded life she and her sisters had led in her father's house. Each day, she would be on the look out specially to catch a glimpse of the master's oldest son, as he passed by the kitchen on his way to the stables. Every time she saw him, she felt her heart skip a beat. He was so handsome and dashing, just like someone out of the fairytales she had been fond of.

One day there was a lot of activity in the kitchen. Everyone was working feverishly.

'What is happening? Why is everyone so busy?' Kees asked one of the maids.

'Haven't you heard? The master is giving a big party for his son, who has just won the biggest prize in the horse races,' replied the maid.

'Everyone is invited, including the servants,' the cook added as she passed by, 'There will be music and dancing. You must come too. Get washed up and we will lend you a dress to wear.'

'No, no,' Kees seemed alarmed at the prospect, 'I have been forbidden to go into the house. I don't dare enter the majlis. Don't worry about me. All of you have a good time.'

When everyone had gone off to the party, Kees decided on a plan. Quickly she took off her dirty sack and washed herself in the kitchen. Then she dug inside one of her sacks, in which she had hidden some dresses she had brought with her when she left home, and took out the prettiest one. She took out her gold jewellery from another sack and put on all of it. She looked beautiful, like a princess in a fairy tale, and walked with an air of confidence into the glittering hall.

When she entered the hall, all eyes were upon her. 'Who is this lovely lady?' asked many young men struck by her beauty but, she didn't bother about them and strode towards the handsome host, in whose honour the party had been arranged. He was surrounded by a number of beautiful maidens. As she approached he looked up and their eyes met. Suddenly no one in the room mattered to him, except this charming woman, walking towards him. He got up and taking her hand, led her to the dance floor. The musicians began to play and Kees and the host danced for a long time. He found himself inexplicably drawn towards those enchanting eyes. When he left her for a moment to talk to his father, Kees took the opportunity to slip out. She ran back to the kitchen, and getting out of her fineries, once again stained herself with coal dust and donned the sack. She once more hid her fine dress, got into her bed and later pretended to be asleep when the other servants returned from the party.

The two kitchen maids with whom she shared the room shook her awake, 'My God, Kees, you really missed something incredible. A princess just like out of the fairy tales attended the party and she stole the young master's heart. He left all the glamorous women, who were vying for his attention, and danced only with her and was clearly smitten by her. Then she disappeared into thin air. Nobody seems to know who she was or where she came from? The young master was very upset. He kept looking for her and when he couldn't find her, he left in a huff. Indeed, the woman was a sight to behold.'

Kees listened to the maids and smiled to herself.

'Let me sleep. What do I care about your fairy princess or the young master,' she pretended to grumble

'Come on. Don't you wish you could be like that mysterious lady?' one of the maids commented.

'Let me sleep. I have a lot of work to do in the morning,' Kees replied, and turned around to go back to sleep.

Life went on as usual in the mansion, until a week later one of her roommates, who worked inside the main house, told them that there was going to be another party.

'This is one event you would not want to miss, Kees. Omme Kulsoom, the famous singer, is coming all the way from Cairo to perform in the house. The master has invited everyone to attend. The mistress is so excited that she has forgotten that she asked you never to set foot in the house and says you can come also. She feels that you have been very diligent in your duties and deserve a reward and has even sent this dress for you, so that you will have something proper to wear on the occasion. She has only worn it twice.'

'No! No! I don't want any clothes. Please do not bother about me. At the end of the day, I feel too exhausted to go anywhere, all I can think of is my warm bed. When you come back you can tell me all about it,' said Kees very calmly, while her heart danced with joy at the prospect of seeing the young master again.

On the day of the concert, Kees waited until the kitchen was empty and once again got into one of her lovely gowns. This time she wore a *thobe* of the finest silk money could buy, and looked truly ravishing. When she entered the ballroom, she immediately spotted the young master standing alone on the far side of the room. His eyes seemed to be looking for someone. When he saw her coming towards him, his face lit up and at once he strode towards her. They exchanged greetings, she smiled enchantingly and he looked meaningfully at her. Taking her hand, he guided her to a chair next to him. Omme Kulsoom began her performance. Kees was bewitched by her voice and by the haunting music. Throughout the performance, the young master kept asking her, 'Who are you? What is your name? Where do you come from?' Kees left all his questions unanswered and concentrated on the music. Finally the violins struck up a dance interlude and Kees danced in his arms. She seemed to float on air. But as soon as the young master went up to the famous singer, to ask her to sing a special song for them, she slipped away and ran towards the kitchen.

Before long, Kees heard the chatter of the other maids returning. They were very excited.

'Kees, you are a fool for missing such a wonderful event,' one of them said to her in mock exasperation, 'The mysterious princess came again. She has utterly captivated the young master. When she left he was really sad. He hardly spoke to anyone and didn't smile throughout the evening.'

Kees felt elated and kept dreaming about the events of the evening over and over again in her mind. Her face, however, remained impassive.

A few weeks later, preparations for another party were underway. The gossip in the servants quarters was, that this time it was to entrap the lovely princess, who had the habit of disappearing. Once more Kees made her appearance at the party in the same manner. This time she looked even more beautiful. She saw the young master waiting impatiently in a corner. She quickly slipped in from the side, beckoned the music master and instructed him in the accompaniment she wanted. Then she stepped on to the stage and began to sing in her melodious voice. Everybody turned and began to listen. She sang so beautifully, the young master and all the guests were intoxicated by her performance.

Afterwards, the young master came up to her and gave her a ring as a token of his love, and whispered, 'Please do not leave me again. My life has no meaning without you.'

But the minute his back was turned, Kees made her clandestine exit once more and hurried back to the servants quarters.

This time she had truly broken the young master's heart. He searched high and low for the lovely maiden. There was no trace of her anywhere. His health began to deteriorate and he took to his bed. He lost his appetite and would not eat for days. All the doctors and healers failed to cure the young master. Kees began to feel guilty for the effect she had had on her beloved. She was miserable and felt quite helpless, but how could she divulge her true identity. All day long, while at work scrubbing the dirty pots and pans, she would try to think of some way to help him.

One day she heard that an important doctor had been summoned from abroad and he had advised that the patient be fed only chicken soup. The cook rushed about making the soup, grumbling to herself.

'May God strike the she-devil that has broken the master's heart. To think that she looked like an angel, how can she be so hard hearted?'

Kees was very upset at this. Then an idea struck her. When the cook filled the bowl with soup and put it on the table for the maid to take it up to the young master, Kees quietly slipped the ring he had given her into the dish.

When the soup was taken to the young master, at first he refused to drink it. Then his mother coaxed him to take a few sips. While drinking, his spoon clinked against some object in the bowl. He fished it out with his spoon, and to his surprise found it was a ring.

He recognized it at once and sat up with a jolt and shouted, 'Who has made this soup?'

'Why do you ask, son? It was our cook who made it,' replied the mother quite astonished.

'Who else was in the kitchen besides the cook when this soup was made?' asked the young master getting very agitated.

'Yes, yes there is a young, dirty, miserable girl in the grease kitchen, who I felt sorry for and let her work there,' said the mother.

'Call her at once,' the young man ordered, 'I want to meet her.'

The mother thought it was a strange request, but nevertheless, to oblige her ailing son she told the maid to call Kees,

'Kees! Kees! The mistress is calling you in the house,' the maid ran in, all out of breath.

'But I am not allowed to set foot in the house. The mistress will not like this,' replied Kees.

'These are direct orders from the mistress herself. Wash your silly face and come with me.'

Kees followed the maid into the young master's room. When she saw how thin and emaciated he looked her heart bled for him.

'Were you the only one in the kitchen besides the cook when this soup was made?' asked the young master.

'Yes, I think so,' replied Kees in a frightened voice.

'Then it was you who put this ring in the soup. Tell me where did you get it?' he asked her very gently, so as not to scare her too much.

'Someone gave it to me,' replied Kees.

The young master looked closely at her and then the truth dawned upon him. This wretched kitchen girl standing in front of him was actually the mysterious princess who had captured his heart.

'It's you! I knew I would find you the minute I saw the ring. You were sending me a signal. I have been looking all over for you. This time you are not going to disappear,' said the young master, now glowing with happiness.

'I, too, do not want to leave you again,' replied Kees in a soft voice.

So it was that Kees and her handsome young master were betrothed. The entire household joined in the wedding preparations. All of them were extremely happy that the young master's health had been restored and that he was marrying such a beautiful woman. Kees divulged her family background to her prospective in-laws and they were happy to know that she came from a distinguished family. However, she requested them to keep this a secret for the time being and explained to them what had happened between her and her father.

When the time came to make out the guest list, Kees added the name of her father and sisters. Since she was soon to become an important member of the family, she requested that she should be allowed to select the menu for the pre-nuptial feast, to which her own family had also been invited.

On the day of the feast, all the guests were seated very graciously and formally. Dinner was served. It *looked* delicious and impressive. Trays and trays of food were placed in front of the guests and they soon started to eat. But they took the first bite and stopped.

'Please do not be upset at the food. There is no salt in any of the dishes,' the host explained to his guests. 'This was done to prove that salt is the most essential ingredient in any food. Despite all the spices in the world, food is tasteless without the humble salt.'

Abu Ameen, who was sitting at the table, at once realized his folly.

Quickly he got up and addressed the gathering, 'I have a confession to make,' he said, 'Once I had a beautiful daughter who said she loved me as much as meat loves salt. I am afraid I felt insulted at being compared to meat and banished her from my house. For the last year I have regretted my behavior, and have looked high and low for her but to no avail. I am afraid some wild animal might have devoured her and I am to blame for her death. Today, after eating this bland food, I was reminded of the merit of my daughter's statement. What indeed is meat without salt.'

Bilquis, who had been standing in the shadows, came forward and stood before her father.

'My dear father, your daughter is neither lost nor has she been devoured by wild beasts. She is right here, standing before you.'

Abu Ameen hung his head in shame, 'Could you ever forgive this foolish father of your?'

Bilquis embraced her father and sisters and invited them to meet her new family.

Then the tasteless food was removed from the table, and swiftly replaced with proper salted delicacies. Great celebrations ensued and Kees lived happily ever after with her young master.

THE APPLE TREE

There once was a tree that stood on a hill, all by itself—a lone tree, which neither blossomed, nor bore fruit. Despite the fact that it was barren, the tree was quite content, and almost arrogant in its solitude. The surrounding mountains protected it. The sun shone on it during the day, and a fresh stream running at the base of the mountain, provided it nourishment. The dawn dew washed its branches and trunk, and refreshed it. The tree was extremely self-sufficient and comfortable, and was confident that there, high up on the hill, it would never be disturbed. It would look down at the world and almost snicker at people it saw, working hard to eke out an existence.

'All I have to do is stand here and my needs are taken care of. I do not need to give anything to anyone like those poor people. Look at them working and working, to earn their living,' it would often think to itself and be happy.

Even the other trees, growing some distance away, had to struggle in their own manner to exist. In autumn all their leaves would fall off and in the winter their branches would remain bare. In the spring, the branches would touch the ground with their load of fruits, and people would come and pluck these from them. Animals and children would be playing around them all the time. The tree just could not understand why everyone was struggling so much. It had sunshine, wind and water. It became so selfish in its love for seclusion, it even abhorred birds alighting on its branches and would not let them build their nests in the springtime. It would always find a way to drive them off.

The tree's life of solitude continued undisturbed, until one day it saw a man coming towards it. The tree was very displeased at this.

'Why is this creature coming towards me? Doesn't he know he is invading my privacy?'

Of course it could not stop the man from sitting under its branches with his back resting on the trunk. How the tree hated this! The man seemed to be very pleased at the scene he observed all around him. The valley was indeed very beautiful and had not yet been touched by civilization. The tree shook its branches and even threw down one of its larger limbs to frighten the man away, but to no avail. As a matter of fact, the man sat for a long time and even dozed off for some time. 'I wish he would leave,' the tree kept repeating to itself.

After quite some time the man got up. He decided that he wanted to remember this beautiful spot.

'This useless tree won't do, it doesn't have any fruit. I will plant another tree here. With the stream nearby it will surely flourish,' he said aloud.

The tree was getting very, very angry, it shook and it shuddered, 'I don't care, let him plant his precious tree. I just don't want anything next to me. Why is he spoiling my life?'

The man was determined. He was soon digging into the ground to test the soil and seemed to be pleased with what he found.

'I know exactly the kind of tree that would look beautiful here and flourish,' he said in a happy tone.

A few days passed and the man returned with a sapling, which he planted in the spot he had selected on his previous visit. Much to the tree's dismay it was very close to it. The man made a small channel to ensure that the young plant got plenty of water.

'Soon this will grow into a fine tree,' he remarked before leaving.

As soon as he left, the old tree began to badger the sapling, 'Young one, aren't you angry that you have been uprooted from your family and friends and brought here. The weather here is terrible, with thunder and lightning and pouring rain. Do you really wish to be so near me?'

The little tree would reply quietly, 'It was the wish of my master, the gardener. He knows all about trees and if he thinks this is the right place for me, then it must be.'

As the days passed and the seasons changed, the little tree continued to grow and the older tree continued to try and harass it. Now the thriving young tree was able to answer back, 'Well! you seem to have survived the thunder and lightning, and the pouring rain does not seem to have done you any harm.'

'But I am old and strong and can take care of myself, whereas you are weak and small,' the tree would counter.

As the days passed, the little tree continued to become even more handsome.

One day, when the older tree had really harangued him he said, 'You seem to have thrived, although you are a bit unfortunate not to be able to bear any fruit. If you haven't been harmed, then why should I worry?'

'Me, unfortunate! Why that is ridiculous,' replied the older tree rather gruffly, 'As a matter of fact, I am the most fortunate object on the face of this earth. Everyone leaves me alone. I do not give anything to anyone, so no one comes to disturb me, and I have everything I need provided to me right where I stand.'

As the young tree matured, it blossomed with leaves and myriad flowers.

'Just wait and see how the birds sit on your branches and hurt your tender twigs,' the older tree taunted.

But whenever the birds would sit on its branches the young tree would be delighted, as they would trill with the joy of the beautiful spring days. The young tree continued to grow, and one day it's flowers turned into fruit. At first they were small, but they slowly grew to be red and luscious.

'Look. Look. I am an apple tree. Just look at my branches laden with apples,' the young tree was very excited.

'Just wait when they come to pick your fruit. There will be nothing left when they are through with you. All your efforts would have been in vain.' As usual the older tree tried to put a damper on his enthusiasm.

This time the young apple tree became a bit rude. 'At least I am of use to someone. I am not standing around uselessly like you. Why, you are just a plank of wood.' But soon he regretted being so hurtful, 'Come now, old friend, let us bury our differences and live together in harmony. It is no use quarreling all the time. We each have our destiny to fulfill.'

The older tree was not impressed.

Time passed by. The apple tree became more and more beautiful. Laden with fruit it looked like it belonged in the Garden of Eden. Soon birds began to nest in its branches, and children from the village would come and play in its shade Whenever they were hungry they would simply pluck an apple from its branches and munch on it, with the sweet juice running down their chins.

One day there was a lot of noise. 'What is happening?' the apple tree asked.

'Don't ask me. You are the one everyone comes to admire,' said the old tree rather irritably.

Indeed the same person, who had planted the sapling, had come by with a large group of people for a picnic under its shade.

'Look at this magnificent tree. I knew this was the right place for it. Even a useless tree like this old one flourished here,' the man told his companions. He then continued, 'Look at that old thing. It is so bare. It has no fruit or even many leaves, yet it seems very proud. Because of this tree, I realized the potential of this spot.'

'See, I told you everyone has a purpose,' the apple tree whispered to his senior.

Soon winter came and cold winds began to blow. The trees shed their leaves, the river froze over and a mantle of snow covered the countryside. One day, the two trees saw a couple of people approaching them. They were looking for firewood, as was apparent from the axes they were carrying.

'Look, there are two trees. You chop one while I deal with the other,' one of them exclaimed loudly.

As they came closer, the other man said, 'This tree is too big for me to chop alone. We'll have to do it together.'

So they set about chopping the old tree down. When they had finished they were exhausted. The first man then realized that the younger tree was an apple tree, and although barren now would surely flower again in spring. They decided to leave it alone. In any case the old tree had provided them with more firewood then they could carry. They loaded the logs in a cart and began to leave.

'I will miss you, old friend,' said the apple tree, 'But everyone has a purpose in life. Apparently yours was to make sure that I survive another spring and bring joy to many.'

The rustling of the branches of the apple tree attracted the men, taking away the logs of the old tree. When they looked back it seemed as though the tree was waving its branches in a silent goodbye.

HOT PEPPER

The humble deeds of innocent children are as worthwhile as the deeds of mighty men.
The following story is based in Turkey.

Usman was very excited. Tomorrow was to be a special day for him, but right now it was time to sleep.

'Mother, mother, you must wake me up early tomorrow morning,' he told his mother.

'Wake you up early? What if I can't wake you up?' his mother smiled.

'Oh! But you must,' cried her son, 'Do anything to wake me up, please. You can pinch me, smack me pull my hair, even throw cold water on me; but please wake me up! I have to get up early, I just have to!'

His mother was touched by her son's eagerness and said, 'My darling, you know how difficult it is for you to wake up in the mornings. What should I do if nothing works?'

'I have a great idea,' said Usman, 'Put hot peppers in my mouth. That ought to make me open my eyes!'

His mother looked at the serious face of her beloved son and took him in her arms, 'Oh my precious little son!' she murmured softly.

But he persisted, jumping up and down, 'I have to get up early. Put hot peppers in my mouth.' He kept repeating this until finally he went off to bed.

It was a warm and humid night. Usman could feel the damp sheets clinging to his body. He curled up and closed his eyes and tried to sleep. Suddenly he had an idea, 'Why don't I stay up all night?' he thought, 'Then when mother comes to wake me up in the morning I will surprise her. I don't really need to sleep.' He tossed and turned in bed, until his mother came to sleep beside him.

She hugged her son and whispered, 'Little Usman are you sleeping?' He remained silent and pretended to be fast asleep.

She looked tenderly at the still form of her son. As usual she prayed for his health and happiness. Unknown to his mother, Usman struggled to stay awake. After a while he turned around and looked at her. She was bathed in the light of the full moon. It seemed as though he was looking at a silvery angel lying next to him, and he knew she must be the best mother in the world.

As the night wore on, Usman kept repeating to himself over and over again, 'Hot peppers, hot peppers, red chillies, red peppers—so mother will put peppers in my mouth to wake me up—but I will fool her. I will not sleep.' His eyelids became heavy and he struggled to keep awake. He looked up at the sky and saw the bright stars twinkling. He began to count them in an effort to keep awake. He then peered through the trellis on his side and saw the cows there in the dark. He counted all his fingers and toes, but finally he lost the battle, and drifted off into dream-land.

When the sky began to lighten, all the animals in the courtyard began to stir with the first rays of the sun. Usman's mother woke up, and as soon as she heard the *muezzin* calling the faithful to the mosque, laid out her prayer mat. She fervently prayed to the Almighty for His blessings for her son. After praying, she went to check on Usman, who was sleeping soundly. She gazed at him adoringly and gathering him in her arms said, 'My darling, what wondrous world are you in now, in your dreams? I can never put hot peppers in your mouth to wake you up. Do you want to get up now?'

Usman stirred in his sleep. She lifted him up and his arms slipped from under the cover.

'How thin he is. I cannot even give my poor son enough to eat. But even if we die from lack of food, I don't want him to be forced to work. I just don't have the heart to wake him up,' she said quietly to herself, looking at the angelic face of her sleeping son.

Today was the first day Usman would be going to the fields to work for daily wages. The little fellow was so excited by this, but his mother knew what this entailed. She decided not to wake him up.

'Has he woken up yet?' her husband shouted from the courtyard and suddenly broke her idyll.

'Wake up the lazy brat and send him down immediately. Agha Mostafa will be here any moment to take him to work.'

'Please don't wake my son,' she begged her husband, 'Please don't send him to work. He is so small and thin. Please show some mercy.'

'Shut up, you old woman,' was the rude reply, 'So you want him to live like a young lord! Indeed! In my house he will have to work for his food. I'll soon wake him.'

She continued to plead with him, but he grew angrier and finally he rushed up the stairs, grabbed Usman and threw him on the ground. The mother quickly tried to shield him, whispering to herself, 'May God never make one give one's child into the hands of strangers.'

Usman was aroused from his dreams. He got up groggily and the first thing he asked his mother was, 'Did you put hot peppers in my mouth, mother?'

But before she could reply, Agha Mostafa's cart arrived at the gate and Usman ran out excitedly, all the sleep vanishing from his eyes, and jumped into it. He was bubbling with energy and raring to be off on his first day of work. His mother ran after him. She saw a neighbor, Zeinab, in the cart who also worked for Agha Mostafa.

'Please look after my Usman. He is just skin and bones, and the heat is terrifying. Please look after him,' she pleaded with her friend.

'Don't worry sister, I will take care of Usman,' Zeinab assured her.

As the cart trundled away, Usman was singing happily to himself. Zeinab was happy to see him looking so animated and full of energy. It was still dawn when they reached the field. The reapers had made bundles of the harvest, ready to be collected. These were still damp with dew and filled the air with the lovely aroma of fresh grass and wet corn. All the workers got down from the cart. They harnessed the horse and began loading the bundles. Usman led the horse away when the cart was filled. Mostafa preferred to have little boys work for him, because they were so agile and full of energy. What an adult did in half an hour, a boy like Usman could complete in fifteen minutes. Agha Mostafa praised Usman for being so quick and his little heart filled with pleasure.

Soon the sun rose from behind the mountains and first it appeared above the outline of peaks like a crimson ball of fire. Steadily it climbed higher in the sky and began to grow hot and dazzling. Usman was oblivious to the rising temperature and continued to work, running back and forth carrying the bundles to the cart.

Zeinab saw him and said with concern in her voice, 'Usman you are like a little lion. But it's growing hot. Take it easy. Don't wear yourself out.'

'I'm not tired, Auntie,' said Usman cheerfully, 'This work is fun.'

'But look how thin you are. You must take care,' Zeinab felt sorry for the little boy, forced to work in this heat, but such is the lot of the poor.

At midday, the sun was high in the sky. Everything was shimmering in the hot rays of the sun. The workers in the open field were bathed in sweat. Usman's face had taken on a red tinge. He hadn't even slept properly the previous night and his eyes were half closed in the glare of the sun. His shirt was dripping wet with sweat and stuck to his tender skin and his throat was so parched that it was hard for him to swallow.

As the temperature soared, Usman's feet felt the heat of the ground, prickling uncomfortably through the thin soles of his shoes. Nevertheless, such was his youthful ardour that he continued to work energetically, though somewhat slower now. All he could think of was the hot peppers he had asked his mother to put in his mouth to wake him up. Was it some searing hot iron, passing like a lance through his body, or was it just the effect of the red peppers still in his mouth? 'Red hot peppers—red hot peppers.' That was all he could think of. Now his legs were beginning to buckle under him. Zeinab saw the state he was in, and picked him up and sat him upon one of the horses, but Usman's legs would not stop shaking. Unconsciously, he tried to urge the horse to move forward. Zeinab rushed over to him. She could see that the heat had made him light-headed and he began to babble, 'Auntie Zeinab, when I grow up I am going to buy you a pair of the finest gold earrings.'

All the workers were hard at work under the blazing sun and Usman was the tiniest of them all. A small, eight-year old, weak and emaciated from deprivation and hunger, he continued to do his share of the work. Zeinab finally could not stand to see his condition any more. She took him to a shady spot, by the stack of corn he had helped to pile and urged him to rest.

'Little one, you must lie down for a while. You have done more than your share of the work. I am sure Agha Mostafa will give you a bonus."

'Do you really think so?' Usman said, still excited. 'Maybe with that I can buy something pretty for my mother.'

'Yes you can and now you must rest,' Zeinab insisted. Soon Usman dozed off and in his sleep, for some reason he kept dreaming that someone was putting red hot peppers in his mouth.

The sun went down in the west and the shadows lengthened across the fields. Everyone was now relaxing. The horses had been unhitched and given fresh grass to eat. All the workers were eating and joking. Usman got up with a start. All he could think of was the bonus. No one seemed to notice him as he sat in his corner. He kept staring intently at Agha Mostafa, as though willing him to pay him his wages. At last, Zeinab remembered the little boy, and came over and gave him some water to drink and something to eat. Agha's wife also noticed the lad.

'Why have you stayed on so long. Your mother must be worried sick. Go on home.' she said solicitously.

Usman felt very uneasy and seemed to want to say something. The woman understood and leaned over and whispered something in her husband's ears. Everyone began to laugh at him. Usman felt embarrassed and was getting very angry. He wanted to run away.

But just then, Agha Mostafa said out aloud, 'Well, well! Look at me. I have forgotten to give my best worker his wages.' He then held out a twenty-five kurush coin. Usman was delighted. He snatched it from Agha's hand and ran home.

When he reached home, he found his mother waiting anxiously at the door. He handed her the twenty-five kurush. His mother was delighted and kissed her son. 'For my mother's smile, I am willing to endure all the hot peppers in the world,' Usman thought proudly, as he looked up at his mother passing the coin three times around his head, as a blessing and to ward off the evil eye from her beloved son.

UNCLE AQUAN'S ORANGES

The oranges growing on the trees in Uncle Aquan's small orchard had ripened and presented a truly glorious sight. The brightly coloured fruits, hanging amidst the lush deep green foliage, gave a look of distinction to the small, humble cottage in which Uncle Aquan lived with his family. Ding Dong, who was almost six years old, loved the sight of these trees. Oranges were his favorite fruit and he felt it was his duty to look after them while they were ripening on the trees. He would become very anxious when strong winds blew and caused the branches to break. He would pray for the wind to die down before they harmed his beloved oranges. On such days he was very nervous indeed.

It was on one such cold, windy day, that Ding Dong was sitting inside the cottage, watching his mother spinning cloth. Every now and then, he would rush to the window to make sure that the oranges were still hanging safely on the branches.

'Don't worry, Ding Dong,' his mother tried to reassure him, 'The wind will not be able to blow down the oranges. They are not as fragile as they look.'

She took his tiny hands in her own, 'My goodness how cold your fingers are. Come nearer the brazier. It will warm you up a bit.'

'But I don't want to warm my hands,' said Ding Dong in a distressed tone, 'All I want are some oranges.'

'What? Again?' His mother pursed her lips, 'Ssh, your grandfather is asleep. We must not disturb him. Just wait for your father to come home. He will give you some oranges. My goodness, it's a good thing you cannot reach them. There would be no oranges left on the trees by now.'

Ding Dong heard his father entering the gate and rushed to the courtyard to greet him.

'Be careful, do you want to collide with the bamboo poles?' shouted Gengui, as he unloaded the bundles of bamboo that he had spent many hours hacking down. He was tired and in no mood to tolerate his son's incessant demands.

'Father, mother said you would pick me some oranges,' Ding Dong asked excitedly.

Gengui frowned and said curtly, 'Ding Dong, first fetch me the hatchet to cut up these bamboo sticks.'

Ding Dong had other plans, 'But father, I want oranges. I have been looking after them all morning and now want to eat some. All I want is to eat a few oranges,' he said pouting.

'Do as I say,' his father shouted.

Uncle Aquan woke up with a start at the sound of loud voices, mumbling sleepily to himself, 'Who will come all this way to buy the oranges?'

The road was muddy and slippery from the rain and the weather had taken a turn for the worst. Suddenly, they heard the sound of barking dogs down the road.

Zhu, the family pet Pekinese, also became agitated as if someone was trying to get into the house. In the distance, they saw a man attempting to approach their gate. Picking up one of Gengui's freshly cut bamboo sticks, Uncle Aquan hurried over to the gate. The man entered and came towards him. He was wearing a threadbare, blue cloth gown and carrying a pipe in his hand. Around his waist was wrapped a faded red girdle, with dragons embroidered on it, much like those worn during the New Year festival in the first lunar month. He also wore a black jacket.

The visitor was actually a merchant who came by this way frequently to purchase oranges. His name was Zhang and Uncle Aquan had sent word to him earlier, requesting him to come and discuss the sale of the oranges in his orchard.

'Welcome, my respected friend,' Uncle Aquan greeted him, as he shooed away Zhu, who by now was barking frantically.

He ushered his guest into the cottage. Ding Dong's mother quickly drew the bench from under the table, dusted it with the sleeve of her dress and placed it in front of Zhang. She then silently resumed her spinning. Women in those days were expected to keep away from any matters of business, which was considered a male occupation. Their opinion was seldom sought or given.

Zhang began the conversation, 'I was on my way to Mr Wang's orchard. He has had a good harvest of oranges and has made me a good offer. But seeing that we are such old friends, I thought I'd look you up first. What did you want to see me about?'

'It's nothing much,' Uncle Aquan replied, 'We have a few orange trees, ourselves. In the past, I used to keep all the fruit for my family, especially my grandson Ding Dong, who *loves* oranges. With some I used to make orange candy for my nephew's shop. But sugar is so expensive, that we do not earn anything from that. Times are hard you know, and with the new year approaching. I need some ready cash. I was wondering if you would be interested in buying my fruit.'

He then called Ding Dong and said to him, 'Go outside and ask your father to bring in some oranges for our guest to sample.'

Ding Dong ran outside and helped his father gather ten of the juiciest oranges in the skirt of his gown. His mouth watered at the sight of these morsels, but he knew that he was not supposed to eat any without his grandfather's permission. He saw him hand over the oranges to Zhang,

'Try them. See for yourself how delicious they are.'

Zhang toyed with the oranges, studying one, measuring it and then, breaking off some slices, tested them by biting them with his teeth. He screwed up his face, as if to show the oranges were sour. This was an old merchant tactic. The oranges were in fact very sweet and juicy.

After a few minutes silence he said, 'Uncle Aquan, in what way do you want to sell your fruit?'

'Do you mean the price? Well I will sell them at the market price,' Uncle Aquan's replied.

'No, no That is not what I meant!' said Zhang, while his fingers kept feeling the plump oranges, 'I mean, would you like to sell them by the weight or by the lot?'

Uncle Aquan was a straightforward man and the merchant's tactics puzzled him.

'Selling by weight is always better as no one loses. After all, a pound is a pound,' he answered in a pleasant way.

Zhang did not say anything, but got up and went outside to inspect the trees. He counted twenty trees in all. Five by the threshing floor, and fifteen by the vegetable plot. The branches of all the trees were almost touching the ground under the weight of the fruits.

Actually Zhang was pleased with what he saw, but took care not to show his pleasure. When he finished inspecting, they stood together under a tree.

After thinking for a few minutes, Zhang finally said, 'Uncle Aquan, You are like a friend. But business is business. I must inform you that the price of oranges has drastically fallen this year. There is a glut in the market and no buyers. With such a small number of trees, you are hardly in a position to bargain. Mr Wang has hundreds of trees and merchants rush to him, because we can pick and choose the best. Frankly speaking, your oranges do not have the same quality as his.'

'I understand what you mean. But I know that you are a friend and will not cheat me. Tell me what I should do,' Uncle Aquan replied humbly.

'Relax my friend. We will come to a mutually beneficial agreement. I am willing to buy your whole stock and I will give you three dollars a load, for your lot of four loads,' Zhang offered.

With this he fished out six silver dollars and placed them on the table saying, 'I will give you the remaining six dollars when the oranges are delivered.'

'Three dollars a load and only four loads?' Uncle Aquan was surprised at how low the offer was. He knew what the merchant was up to but felt unable to do anything.

Ding Dong's mother was listening to the whole conversation, while appearing to be busy at the spinning wheel. She was not at all pleased at the way the merchant was dealing with her simple father-in-law. She quickly got up and sought out her husband Gengui.

'Look at your father. He is such a simple soul and the merchant is taking advantage of him. He is talking him into selling all the oranges for only twelve dollars. That is entirely unfair. Do something, before your father finalizes the deal.'

Gengui hurried to the spot where the two were talking. He heard Zhang tell his father, 'Well, it's all right by me if you are not interested in the money I am offering you. We can still part as friends.'

'What's going on? Have the two of you agreed on the deal?' Gengui interjected.

'No, no,' replied Zhang, 'We are still negotiating. After all we are old friends.'

'So then since nothing has been finalized, I hope you don't mind if I say something. Uncle Zhang, the three dollars per load that you have offered is really not enough. What would you say to seven loads of our entire crop and you pay us for six,' Gengui suggested.

'Sorry,' said Zhang firmly, 'Twelve dollars is all I am prepared to offer. Take it or leave it.'

Then father and son agreed, although they knew that the merchant was not being fair. They were not sure they would be able to get another buyer and the New Year festivities were round the corner.

Zhang gave a triumphant smile at the conclusion of a most satisfactory deal—from his point of view. This was not lost on Uncle Aquan. Even little Ding Dong was able to guess that the stranger had been unfair.

'Come on all of you, let's fill the crates for Uncle Zhang,' Uncle Aquan called out to his little grandson.

Ding Dong was not at all pleased with the situation. The stranger with the red sash was going to steal all his precious oranges. He ran to his grandfather and threw himself in his arms.

'Grandfather, please do not let this man steal our oranges. I want some. I haven't eaten even one all day.'

'Come, come, don't be such a spoilt baby. Help us load these oranges,' said his father.

Uncle Aquan could understand the little boy's distress. He knew that the child liked to eat oranges more than anything else, and all his life he had been told that these oranges belonged to him.

Uncle Aquan took the little boy to the vegetable patch and pulled down a branch full of beautiful ripe oranges, so that he could give one to his grandson. At that moment, he heard the merchant's voice and was embarrassed by the little act of dishonesty he was about to commit. He was a God fearing man and believed it was wrong to take something that did not belong to him.

But in his heart he wanted to see little Ding Dong smile. 'Maybe twelve dollars are not worth hurting his feelings. After all I take care of the trees. Why can't I give my grandson a couple of oranges?' he thought, convincing himself, and was on the verge of picking a fruit once more, when he heard Zhang's voice again and stopped.

'Grandfather, can't you hear me? Please give me an orange,' Ding Dong kept begging him.

Uncle Aquan could not bear to see his grandson so upset, 'Okay, I'll get one for you.'

Two oranges tumbled down from the branches and a delighted Ding Dong ran over to pick them up. The merchant now approached the trees in the vegetable patch. He had a high stool with him to reach for the oranges higher up. He smiled at Uncle Aquan, but the old man's cheeks burnt with shame. He sat down with bowed head.

'I know I have stolen two of your oranges,' he muttered in a low voice, almost as if to himself, 'I know they are not mine anymore. Okay, I will give you your money back. After all, it is my fruit if I want to sell it or not.' However, nobody heard him. In the meanwhile, all twenty trees had been stripped clean of oranges.

Ding Dong held his two oranges, laughing gleefully.

'Two oranges are enough to gladden his little heart,' he thought to himself.

Then suddenly he got up and said loudly in a trembling voice, 'I can't do this. Please Ding Dong put down those oranges. They don't belong to us anymore. Put them down, I say.'

Ding Dong stared at his grandfather. He had never heard him speak in such a harsh voice before. He let the oranges slip through his little fingers and fall to the ground.

Zhang, who was watching all this, waved his hand magnanimously and said, 'It's alright, Ding Dong. You can take those two oranges.'

To his utter surprise the little boy left the oranges lying there and walked away.

THE GHOUL-I-BIYABANI

The Persian word 'ghoul' is probably the root of the English word, as they both have the same meaning. This story is about the wild giant of the desert and was narrated by an old man as his own experience.

This happened when I was twelve years old. I lived with my large family in a huge house. It had a courtyard surrounded by rooms. There was one family room in which all of us would gather to spend the evenings. As is common in Iran, our family room had a huge oblong *korsi* (a low, oblong table) in the middle. In winter, which is very harsh in this country, there was usually a large brazier filled with hot glowing charcoals placed under the *korsi*. Everyone would gather around to keep warm, as well as enjoy family togetherness. Teapots set on small *samovars* would provide hot drinks for the elders, and for the children, huddled together under quilts, there was always plenty of fruit, nuts and sweets. Here the adults would discuss family matters and the children would do their homework.

On the night my adventure occurred, it was extremely cold and a fierce wind was blowing. All the women and children had gathered in the room. There was a pile of snow outside but inside the family room, we were warm and cozy, without a care in the world. There was pleasant conversation and everyone was listening to a story recounted by an old aunt. Suddenly the door of the room flew open and my grandmother strode in. She looked worried.

'Zeevar is about to have her baby and we need the midwife,' she announced, 'Someone will have to go and fetch her in a hurry.' She strode up to me purposefully, 'You will have to go immediately. Go to your aunt's house and ask her to accompany you.'

My aunt lived several lanes away. I guess the task had fallen on me as I was the eldest boy around. I set out in the snow and bitter cold. My grandmother had taken care to wrap a warm scarf around my ears and tucked it under my chin. But nothing could keep the cold away. Besides, it was really dark and gloomy. I only had a small lantern to show the way. My shoes made a strange, scratching sound as I walked. The street was deserted, only occasionally a muffled figure would pass by. I hurried on through the Jewish quarters, about which we children had heard all sorts of frightening tales. The trek seemed to take forever. At last I reached my aunt's house, and lifted the huge knocker and banged on the door as loud as I could. My hands were freezing.

The door was opened by my aunt. 'Good God! Manoocher! What are you doing out of doors at this time of the night. Come in quickly or you will freeze.'

'Grandma has asked me to take you along to fetch the midwife quickly, for my mother,' I told her.

'I need to get ready, so why don't you take off your coat and eat something and sit by the *korsi* in the meantime,' she told me and hurried to get ready.

I sat down with my cousins who were listening to an old woman tell a hair raising tale of a *ghoul-i-biyabani*. The children were all listening wide-eyed as she continued, '...this ghoul is everywhere. He eats up all the animals and is especially fond of little children whom he really relishes.'

I asked if it was really true that he gobbles little children, feeling a shiver down my spine.

The old woman cackled loudly with a toothless grin, and said, 'Of course. And you would be a tasty morsel for him, young man.'

'How large is he and what does he sound like?' asked a cousin in a quivering voice.

'He is gargantuan, taller than this house and when he speaks his voice cracks and sounds like the roar of a lion.'

That is all I had time to hear, as my aunt came in, ready to go.

'Come on Manoocher, lets go and fetch the midwife.'

I quickly put on my scarf and coat and followed her, holding the lantern.

Outside it was pitch dark. The light from the lantern cast long shadows on the snow-covered ground. It was hard to imagine that this was the same place that was filled with the hustle and bustle of the market in the daytime. We walked quickly and reached the midwife's house and knocked. An old man, who seemed to be annoyed at the intrusion at this late hour, opened the door.

'What do you want?' he asked gruffly.

'We have come to fetch Safoora. She is needed urgently, as my sister is having a baby,' explained my Aunt.

'Well, Safoora can't go with you.'

'Why not? Please call her. This is an emergency. We have walked in the cold to get her,' I pleaded, almost in tears.

'She isn't here. She has gone to the neighbouring village to attend to an emergency and will not be back tonight,' said the old man quite annoyed with us.

We could do nothing but go back home with the bad news and hope some other arrangement could be made for the birth of my little brother or sister.

When we reached her house, my aunt bade me goodbye and told me to hurry on home. The thought of passing through those dark lanes terrified me. 'How am I going to go through the bath area? It is infested with *djinns*. But I must not be afraid. I must prove that I am the man of the house,' I told myself, trying to find some courage. I began to run. It was difficult to move fast over all that slippery snow, and soon I was out of breath and sat down on a nearby bench to recover. I was breathing hard and closed my eyes to relax.

When I had rested sufficiently I opened my eyes— and screamed. There in front of me, just a short distance away, confirming my worst fears, was the *ghoul-i-biyabani*! He was huge and furry and there was a fiery glow emanating from him. He was coming down the lane straight towards me, with his arms outstretched. He looked famished and surely he was going to swallow me in one gulp, small as I was. I got up and tried to run. 'Maybe he cannot run as fast as me because he is so big,' I reasoned.

But my heart was in my mouth and I could barely lift my limbs. I began to feel myself shaking uncontrollably and tears began to flow down my cheeks.

'The old woman was right! He is ferocious!' I thought.

The ghoul kept coming closer and seemed to be growing larger by the second. I could see his mouth was open to swallow me. 'This is definitely the end of me,' I thought, my teeth beginning to chatter.

I fell on the ground, on my knees, and began to plead with the ghoul, 'Please Mister, spare me. I am but a tiny morsel for you. You won't even know you have eaten something. It is the coat that is making me look big. Inside I am really all skin and bones.' The words came out desperately, 'Please Mister Ghoul-i-biyabani, Have mercy on me.'

I closed my eyes preparing for the worst. My hands were clenched tight, and I braced myself. I then heard a gentle voice, 'Who is this *ghoul-i-biyabani* you are talking to? I don't see any such thing around here, young man.'

I quickly opened my eyes. Through my tears and fear I saw the same ghoul standing in front of me, but he was talking to me kindly.

'Who are you and what in the name of good heavens are you doing out in this cold night?' he asked.

'I am Manoocher and I had gone to fetch the midwife,' I answered in a quivering voice.

'Well, look at me,' the ghoul commanded, 'Do I look like a monster to you?'

I looked up to see our neighbourhood policeman standing in front of me, a nice normal sized man once he had taken off his thick furry coat.

'Come with me, young man. I will take you home.'

As we walked down the lane, I saw the *nanwai*, baking bread in the fiery glow of the *tandoor*. It was the same glow which I thought had come from the ghoul-i-biyabani. The mind can really make up anything in a fit of terror. But I was really glad to be home and it would be a long time before I ventured out in the night again. In the meantime, my father had returned and taken the carriage to get another midwife. Ghoul or no ghoul, I was not going to take any more chances.

SHAH ABBAS AND THE THREE SISTERS

Shah Abbas was the King of a far away land, somewhere in Azerbaijan. He and his wazir, Allahwardi Khan, had the habit of disguising themselves as dervishes and travelling through the land, mingling with people, but not for the purpose of seeking to learn of the citizen's problems in order to aid them. The King's objective was somewhat less noble—to spy on his subjects and find out what they were saying about him. A sort of self-serving intelligence system.

One day, while on such a 'mission', they spied three beautiful maidens, who seemed to be sisters, sitting in a courtyard of the house of a groom (*mehtar* in Persian) of the palace. They were discussing something among themselves. The King was eager to find out what these fair maidens were talking about, so he and the wazir sneaked into the house through the open gate and positioned themselves secretly to eavesdrop on the sisters. The open gate was not incidental. In those days an open door was the symbol of a hospitable household.

They heard the eldest sister saying, 'I wish I could marry the wazir's son. I have seen him many times and think he is the most handsome man in town. If

only this dream of mine could come true, I would be the happiest girl in the entire world.'

'That can be easily arranged,' thought the King, looking at his wazir, who was not too pleased with the idea.

Then the second sister spoke, 'If the Judge were to bring a proposal to our father for his son for me, I would willingly accept. He is rich and very good looking. If only this dream of mine could come true.'

'That too, can be easily arranged,' thought the King.

Then the two sisters turned to the youngest. She was easily the most beautiful of the trio.

'Jehan, now it is your turn to tell us who is the man of your dreams?' they asked her.

'Well, my wish is really quite different from yours. I wish to marry a man who is honest and good. Someone who has drunk only the pure milk of his mother —a *sheer-e-pak khorde*. I would marry such a man, even if he be only a poor shepherd and ugly as well.'

The King was perplexed at this. Jehan continued, 'Do you know what I would really like to do?'

The two older sisters were eager to know.

'I wish somehow I could force Shah Abbas and his pompous courtiers to do our bidding. I would make them carry our luggage, while we roam the world. Carrying large and heavy sacks on their backs would teach them a lesson or two, and make them realize what the poor people in the country have to bear for a pittance. Why does Shah Abbas expect everyone to bow and scrape before him? Isn't he a human being just like the rest of us? Is he not going to die one day? Does he think he can take all these riches with him to the other world? He is really a vain man,' she concluded.

Shah Abbas' blood was boiling, 'How dare this chit of a girl criticize me. I will teach her a lesson she will never forget.'

The King and his wazir returned quietly to the palace, seething with anger. Shah Abbas lay awake all night thinking of what the girl had said, and resolved to punish her impudence. Early the next morning he donned his red, embroidered, royal gown and summoned his wazir.

'Fetch the *mehtar* and his three daughters immediately,' he commanded, 'I also want to see your sons,' he ordered, turning to his wazir and the judge.

When they all presented themselves before the King, he ordered the wazir to announce the betrothal of his son with the eldest daughter. Then he ordered the judge to take the second daughter as his daughter-in-law. The grooms elder daughters were overjoyed. However, at that moment the King was hardly in a benevolent mood. Then, in all his fury, he turned to the youngest.

'You are a rude and ungrateful girl! You don't think I am a pure and honest man! You want to make me carry your luggage, while you travel far and wide with that ugly shepherd of yours,' he roared at the top of his voice. He then ordered the executioner, '*Jallad!* Lop off her head in one clean sweep.'

Jehan realized that the King must have eavesdropped on their conversation the previous evening. But she was unafraid.

'As I have nothing to lose anymore, I want to tell you that you are a petty and insignificant man, who is not worth even being afraid of,' she said to the King,

'What! You have the nerve to stand before me and call me names! In my own palace!'

'Yes. I have the courage to tell you what you really are. A mean, despicable person, who has nothing better to do than to eavesdrop on people. You ought to be ashamed of yourself.'

Needless to say the King was ready to burst with anger, '*Jallad*! Cut off her impudent tongue before you behead her.'

Jehan had thrown caution to the wind and continued her tirade, 'You sir, are worse than I had thought. Not only are you petty, you are a coward as well. You bully people and cannot accept the truth about yourself. Neither do you want to admit that you can be wrong. I am an insignificant person. You can have my head cut off. But remember, when people hear why you ordered my execution, I will be acclaimed as a person of courage, who was unafraid to criticize you. You will be condemned for not accepting the truth about yourself.'

At this, Allahwardi Khan spoke up and said, 'My Lord, I hate to admit this, but she does have a point. If she is executed merely for criticizing you, then people will feel that you are not a fair and just ruler. That will not be good for us. So, in my opinion, instead of having her beheaded and creating a martyr out of her, why don't we just send her far-away into exile?'

Shah Abbas thought for a while and then said, 'Under no circumstances am I going to let this girl go unpunished. Exile her into the wilderness. Take her deep into the jungle, where there is no water or human being. There the wolves can have her for dinner.'

So this brave young girl found herself in the wilderness, all alone. She wandered for several days, without meeting a soul and was about to drop from sheer exhaustion, when she saw a person coming towards her. As he came closer, she saw that he was a shepherd. He walked in a very lazy manner, ambling along and did not seem to be going anywhere in particular. He wasn't very good-looking either, and was bald. But he had an honest face. Suddenly Jehan realized that he had all the characteristics of the kind of man she hoped to marry.

'Young man, I am lost and lonely,' she called out to him, 'Will you help me. I haven't eaten in days.'

The shepherd stopped and looked surprised at finding such a beautiful maiden in the wilderness.

'Who are you and what are you doing in a place like this?' he came up and asked her.

'It's a long story and I will narrate it to you as soon as you give me something to eat,' replied the girl.

'I will have to go home and fetch something for you,' said the man.

'If you live close by, why don't you take me there?' asked Jehan.

The young man thought for a while and said, 'I will have to first ask my mother if you can come to our house. Wait here, while I go and ask her.'

So she waited and thought about the simplicity of the man. She decided that he was the man for her. Soon the shepherd returned with the news that his mother had said that she could come and stay with them.

Thus, the young girl went to live with this simple shepherd and his mother. While staying there she observed that the young man was quite lazy. But he was very obedient and loyal to his mother. 'He probably never made a decision by himself in his entire life,' thought Jehan.

One day, she said to the mother, 'You have been very kind to me. I want you to accept me as your daughter-in-law.'

The old woman was delighted, 'Nothing would make me happier. But I could not imagine that you would actually agree to marry my lazy Kuchal (which means bald in Persian).' She had never thought that her simple, lazy son would be able to find such a beautiful and intelligent bride. The young man also had secretly dreamt of making her his wife, and he was overjoyed. So Kuchal and Jehan were married in a simple ceremony.

The young man proved to be a very loving and loyal husband. Jehan knew that she would have to make all the decisions in the family and she happily took over the responsibility of running the house as well as taking care of the fields. She sent her husband to the market to purchase a pair of bullocks, to pull the plough. Together they tilled the land and had to work very hard. Her husband overcame his lazy ways and became a very diligent worker. They were very happy.

One day, the young man was working alone in the fields, clearing a patch of land for planting when suddenly his spade hit a large rock. The man tried to remove the rock, but it was very heavy. After great difficulty he managed to shift it and underneath, he discovered the mouth of an old, unused well. But a staggering sight beheld his eyes. The well was filled to the brim with shiny round discs. He picked one up and examined it carefully, however, he could not make out what it was. Quickly he covered the mouth of the well and ran home excitedly to show the disc to his wife.

'Jehan, look at this pretty round piece of metal,' and he told her about the unused well he had found. When Jehan saw the shiny gold piece, she knew at once that he had discovered a well full of buried treasure. Now they would be rich and be able to fulfill their wildest dreams.

'Shush, keep your voice down. No one must hear of this,' Jehan calmed down her husband. She then instructed him, 'Fill the bags with the gold and load it on the backs of the bullocks, but just enough for it to seem like a normal load and slowly, very casually, bring them home.'

In the meantime, she dug a big hole in the ground in the garden to hide the treasure. Slowly, the gold was transferred to the house over a number of days.

When all the gold was safely buried in the house, Jehan asked Kuchal to go into town and fetch the best architect and builder. She seemed to have a plan up her sleeve. Remember, she had not forgotten the treatment meted out to her by Shah Abbas. When the architect and the builder arrived, Jehan told them what she wanted.

'Build me a palace with forty rooms,' she instructed them, 'Each room must lead to the other. There must be only one entrance and the exit must be only after the forty rooms have been traversed. Each room must have it's own color scheme, different from the other. Do you think you can construct such a palace for me?'

'Madame anything can be built on this earth, if you have the money to do it,' the architect replied.

'Spare no expense. Make it the most magnificent mansion in the land,' ordered Jehan.

Soon the palace was completed. It was a magnificent structure. News of its grandeur began to spread far and wide. Jehan laid out the gardens with flowers of all hues and fragrance. There were nightingales and peacocks everywhere. The fruit trees had been brought in from faraway lands and they flourished under her care. Jehan then hired many *kaneezes* and taught them the niceties of looking after guests. Each *kaneez* was dressed in the same color as the room she was assigned to. The rooms were decorated with priceless carpets, paintings and jewel encrusted vases. She then opened the gates for visitors.

People flocked to this splendid palace and each one was treated with the utmost hospitality. They were wined and dined and made to feel really welcome. Many people thought that this was more opulent and magnificent than even the royal palace. When Shah Abbas heard of this beautiful mansion, famous for its hospitality, he was consumed with jealousy and curiosity. So, along with his wazir, Allahwardi Khan, the King set off to see the place for himself. Of course, they disguised themselves as dervishes, as they always did.

After wandering for many days, they came to the palace and were awestruck by its splendour. While they stood outside gazing at the view, Jehan saw them from a window and recognized them at once. She had been expecting them to come, sooner or later. At once, she sent a *kaneez* to them.

'Can I help you?' the maid asked them.

'We are two guests of God from Isfahan,' replied Shah Abbas.

'This is a place where the gates are always open to guests, especially for guests from God, *mehmane Khoda hasteed*,' the *kaneez* said as she led them inside.

When the two entered, they were amazed at the luxury and the opulence they saw around them. They were fed the most delicious food in beautiful gold and silver platters. The colours and the music were a delight and soon the two began to enjoy themselves thoroughly.

'I am the King and even I have not seen such lavish hospitality, such splendour and opulence,' said Shah Abbas to his wazir.

The wazir agreed, 'The mirrors, the crystals, the filigree, and the gold and silver encrusted objects are dizzying. Its enough to make one's head swim.'

They remained in the palace for many days, going through the myriad of rooms, each more splendid than the last. 'Each room is a *behesht* (paradise). If this is earth, what must the next world be like,' thought the King, by now totally intoxicated by the sights and sounds he saw around him, as they wandered from room to room. When they came to the thirty-ninth room, a *kaneez* came up to them.

'My mistress would like to know if there was anything more your hearts desire,' she asked them.

'The owner of this magnificent palace is a *woman*?' the King said surprised, 'I must meet her. Please tell your mistress that it is our desire to meet her.'

The *kaneez* went inside and came back with the message, 'My mistress says that since you have not yet seen the gardens, she would like to invite you to meet her there. But if you would be kind enough to carry those two sacks with you to the garden, she would be most obliged.'

The duo agreed and bent to pick up the sacks. Each weighed at least five maunds. They lifted them with great difficulty onto their backs and began to follow the *kaneez* to the garden. Shah Abbas and Allahwardi Khan were not accustomed to lifting anything heavier than their wineglasses and they staggered under the weight. Soon they were ready to drop with exhaustion. By the time they reached the garden, which proved to be a long walk through thirty-nine rooms, they were bathed in sweat and their limbs were stiff with exhaustion.

In the garden, lavish arrangements had been made for them, with platters full of delicacies and maidens dancing to exotic tunes played by musicians. They were requested to sit under an arch, entwined with vines laden with grapes. They could see pomegranates, apples and all kinds of luscious fruits growing around. They were truly intoxicated by all this.

Then the *kaneez* came back with a message, 'My mistress would like to speak to you in her chambers after all,' she told them. Then added, 'Would you be kind enough to bring the two sacks along?'

So off they went once again, staggering along, through all the rooms to the mistress' private chambers. This was obviously the fortieth room of the house. The sacks on their backs now seemed heavier than ever.

When they entered the last room, they were confronted with a scene like something out of a dream. The room was decorated more beautifully than all the others. In front of them sat a veiled woman, among freshly, blooming flowers. The chair she was sitting on was studded with rubies, diamonds, sapphires and pearls. It was a heavenly sight and Shah Abbas and his wazir gasped in wonder. Jehan allowed them sufficient time to look around and admire the surroundings. Then she removed her veil.

'Shah Abbas and Allahwardi Khan, welcome to my humble abode,' she said with a sweet smile.

Shah Abbas was taken aback at being addressed by their real names. 'We are only guests from Isfahan. We are not who you say we are,' he replied unconvincingly.

'All right, if you two want to conceal your identities, I have no problem with that. But you should know that I am aware of who you are.'

Shah Abbas realized that this woman had seen through their disguises and asked, 'How do you know who we are?'

Jehan stood up and said, 'Do you remember the three sisters you summoned to the royal court after eavesdropping on them?'

'Yes, I do' replied the Shah, 'The youngest girl was rude and impertinent and I had her exiled. But, what does the mistress of this heavenly palace have to do with that incident?'

'Don't you recognize me? I am the girl you banished into the wilderness to die.'

The Shah was absolutely speechless.

Jehan continued, 'Do you remember. I had said that I would marry a man with a pure heart and would make you and your wazir carry heavy loads on your backs, just like the poor of your kingdom. Well I have succeeded in my plans, but you failed, as I was not devoured by wild beasts, as you well wanted me to be.'

Jehan then introduced her husband to them and said, 'He is kind and pure and a better man than you will ever be.'

The young girl had properly humbled the King.

Then his wazir also spoke on her behalf, 'Sire, I do not blame her for teaching us this lesson in humility. What I am really worried about is that if the people find out how you have been outwitted by a mere girl, you will be the laughing stock of the whole kingdom. That will not be good for your image.'

Shah Abbas realized the truth in what his wazir had said. He could not afford that anybody should find out what had happened to them. 'Please do not tell a soul what you have reduced me to. I shall forever be obliged to you,' he begged Jehan.

Jehan stipulated her conditions for remaining silent, 'I will not tell a soul, if you promise never to eavesdrop on people and never ever to trample on their rights. If you do not live up to your promise, then the whole world will hear of this episode, where a 'mere chit of a girl' humbled the mighty King.'

Shah Abbas readily agreed.

The King and his wazir returned to the royal palace. After that, never again did the two spy on people or abuse anybody's right to privacy.

THE JACKAL'S SPELL

Once upon a time, when Brahmadatta was King of Benaras, a wise man called Budhisatta was the royal family priest. The priest had learnt the three vedas and the eighteen branches of knowledge. He knew a spell that could subdue wild animals and cause them to obey him. But such a spell was not to be used lightly and Budhisatta kept it a close secret, lest someone overhear it and use it unwisely. To remember the spell it was necessary to practice religious meditation regularly.

One day, Budhisatta went to the jungle nearby, so that he could meditate and recite the spell in seclusion, away from the ears of eavesdroppers. He sat on a flat stone, leaned against a tree trunk and got into the proper trance-like state and kept on reciting the spell. Unknown to him, a cunning jackal was resting in his hole, very close to the tree. He heard the spell and being clever, he started to recite it along with the priest and soon knew it by heart. You see jackals have a sharp mind and can learn things very quickly. When Budhisatta ended his ritual, he rose to leave; the jackal could not contain his glee at having mastered an ancient charm and came out of his hole.

'Oh noble priest, I have learnt the spell better than you know it yourself,' he said loudly. Having said this he ran off into the deepest part of the jungle.

Budhisatta was extremely distressed at this unfortunate development and ran after the jackal crying out, 'You jackal, listen to me! You will do great mischief if you do not know how to use the charm wisely. Come back and listen to me.'

But needless to say the jackal was in no mood to be wise or noble, and did not listen to the priest. After some time Budhisatta gave up the chase and went back to the palace full of misgiving.

Now the jackal wanted to use the charm. He sought out the she-jackal he had been eyeing for some time and who had spurned him. When he got near her, he gave her a sharp nip in her tail.

She was surprised and looked annoyed, 'What is it?'

'Will you be my companion or not,' he asked her quite gruffly.

'Go away, I do not want to have anything to do with you,' she replied with a toss of her head.

The jackal smiled to himself, a very knowing smile and quickly recited the charm. The she-jackal immediately became enamoured of him and readily agreed to be his mate. The jackal was delighted, not only with his conquest, but also with the fact that the spell really worked. Now the entire jungle would be his to command.

First he went to the council of the jackals and subjugated them with the spell. He then worked the charm over the lions, elephants, deer and eventually, over all the four-footed creatures of the jungle. He named himself, Sabbadatta, which means King of Kings, and his consort became known as Sitadatta, and together they ruled over the animal kingdom. Whenever they would go out to survey their kingdom, they would sit on the backs of two lions, who in turn would be riding on top of two elephants. Such was his vanity that he wanted to be on top of the world. Everyone in the kingdom paid homage and bowed as the entourage passed by.

As time went by, the jackal grew more and more conceited. His ambition knew no bounds. He wanted to be monarch over all he could see. He wanted to be the supreme ruler, and wished to see everyone totally subservient to him.

So Sabadatta decided to capture the kingdom of Benaras. With all his four-footed creatures in tow, he marched towards the city and halted at a place twelve leagues away from it. From there he sent a message to the King of Benaras, ordering him, 'Give up your kingdom or be prepared to fight.'

The people of Benaras were struck with fear at seeing such a gathering of wild animals at the city gates, and barricaded themselves in their homes. The King too, grew very worried.

'Why are these wild animals attacking us?' he asked all his generals and courtiers who had gathered around. Each one was perplexed at how such a thing had come to pass. The animals of the jungle had never challenged human beings before. Something was very wrong here. No one seemed to have any clue as to how to deal with this problem.

Budhisatta the priest, of course, knew how the jackal had become Sabadatta. He came to the King and said to him, 'Your Majesty, do not worry about this matter. Leave it to me. I know why this so-called Sabadatta has challenged you?'

The King had great faith in Budhisatta's abilities, and was relieved that he had offered to help overcome this crisis.

Budhisatta went up to the highest point of the palace and called out to the jackal, 'Sabadatta, you evil jackal, how do you propose to take over the realm of His Majesty the King of Benaras?'

'I will cause the lions to roar and with that frighten the multitude that live within your city, and thus I will take over,' the jackal shouted back.

'So this is what he proposes to do,' thought Budhisatta, Quickly he climbed down from the ramparts and called in the town criers. He ordered them to immediately go through the entire length and breadth of the city and proclaim that each and every person is to stuff their own ears and those of their animals with flour. Everybody did as they were bid, so that the roar of the lions would not frighten them.

Budhisatta went up to the tower again and cried out, 'Sabadatta!'

'What is it old priest? How dare you address me! Where is your King?' the jackal replied, getting rather annoyed.

'You do not have to talk to the King. He has bestowed all authority on me to negotiate with you. So tell me again, how will you take over our kingdom?' the priest asked him again.

'Oh! I will cause the lions to roar and I will frighten the people and destroy them. Thus, I will take over your kingdom,' replied the jackal.

Budhisatta laughed, 'You will not be able to make the lions roar. These noble lions with their strong claws and royal mane, will never do the bidding of a mangy jackal like you.'

The jackal was infuriated at this and shouted to the priest, 'Not only will all the lions do my bidding, but this one on whom I sit, will roar the loudest.'

'Show me,' the priest taunted.

The jackal ordered the lion on whose back he was perched, to roar loudly. The lion did as he was bid. But nothing happened, as no one could hear it, since their ears were stuffed with flour.

'Make him do it again, you old jackal. Is that the loudest he can roar?'

The jackal nudged and kicked the lion again and it let out another mighty roar. The elephant, on which the lion was mounted, grew frightened by the sound, panicked and reared up. The lion fell off its back, and with him the jackal also came tumbling to the ground with a thud. Then the elephant ran, trampling the jackal in the process. On seeing the fate of the lion and the jackal, all the other animals grew frightened and ran, helter skelter, towards the jungle. Many animals perished in the stampede, including the consort of the jackal.

After the dust subsided, Budhisatta ordered all the people of the city to remove the flour from their ears, as well as from the ears of their animals. Thus it was his wisdom that saved the day.

MEHMANE NAKHONDA

This story is called Mehmane Nakhonda, which means guests who are uninvited, but who are welcome.

Once upon a time, in a small village in Iran, there was an old woman who lived in a tiny one room house just big enough for one person. However she was so hospitable, that she welcomed everyone, especially children, to her house, despite the lack of space.

One evening as she was sitting outside telling the children stories, the sky darkened and it became pitch black, as if a storm was going to burst. She quickly told the children to go home. Suddenly there was thunder and lightening and her whole house started shaking. She hurriedly locked all her doors and windows and got into bed, to try to keep warm and sleep.

As the rain started to pour, she heard a knock on her door. She wondered who it could be, in this driving rain.

'Who is it?' she asked. She heard a chirping sound.

She opened the door and found a tiny sparrow.

'Please let me in, its really cold out here, I'll die,' said the drenched sparrow, shivering. The old lady, being the kind-hearted soul she was, let the sparrow in and bundled it up in a piece of cloth and put it on her shelf and went back to bed.

Shortly thereafter, there was another knock on the door. The old lady opened the door and this time found a hen shivering in the rain.

'Please *khala jaan*, let me in, I'm getting all wet outside,' said the poor hen. The lady let her in too and covered her with a piece of cloth, so that she could dry off.

As she was heading for her bed, she again heard someone tapping at the door. She ran to open the door and this time found a crow, soaking wet, outside.

'I'm *kalagh siyah*, its really very cold out here, please let me in, auntie.' The gentle hearted old lady let the crow in as well, and wrapped him up in another piece of cloth and put him in another corner of the room, so he wouldn't wet the other two birds.

Soon there was another knock at the door.

'Oh my goodness! Who could it be now?' She opened the door to find a cat dripping from head to toe.

'Please let me in, its freezing outside,' said the cat shivering.

'Oh, all right, you can come in too,' said the kind old lady.

But as she let the cat in, the birds were extremely alarmed. The cat seeing this said, 'Don't worry I won't harm you. As we are all guests here we shouldn't be hostile to each other.' The birds calmed down, and the lady put a sweater around the wet cat.

As they were all dozing off, there was yet another knock on the door. By now the old lady was very tired and wanted to rest. However, she got up once more and opened the door and found a dog outside.

'I am your neighborhood watch dog, please let me in, I am getting drenched out here.'

The old lady let him in too and tied a scarf around him to keep him warm. Again, all the animals got a bit worried at the dog's presence in the room. However he gave them all a kind look and went off to sleep.

Suddenly there was a very loud knock on the door. When the old lady opened the door once again, she saw a donkey outside.

'I am getting wet and I am very scared of lightening, so please let me in,' implored the donkey. Even though her house was already very crowded, she let him in and covered him with a quilt to keep him warm.

She then went to bed, and hoped that that was the last interruption. However, she heard another knock on the door. This time it was a cow.

'I am the black cow, please let me come in too,' pleaded the cow.

'Oh alright. You can squeeze in too,' said the old lady, and she led the cow with much difficulty into the room, which was already quite crowded. She put a mat on the cow and said, 'Now for God's sake let me rest, I'm very tired.' Then she got into bed and finally managed to go to sleep.

The next morning when she woke up, there was the aroma of hot tea. She saw the cat pouring tea and the donkey was building a fire. She looked around and saw the dog cleaning up her little compound outside. Everyone seemed to be busy doing something or the other. The crow was bringing in sticks for the fire and the cow was cleaning the roof. The old lady was delighted, and she went out quickly and got bread for all of them, and they all sat around the fire sipping tea, eating bread and chatting.

When everyone was finished with breakfast, they all thanked her for her hospitality and asked her if there was anything they could do for her. They were all very sad to leave each other and told the old lady that they would be happy to help her around the house, clean up, and build fires whenever she wanted.

'I wish I could accommodate all of you in my house, but as you can see it is too tiny for that,' the old lady said to them. However, she then turned to the sparrow and told her, 'Since you are so small I suppose I can keep you at least.'

At this, the black cow turned around and said, 'I may be big in size but if you let me stay I can plough land for you and bring you things you need.' The old lady asked the cow to stay too.

Then the crow said to her, 'I can also do small chores for you; I can bring you sticks for the fireplace and do other odd jobs, so please let me stay too.'

'All right, you don't take up much space either, so you can stay too,' said the lady to the crow.

The donkey looked at the old lady with sad eyes and said, 'Auntie, please let me stay too. I can carry you when you want to travel long distances and I can tell you all the gossip of the neighborhood.'

'Oh, all right, you can stay too,' said the old lady to the donkey.

'What about me?' asked the cat. 'I can protect your food from rats, please let me stay too.'

'Okay. You can stay as long as you don't bother the other animals, by pouncing on them and teasing them,' said the old lady to the cat.

The hen said that she could lay eggs for her, and the dog said he could protect her from thieves and look after all the other animals. So the old lady let them stay too.

All these animals lived altogether harmoniously, under one roof. Thus, this little tale goes to show that if animals of different species can all live together peacefully, therefore, so can people of different castes and religions.

MULLAH NASRUDDIN

Mullah Nasruddin is a very popular folklore figure in our part of the world. Every child has heard some tale or the other about the clever deeds of this Mullah. There is also an element of simplicity and naiveté in his character which is actually very endearing. My favourite tale is this one, which my grandfather would relate to me as a child. The story is set in the sixteenth century and my grandfather gave it the name, 'The Professor and Mullah Nasruddin'.

When Mullah was a student, one day his class was informed that a very renowned professor from the Al-Azhar University in Egypt, was coming to examine them. This professor had a formidable reputation and was known to be very strict. Also it was said that he was not easy to please. The students were very worried and quite scared. So they put their heads together and concocted a plan, whereby they would be able to fool the professor. They decided that they would dress up as labourers, millers etc, and when the professor came into town and asked for directions to the *madrassah* they would talk to him in gibberish. He would thus become confused, and believe that the people of this town did not speak Persian. Maybe then he'd return to where he came from.

So on the appointed day, the professor rode into town on his donkey. To the students, waiting there in disguise, even the donkey looked very serious and

regal. The professor, being a stranger to the town, had to stop and ask the way to the *madrassah*. He called two labourers working in a field nearby, who were in fact two students in disguise. They answered the professor, in a sort of gibberish they made up on the spot. The professor obviously could not understand what they said. 'Maybe this is the local dialect,' he thought to himself.

He rode on. After a few yards he stopped again to ask directions. This time too, he encountered a disguised student, who answered him in whatever nonsense he could utter. But this was different from the one used by the two field workers. The professor was puzzled. 'Now this is a dialect completely different from the one I heard earlier. Don't these people speak a common language?' he wondered.

This scene was repeated several times and each time it seemed he heard what seemed to be a different dialect. The professor was thoroughly confused, as indeed was what the students intended.

'Is it some ancient language that these people are speaking, and I, a learned professor, know nothing of it?' he wondered getting more and more anxious. 'How in the world am I going to examine the students of the local *maktab*. I cannot let them know that I am ignorant of the language they speak here.'

So it was that the tables were turned, and instead of the students, it was the professor who was nervous about the impending examinations. Then the professor hit upon an idea, which would cover up his ignorance, 'I will use sign language to question the students. Surely that is a universal language.'

Thus, it was announced that the respected professor had decided to examine them in sign language.

The students braced themselves for the test. Each one was worried, but the one most perturbed was a one-eyed scholar, who was brilliant and tipped to come first in the class. He was nervous at the prospect of taking an examination in sign language, because he had no knowledge about communicating in signs. He was pacing up and down the corridor outside the examination hall, waiting for his turn. The hall was filled with students, as well as teachers, and he was getting very jittery indeed. Then along came another student—a late-comer.

'What is the matter with you? Why are you looking so worried? You, of all the people should have no difficulty,' the late-comer asked the nervous scholar.

'Please, dear friend, help me. I cannot face the professor and my teachers. I know I will make a fool of myself,' pleaded the brilliant student.

'Okay, I have an idea. You know how daring I am, I will take your place. What is there to fear? At the worst you will not get a prize. No one will throw you out of school. So let us exchange robes and I will take your place. I will even pretend to have only one eye.'

So the brilliant scholar waited outside, and the late-comer went inside to face the professor in his place. There was pin drop silence inside the hall. To the scholar waiting outside, it seemed as though an eternity had passed, then he heard thunderous applause.

His friend ran out and said to him, 'Come on! Quickly change clothes! It seems as though I have won. Go inside, they are going to announce you as the winner. The professor is about to speak.'

The scholar immediately got into his clothes and ran in and took his place in the audience. The professor announced his name.

'Now this is the student who deserves the first prize. His understanding is remarkable. I have never come across a student who could follow my train of thoughts so precisely and give such apt answers,' the professor then went on to explain what had happened.

'I took out an apple to show that this was the cause of the downfall of man. Without faltering, the young man took out a crust of bread, to show that it was the bread of life that has been mankind's redeeming feature. I then held out one finger, to show that there was only one Allah. He held out two fingers to show that we must not forget Rasul Allah, his messenger. I then made a round circle, to show that everything in the universe had been created. He clenched his fist and showed a threatening finger to reply that, 'Yes, everything in the universe had been created but everything depended on one Being, the Creator of the universe. It is amazing. I have never come across such a brilliant student before.'

Everyone began to clap and came over to the one-eyed student to congratulate him. The scholar was perplexed, 'How did my friend, who at the best of times does not understand the simplest problems, happen to interpret the professor's questions and answer so wisely? I must go and ask him.' His friend was waiting outside.

'How were you able to understand the professors signs?'

'Well, to tell you the truth, this professor of yours is very quarrelsome,' the friend replied, 'But you know me, I fear no one. I gave him as good as I got.'

The one-eyed scholar was perplexed, 'Go on. How did you do that?'

'Well,' replied the friend, 'The professor reached into his pocket, took out an apple and shook it under my nose in a threatening manner. I too dived into my pocket and took out the crust of bread, the remains of my breakfast, and shoved it under his nose. If he was going to throw the apple at me, I was not about to take it lying down. I would have thrown the bread at him.'

The one-eyed scholar was amused, 'But then why did you raise two fingers when he raised one?'

'Now look here,' said the friend, 'If the professor shows me one finger to tell me that he is going to take out my one eye, since I was supposed to be you; I showed him two fingers to show him that I would take out both his eyes.' His friend was getting angry as he narrated the events, 'This professor of yours thinks he is very ferocious. He continued to threaten me. He then started to wave his hand round and round, so as to tell me that he was going to push me and scratch my face. But I shook my fist at him and admonished him with a raised finger, daring him to come closer. What do you know? That really frightened him, for he started to clap. He was all smiles from then on.'

No marks for guessing that the late-comer friend and hero of the story was Mullah Nasruddin.

HAZRAT EBRAHIM
(KHALIL-ALLAH)

Hazrat Ebrahim, Khalil-Allah, (the Prophet Abraham) was one of the divine messengers of Allah. He was known for his hospitality, and not a day would pass without someone coming to his house, to share his meals with him.

Once a whole week passed by without a single guest coming to visit him. This made *Hazrat* Ebrahim so sad, that he stopped eating and became ill. His entire household tried to convince him to eat, but to no avail. *Hazrat* Ebrahim could not bear this state of affairs and decided to go and look for someone to invite to his table to share a meal. Consequently, he left his house in search of someone who would share his hospitality. He wandered here and there and even climbed mountains, praying to God asking Him if he had done something to displease people, as it seemed they didn't want to come to his home anymore.

Then, *Hazrat* Ebrahim spotted a shriveled up, old man, sitting all alone shaking his head.

'*Assalam-u-aleikum,*' greeted the Prophet.

The old man looked up and asked, 'Who are you?'

'I am Ebrahim,' he replied.

'Oh Sir! I have come all this way to visit your house, as you are famous for your hospitality and

generosity to travellers. I have not eaten for days and I cannot walk anymore. Please give me some food,' said the old man.

Hazrat Ebrahim was overjoyed, and he helped the old man walk to his house.

Everyone in his house was happy to see him back to normal and prepared many different kinds of dishes. Then they all sat down at the elaborate *sofra* to eat. According to tradition, everyone said '*Bismillah*' before starting the meal. However, the old man remained silent.

Hazrat Ebrahim looked at him and said, 'We have so many blessings to be grateful for. Surely, at your age you should take *Allah's* name before you begin your meal.'

'No, I am a heathen, I don't believe in God; it is so meaningless. I thank you for providing me with this food,' said the old man.

Everyone gasped, and Hazrat Ebrahim was beside himself with anger. He told his guest, 'I am sorry, I do not want to bring impurity upon my house with a non-believer. Get up and leave before I throw you out.'

The old man got up with much difficulty and left the house.

All of a sudden a *Vahy* or revelation came upon Hazrat Ebrahim.

'Ebrahim, why did you send a guest away from your sofra? A guest is a mehboob-e-Allah. He eats his own share. I have tolerated him for over ninety years, whatever the nature of his faith and beliefs, and you couldn't tolerate him for a few minutes?'

Hazrat Ebrahim hung his head in mortification, and thinking about the greatness, magnanimity, tolerance and forgiveness of Allah, all he could say was, *'Allah-o-Akbar!'*

THE BENEVOLENT PHILANTHROPIST
SHEIKH MOSTAFA BIN ABDUL LATIF

Bastak, the home of my ancestors, is a small town in the province of Hormozgan, in southern Iran. It has an interesting history. This small, insignificant, far-flung, neglected town has produced many great men of letters, religious scholars, philanthropists, architects, calligraphers and successful businessmen of international repute.

There are several theories as to how Bastak came to be inhabited. One of these is that people from Hejaz and Najd, fleeing from religious persecution, wandered around looking for a safe haven. It is said that eventually these fugitives reached Lingah and Bastak, high up in the mountains. The climate here is salubrious and similar to that of Hejaz. Also it is very green. They felt welcome here and many of them decided to settle in this place.

Another version is that Bastakis originally came from Kashmir. Those who have visited both these places have found many similarities between the two. I was pleasantly surprised to learn that people from an area close to Bastak speak in a language, which is a mixture of Urdu and Bastaki.

Here I want to record the contributions and indeed the legacy, of one of the greatest personalities of

Bastak, Haji Sheikh Mostafa Bin Abdul Latif. Sheikh Mostafa belonged to a family of religious scholars and *khans* or chieftains who hailed from the Bani Abbasi tribe of Najd. He passed away at the age of ninety-eight in 1964, but of him one can truly say 'never will a man die whose heart is filled with passion for the truth and service for mankind'.

hargiz na mirad onke dilash zindah shod be ishq
sabt ast bar jareedae Alam dawame ma

Over one hundred years ago, Bastak was a small, primitive village, where barefoot children played in dusty lanes. At that time one might have seen a lean, twelve year old boy with a stick over his shoulder, walking briskly down the street, with a purposeful expression on his face. This young boy was none other than Sheikh Mostafa. He was deeply concerned about the backwardness of his village. His wish was to somehow improve the lot of his home-town. But he knew he would not be able to achieve anything by staying in Bastak. There were no opportunities here. He had heard of lands far away, where there were plenty of jobs. He dreamt of going to one of these places to seek his fortune so that he would be able to help his fellow Bastakis. He considered this to be his mission in life.

Sheikh Mostafa was not afraid of the hazardous journey he would have to undertake. Travelling in those days was not easy. Passing through the Gardane Hirang, on the narrow, zigzagging, unpaved mountain roads was especially dangerous. Often landslides would render crossing virtually impossible. But Mostafa was determined. He was devoted to his hometown where he had seen more than his share of misery and deprivation.

He began his journey to Lingah, a town 110 kilometers away, on foot. After he had walked a considerable distance he was exhausted and sat down to rest. He realized that walking would not get him very far, especially since he had a very small supply of food and drink. While he was pondering his dilemma, he heard the jingling of bells and knew that a caravan was approaching. Perhaps they would provide him with transport and also some company. Travelling alone was fraught with danger. He was lucky that someone in the caravan recognized him and being familiar with his serious bent of mind, offered to let him join the caravan despite his young age. Mostafa reached Lingah. But this was not his final destination. He was planning on going to Bombay, where there were untold opportunities for education and employment.

Mostafa bin Abdul Latif's family was well-known in Lingah. The people of this town were very impressed by his strong personality and his determination to seek a better life for his people. In spite of his travails he had a cheerful disposition. Nothing seemed to deter him and he literally knocked on every door to find someone who would give him passage on a boat to Bombay. Ultimately, he found a friend of his father's, who was going on a sailing boat to Bombay and he agreed to let Mostafa sail with him. It was nearing the monsoon season and the sea was bound to be rough. There was even danger of torrential rains on the way. But all this did not daunt him from his mission. In those days he would often dream of bulding a school, a hospital with proper medical staff and a library in Bastak. Later he established all that he had dreamt of in those days.

Thus it was that the young boy reached Bombay. There he met a man called Ahmed Muqadam, who was from Kuwait and was in the custom clearance business. He hired Mostafa and the young man worked for him for many years, with total dedication and honesty. Ahmed grew to rely on him completely and whenever he left Bombay he would leave the young man in charge of his entire business. Whatever Mostafa earned he would send home to his father and family in Bastak.

One day, when Mostafa was nineteen years old, Ahmed suggested that he would like him to marry his daughter and manage his very extensive business. Ahmed said that he was getting on in years and was finding it difficult to handle his affairs, and Mostafa's integrity, intelligence and hard work had impressed him greatly. Therefore, he wanted to make him his son-in-law. Mostafa agreed and was married shortly thereafter. He managed the business diligently and was able to expand it far and wide. He was blessed with several children. He was now in a position to help his entire family. In fact, he even sent messengers to far away villages around Bastak, to search out distant relatives who were needy and he helped them as well. Soon he was able to set up his own pearl trading business and became a successful trader.

Mostafa bin Abdul Latif constantly looked for ways to help his native Bastak. When he had left, the village didn't even have the basic amenities of life. He appointed a permanent representative in Bastak to help in developing the village. He was responsible for supplying kerosene for the lamps in all the mosques, and for building *aab ambars (berkahs)* for storing rainwater for general consumption. He also set up primary schools in Bastak and the surrounding areas and provided the money for burial of the destitute. He established the famous cooking pot known as the *deege Haji Mostapha*, to feed people on *Eid*. The pot could contain forty to fifty kilos of rice, and *hareesa* (a combination of wheat and meat) was cooked for breakfast, and rice and curry for lunch. The practice of providing food on *Eid* holidays still continues to this day. Young immigrants from Bastak, who came to Bombay for education or for employment, would visit him in droves. He would employ them if he had a place, or else they were welcome to stay in his house for as long as they needed, sometimes even for months.

On my last trip to Bastak, I visited the primary school Mostafa bin Abdul Latif had set up. It was later upgraded to a secondary school called *Mostafavia*. Everywhere in Bastak one can see some proof of the philanthropy of this magnanimous man. Indeed, few have contributed so passionately and selflessly to their birthplace. No request from the people of Bastak was ever ignored or overlooked by him. Clinics and hospitals received generous support for the purchase of modern equipment.

Mostafa bin Abdul Latif visited his homeland only once after he migrated, but his links with his past remained alive, and he remained committed to the improvement of conditions in Bastak. His children, especially the late Sheikh Muhammad, are the torch-bearers of their father's noble legacy. Muhammad's loss left a painful void in the lives of the many that he helped in his own quiet way. His sad demise has been an irreparable loss and widely mourned in the Gulf region—especially in Dubai, Bahrain, and in Bastak. Today, Muhammad's children or Sheikh Mostafa's grandchildren continue to support the many projects that the family sponsored in Bastak, Dubai and other places.

Many Bastakis who are successful and active citizens, spread throughout the world, including the Gulf and especially Dubai, have not relinquished their connections, with Bastak. Indeed, because of their contributions the basic amenities of life are available today to the residents of Bastak, including the vital and long awaited facility of clean, running water. Many of these notable sons and daughters of Bastak are beholden to Sheikh Mostafa for showing them the way to preserving their identity and never forgetting their roots.

SHEIKH SAADI

Sheikh Saadi of Shiraz, who was also known as Sheikh-e-Shiraz, was a philosopher, writer, *hakim*, and above all a good human being. His renowned books, *Gulestan* and *Bustan*, are rich treasure houses of intellectual thought, ethics and morals. His short and pithy tales are popular with adults as well as children, and even today are read with interest and enthusiasm.

To enrich this humble collection of 'stories which I had heard as a child', I have included some of Sheikh Saadi's tales. I used to hear them in the original (Persian) language and often in the Bastaki dialect. The stories, of course, lose some of their charm when translated, but I have tried to keep them as close to the original as possible. Each of Sheikh Saadi's stories has a moral value, which he presents at the end in the form of a poetic couplet. These couplets are beautiful, like pearls in a string, but unfortunately, justice cannot be done to them in translation, so I have merely written them as best I could or omitted them.

Sheikh Saadi, like all other human beings had experienced heartache, grief and even frustration. But he never talks of this unhappy side of life in his stories. His tales are full of hope and aspirations and there is always the ideal of a better life. His faith in the Creator is always evident and inspiring. He refers to the world as a *mosafer khana* (wayside inn), implying the transience of existence, until one is united with Allah.

THE THIEF

A poor man went to the house of a well-to-do friend when he was not in, and picked up an expensive carpet and brought it home. He had never done such a thing before, but he was desperate. He had no money to feed his family, and had committed this act on the spur of the moment, as he could think of no other means to save his household.

As luck would have it, the police apprehended the poor man before he could sell the carpet. Both the well-to-do friend and the thief were presented in the court of the local judge. The case was uncomplicated. The man had been caught red-handed with the stolen goods, and there was absolutely no doubt of his guilt. The judge announced the verdict, whereby according to the law, both the hands of the thief were to be chopped off. The sentence was to be carried out in public, to serve as a lesson for all.

The well-to-do man, however, knew about the hard times his poor friend was facing and felt sorry for him. He realized that if his circumstances had not been so desperate, his friend would never have committed such a dishonest act.

He stood up in front of the judge and addressed the court, 'My lord, I forego my claim. I have forgiven this man, who is my friend, from the bottom of my heart. I have known him for a very long time and can

stand guarantee for his character. His integrity is beyond doubt. Please exonerate him and let him go.'

'I cannot do that. It is against the law and a verdict of guilt has already been passed,' replied the judge, 'He must be punished for taking what was not his. This has nothing to do with whether you forgive him or not.'

Now the well-to-do man was very wise and he was determined to save his friend. Once again he got up and politely spoke to the judge, 'My lord, I appreciate that nothing must come in the way of upholding the law. Justice must be done. But I think it is my duty to inform you that this carpet had been donated to charity, like many other items in my house. It is the property of '*waqf*' (bequeathed to charity) and it does not belong to me. It belongs to anyone who needs it. If you know of any other person who is needy, let him come and take what he wants from my house. There are three other carpets, a cupboard, two tables and some utensils. These have all been donated to charity.'

Without waiting for the judge's reaction he continued to elaborate further, 'This tradition of '*waqf*' runs in my family. In fact, my father, in his declining years dedicated his entire belongings to *waqf*. Any poor person was most welcome to enter our house in his absence, and pick up anything he wanted. Some of the articles I have are remnants from the same collection, your honor.'

The judge hesitated for a few moments. He did not show whether he believed his story or not, but he changed his verdict and the poor man was free to go. Before the man turned to leave. The judge called him.

'However desperate your circumstances, did you have to go and steal from a man of such a generous nature?' he admonished him.

The thief had a ready reply, 'My lord, haven't you heard the maxim, 'It is better to sweep a friend's house clean rather than knock at an enemy's door'.'

SALT AT THE RIGHT COST

A now Shirwan, was a renowned, kind-hearted ruler, with a passion for hunting. One day on a hunting trip with his entourage, he shot a large, beautiful gazelle. Thereafter, the members of the expedition began to roast it for lunch, when they realized that the cook had forgotten to bring salt. Consequently, the cook sought permission to go and buy the salt from a village nearby. The King, knowing the mentality of the villagers, ordered the cook, 'Buy the salt at the market price. Don't pay a penny more!'

This surprised the King's followers, who asked him, 'My Lord, your generosity and magnanimity are well known, so why have you laid so much emphasis on the cost of a small item like salt?'

'Ah,' he said, 'You people do not realize the danger of over-paying. We could give the villagers a purse of gold for the salt, but that would inculcate greed and afterwards they will keep on increasing their prices. Consequently inflation would occur, as man is never satisfied and his demands keep increasing. Thus, it is important to realize that the root of all evil lies in small things.'

That is how the King set an example for his subjects, and Sheikh Saadi concludes with a couplet giving the moral of the story: 'If the ruler eats one apple from the garden, his subjects will uproot the entire apple tree.'

LAILA AND MAJNOON

An Arab Sultan, who had heard about the desperate love story of Laila and Majnoon, was perplexed by the thought of how a sensible, intelligent man like Majnoon, could renounce everything for the love of a woman. He said he would like to meet him and ask him personally. So he sent for Majnoon, who was said to have taken shelter in the mountains and was living amongst wild animals. When Majnoon appeared in front of the Sultan, the ruler asked him, 'What has this woman done to you that you have forsaken everything, and prefer to live amongst wild animals?'

'Instead of asking me, why don't you see Laila for yourself and you will realize my anguish,' Majnoon replied, 'You too will become a Majnoon (meaning mad in Arabic) like me.'

Therefore, to appease his curiosity, the Sultan ordered his men, 'Go bring this Laila to me, so I can behold this bewitching beauty.'

Thus Laila was also brought in front of the Sultan. The Sultan was surprised to see that Laila was just a dark-skinned, frail woman. He couldn't find anything exceptionally beautiful about her, as Majnoon had described.

He turned to Majnoon and asked, 'What! Is this the woman for whom you have become a lost soul? It is unbelievable! She has none of the bewitching qualities that you speak. of. Leave her, you deserve much better!'

To this Majnoon replied, 'My Lord, if only you could see through my eyes the beauty this woman possesses, then you would realize the truth.'

Thus it is said that, 'Beauty lies in the eyes of the beholder,' and this truth is amply borne out by the legendary love of Majnoon for Laila.

MUEZZIN

There was once this *muezzin* who was a source of great irritation to the believers in the neighbourhood. They felt that his voice and his ways were very unpleasant. The *Emam* of the mosque tried to find some way to get rid of this *muezzin* without offending him.

He called the *muezzin* and said to him, 'You know, I have usually paid the *muezzins* of this mosque five dinars, but I will pay you ten dinars a month if you go and give the *azaan* elsewhere.'

The *muezzin* accepted this offer happily and started giving the *azaan* elsewhere.

A few months passed by and everyone was relieved that the funny-looking *muezzin* with the cracked voice had gone away. However, one day the *Emam* saw the *muezzin* entering the mosque again.

'Why have you come back?' asked the *Emam* worried.

The *muezzin*, looked slightly perplexed and replied, 'You have not been very fair to me. You are only paying me ten dinars whilst the *Emam* in the other mosque, where I give the *azaan* now, has offered to pay me twenty dinars if I go elsewhere.'

The *Emam* laughed and said, 'Be wise and bargain with them, don't accept twenty dinars, I'm sure eventually they will be willing to pay you fifty dinars if you go pray elsewhere.'

TWO DERVISHES

Once upon a time two dervishes (holy people) were travelling together. One was lean and ate very little and the other was fat and robust and ate all the time.

On the way, they entered an unknown land. The authorities there were on the look out for some evil spies, who were supposed to be disguised as dervishes. Unfortunately, these two fitted the description, so they were captured by mistake and thrown into a cell, where they were left to die.

However, after two weeks, the real culprits were caught. The authorities realized their mistake and rushed to the prison to rescue the two dervishes, whom they had locked up and totally neglected. To everyone's surprise, when they opened the door they found the lean man was still alive and breathing, whilst the fat man was long dead. The Hakim was brought in to examine the two dervishes.

He explained this strange occurrence to the rescuers, 'You see, the fat man didn't survive because he was too dependent on food, while the lean man did not need that much nourishment and thus he survived the two weeks by praying to the Lord and meditating.'

Therefore the story ends with Sheikh Saadi's couplet, 'The man who eats continuously, finds it very difficult to curb his appetite when there is lack of food.'

WHO WAS AYAZ?

Ayaz was a Turkish slave bought by Mahmood, the Sultan of Ghaznavi. The Sultan was so fond of him, that he always kept him by his side. Some of the courtiers were extremely envious of the love and attention Ayaz received from the Sultan.

One day, a friend of the Sultan finally asked him, 'What is the reason for your devotion to this slave, who apparently possesses neither charm nor beauty?'

The Sultan suppressing his anger replied, 'I am strongly attached to him because of his manners, grace and loyalty.'

'But there are thousands of people in your court who would readily sacrifice their lives for you,' replied his friend.

'But no one is quite like Ayaz,' retorted the Sultan.

The Sultan knew that his friends were not aware of the qualities that Ayaz possessed, and therefore he told them, 'Wait a few days and I'll show you what Ayaz is all about.'

The friend agreed. After two or three days, preparations were being made for a hunting trip for the Sultan and his entourage. Sultan Mahmood ordered one of his slaves to carry a big box of gold coins. He instructed him to wait for his signal, then drop the box and scatter the coins all around.

Consequently, on the day of the hunting trip, the Sultan rode on a grand horse ahead of the others and when they reached a specific spot, he signalled to his slave to drop the coin box. The coins fell out onto the ground, catching everyone's attention.

The entourage offered to pick up the coins for the Sultan and punish the slave for dropping them, but the Sultan said, 'Don't bother with him. I had intended to distribute some charity, so here it is. Everyone is welcome to collect as many coins as he wants.'

When they heard this, bedlam broke loose and everyone fell to grabbing as many coins as possible. The Sultan hid behind a tree and watched the chaotic scene. However, from a distance he saw that one rider seemed extremely anxious and seemed to be looking for the Sultan.

'Oh my Lord, please help me find him. Take my life but let him be safe,' prayed the man.

Seeing the camp follower going mad with worry, the Sultan stepped forward.

'I'm here, Ayaz, don't panic, I am alright.'

When Ayaz saw the Sultan, he threw himself at his feet and said, 'Thank God you are safe my *Valinemat* (benefactor).'

Seeing this, Sultan Mahmood embraced Ayaz and said, 'People forget about their commander and their faith at the sight of gold; why didn't you do the same?'

'My lord, gold is nothing compared to your presence and well being. I will always guard you with my life.'

Seeing the unparalleled intensity of Ayaz's devotion for the Sultan, all the courtiers who had been envious of him, had to acknowledge his fealty and accept that there was good reason for the Sultan's devotion to Ayaz.

I HAVE TURNED TO HIM

There was once a ruler who fell seriously ill. All the *hakeems*, doctors and even physicians summoned from Greece could not diagnose his ailment. However after a lot of consultations, they were determined that the only way to cure the King would be to feed him the fried gall-bladder of a person with certain specific characteristics.

This remedy seemed to be extremely inhuman, but the King ordered his men to search far and wide for a person who would fit the criteria. Therefore, after searching for some time, they found a young shepherd's boy who had all the required characteristics. The boy's parents were brought to the palace, and were bribed with gold to give up their son.

The highest judge of the land was summoned, and the King asked him if there was any law which prohibited killing a subject to save the King's life. The judge, in fear for his own life, told the King that it was absolutely legal.

Consequently the *jallad* (executioner) was called and the boy was prepared for his final moments. The boy knelt, and with a sweet smile, raised his hands in prayer. The ruler was surprised at how calmly the boy faced his death.

'How can you appear so content and peaceful when you are about to be executed? Why are you smiling and not begging to be spared?' he asked.

'Your majesty,' said the boy, 'A child goes to his parents for support and comfort, but mine have sold me for material benefit. A subject goes to a judge for justice, but the judge has forsaken justice for his personal reasons. Finally, he seeks succour from his ruler, but mine wants to sacrifice me for his health. So then whom can I appeal to in the end? To my God, who looks after the rich and the poor, the weak and the strong alike. Therefore I am praying to Him for he is my only saviour.'

The entire court, especially the King, was stunned by the scene they had just witnessed. He got up and embraced the boy.

'I don't mind dying, but I must spare this innocent boy. I don't want his blood on my conscience for the rest of my life,' declared the King.

The boy was set free and rewarded by the King. God also rewarded the King for having been so kind-hearted. He was cured from his illness and thereafter, enjoyed good health and led a hearty life.

THE REUNION

The stories of the Moghul emperor Akbar and his minister Birbal are very popular in the sub-continent. Birbal was the cleverest of all the ministers in his court and Akbar was extremely fond of him. Birbal was a very wise man who possessed a ready wit and good sense of humor.

Once, for some reason, Akbar in a fit of pique banished Birbal from Agra, his capital. Hence poor Birbal left the city and went off to a village, without letting anyone know of his new whereabouts.

After a short period of time, Akbar began to miss Birbal immensely. Birbal was not only his chief minister, but was also one of his closest friends. They used to talk for hours and Birbal always kept him entertained. Without him Akbar found life rather dull. So, he ordered his soldiers to search far and wide for Birbal, and bring him back to the palace. However, no one succeeded in finding Birbal. Akbar became extremely dejected. He kept thinking about his friend Birbal.

One day, Akbar's soldiers ran up to him and announced that there was a saintly man with two disciples at the palace gate, who wanted to meet him.

'The disciples claim that their teacher is the wisest and wittiest person in the world,' said the soldiers.

'Oh, that can't be true. Birbal was the wisest and wittiest person on the face of the earth,' the Emperor replied, 'Anyway bring them in, maybe I can find a substitute for Birbal.'

Hence, the mendicant and his disciples were brought into the court. He had very sparkling wise eyes, a dense white head of hair and a long beard.

'Oh, saintly man, your disciples claim that you are the wisest man on earth. We want to test your wisdom and if you succeed in satisfying us, I will make you a minister, and if you fail, your head will be chopped off. So, do you agree?' said Akbar.

'Yes, your majesty, I agree. However, I do not wish to prove my intelligence to anyone, but I would like to answer your questions,' replied the mendicant humbly.

The minister, Raja Tadamall, posed the first question. 'Who is a man's best friend?' he asked.

'His good sense,' replied the saintly person.

'What is the most superior thing on earth?' asked the minister Faizi.

'Knowledge,' he answered without the slightest hesitation.

Then Abdul Faisal asked, 'Which is the deepest trench in the world?'

'A woman's heart,' came the reply.

'What is the one thing that once lost, cannot be regained?' asked another courtier.

'Our lives,' responded the pious man.

Then Tansen, the legendary musician, asked the mendicant, 'What is undying in music?'

'Its notes,' he answered.

'Which voice is the sweetest and most melodious during the night?' asked Tansen again.

'The voice which prays to Allah.'

The Maharaja of Jaipur, Mansing, who was a guest of the King at that time, asked, 'What travels faster than the wind?'

'Gossip,' retorted the wise man.

'What is the sweetest thing in the world?' asked Tansen.

'A baby's smile,' he answered.

Everyone in the court was thoroughly impressed by the holy man's wisdom. Then they asked the King if he would like to put any questions.

Akbar asked two questions:

'What is necessary to rule over a kingdom?'

'Cleverness and wisdom,' the mendicant replied.

'Which is the greatest enemy of a King?' asked Akbar.

'His own selfishness and rashness,' replied the holy man.

Akbar and the whole court were thoroughly impressed. Then Akbar asked one, last question.

'As you are so wise, surely you can perform miracles.'

'Yes, why not? I can present in front of you any person you desire to see,' responded the saintly man.

At this Akbar said very eagerly, 'Please bring my minister and friend Birbal in front of me.'

Without uttering a word, the wise old man lifted the dense mass of white hair from his head—it was a wig,

and removed his false beard, and standing in front of Akbar was none other then his friend Birbal.

Akbar was overjoyed. He got up and embraced Birbal and the entire court started cheering.

'Birbal my friend, I thought your voice sounded familiar, that is why I asked you to perform this miracle. One may disguise a face, but a voice always remains in ones memory.'

Thus, Birbal returned to the court and Akbar was happy again.

NAMDAR—THE TAILOR

This is another interesting story about Akbar and Birbal.

Once Akbar and Birbal got into an argument. Akbar was of the opinion that no one could steal anything from him and Birbal disagreed. 'People can steal from right under your nose', said Birbal. 'A tailor for example will never stitch anything for you until he can keep a piece of cloth for himself. If you don't believe me ask a tailor to stitch something for you and you will see. Even if your guards watch him, he will steal cloth from you.'

Akbar accepted the challenge and summoned the royal tailor Namdar. He gave Namdar a fine length of muslin, presented to him by a Persian trader and said to him, 'Namdar, this is very unique material and cannot be found anywhere in the world. You are to stitch a blouse for the Queen and you will not be allowed to leave till you have completed it. I don't want you to waste even a tiny piece of this cloth and return whatever is left-over to me.'

Nandar was taken into a huge room with all his paraphernalia and he started stitching. Akbar posted guards outside the room to make sure he wouldn't be able to steal any bit of the cloth. 'No one is to enter or leave this room,' the Emperor ordered.

After a little while, Namdar's son came and wanted to go into the room to see his father.

'Where do you think you are going?' said the guards, stopping him.

'Let me speak to my father please,' he begged the guards.

The guards of course, refused to let him enter. So he shouted from outside, 'Mother said to come home to eat before you get too tired.'

Namdar, however, seemed to get irritated by his son's continuous interference and he threw a shoe at him and yelled, 'Get lost! Go home! Tell your mother I will not leave this room until I have finished stitching the Queen's blouse.'

The son picked up the shoe and went away sobbing.

At last when Namdar finished stitching the blouse, he was escorted in front of Akbar.

'Your Majesty, here is the blouse for the Queen and here are the remaining pieces of cloth.'

'See Birbal, what did I tell you? It is impossible to steal in front of our eyes with the guards around,' Akbar said to Birbal, after the tailor had left.

'Wait and see your majesty, give the matter some time and you will see that I'm right,' was Birbal's only reply.

A week later, a maid came running up to the Queen and said, 'Your Majesty, I've seen another woman wearing exactly the same blouse as the one you have.'

'That is impossible,' said the Queen angrily. 'My blouse is made from the finest muslin from Persia and

is very special. No one else could possibly have another piece.'

'But mistress, I have seen an identical blouse with my own eyes. Namdar's wife was wearing it,' replied the maid.

The Queen was furious and immediately went to Akbar to complain.

'I thought this cloth was supposed to be unique and nobody else had it. So how is it that Namdar's wife was wearing a similar blouse?' the Queen questioned.

Akbar ordered his men to bring Namdar to the court at once. When he was brought before him, Akbar asked him, 'Did you steal a piece of that precious and expensive cloth? How did you do that with all the guards around you?'

'I will tell you how he did it Your Majesty,' said Birbal with supreme confidence, 'He hid the piece of cloth in the shoe he threw at his son.'

Sure enough, it turned out that that was how he had managed to steal the cloth. Namdar fell at the King's feet, 'Please forgive this servant of yours. I admit that I stitched a blouse for my wife, with the material I hid in the shoe I threw at my son. My lord, stealing cloth is in our blood. I could not help myself. Please forgive me.'

Once again Birbal proved to be right. Namdar, however, lost the right to be the royal tailor.

THE PITCHER OF WISDOM

Once there was a time when Akbar was unhappy with Birbal and ordered him to leave his Empire at once. Birbal left quietly as he was used to this happening when he displeased Akbar, and he knew that Akbar would eventually call him back. This time however, Birbal went to a very remote village and did not inform anyone of his whereabouts.

After a few days, Akbar received a letter from one of his Rajas, with a rather peculiar request. 'Please send me a pitcher full of wisdom,' the letter read.

Akbar was bewildered by this strange request, but he knew he had to fulfill the demand otherwise it would harm his reputation as the wisest ruler in the world. On such occasions he missed Birbal, since he always found a solution to situations like these. Akbar was extremely distressed. He dispatched his men to find Birbal, but his men returned empty handed and said they were unable to find him.

'What should I do, if only Birbal was here,' Akbar kept thinking.

After a lot of thought, Akbar devised a plan to contact Birbal. The next day he ordered that a goat was to be dispatched to every village and instructed the headmen of the villages that the goat was to be fed, but to make sure that the goat doesn't lose or gain any weight. If its weight changed, they would be severely punished.

The headmen of the villages were flabbergasted at these orders which seemed impossible to carry out. When Birbal, who was residing in one of the villages heard of this order by Akbar, he knew at once that this was a ploy to trace him. He went to the headman of the village he was staying at, and said, 'Brother, thank you very much for letting me stay in your village. In return I shall help you solve the problem you face in following the Emperor's orders. Is it true that he has sent you a goat and he has instructed that the goat must neither gain nor lose weight?'

'Yes.' the headman replied, 'I am in a fix as I don't know how to comply with the King's orders. It is next to impossible to ensure this goat's weight remains the same.'

'It is not impossible,' said Birbal. 'Do as I say and your task will be achieved. Feed the goat regularly so that it does not lose weight. And, in order to prevent it from gaining weight, every time it is fed, tie it in front of a lion's cage. The constant fear will not allow it to gain any weight and its weight will remain constant.'

'Well, well,' exclaimed the headman, 'That certainly sounds like a good idea and I shall be eternally grateful to you if it works.'

Birbal's instructions were followed, and the goat was returned to the Emperor after the stipulated period of one month. Akbar had the weight of all the goats checked and found only one whose weight was unchanged. He knew immediately that Birbal must be the one responsible for this and quickly sent a message to the headman of that village to ask Birbal to return.

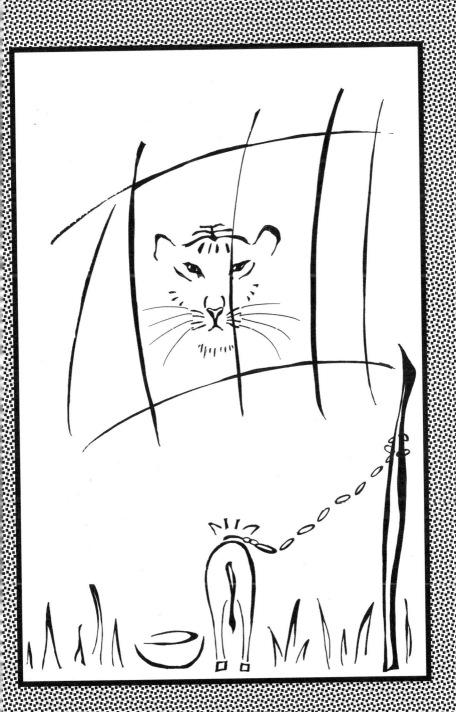

Akbar was extremely relieved to have Birbal back in his court and things returned to normal.

After a while, Akbar showed Birbal the letter from the Raja with its strange request. Birbal read it and tried to make sense out of it. He then said, 'Yes we can certainly send him a pitcher of wisdom, its no problem.'

He then turned to the gardener and said, 'Go get a pitcher and spread some soil in the bottom of it and then plant a pumpkin seed in the soil.'

His order was carried out and the pumpkin soon grew to full size inside it, thereby getting stuck in the pitcher.

Then Birbal closed the lid of the pitcher tightly and presented it to the emperor. 'Your Majesty, send this pitcher to the Raja and ask him to take the pumpkin out, without crushing the pumpkin or spoiling the vessel. In case he fails to do so, tell him to send us one lakh gold mohurs or prepare to face the Royal army.'

The Raja was consumed with immense fear when he heard the orders, as they were impossible to carry out. He fell to Akbar's feet and vowed never to challenge the wisdom of Emperor Akbars' royal court again. The pitcher had indeed made him wiser.

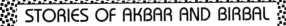

THE HORSE

Birbal's wit and wisdom had made him famous all over the kingdom. He was also renowned for his sagacity and sense of justice. People from all over the country came to him with their problems.

King Afra Tapora had heard a great deal about Birbal and wanted to meet him in person. Therefore, he disguised himself as a merchant and set out on his horse for Agra. On his way, he came across an old man who seemed to have trouble walking. He immediately took pity on the elderly person and asked him to ride his horse and he walked alongside, leading the animal.

When they reached Agra, the King said to the old man, 'We have arrived at the city and I shall be on my way now. Let me help you off the horse and you can go your way too.'

However, to his immense astonishment, the old man refused to dismount the horse.

'What are you talking about?' said the old man, 'Thank you for leading *my* horse into Agra and now you can let my horse go and be on your way.'

'What! Your horse? This is *my* horse. I only let you ride him because you seemed to be so old and feeble. You can't claim this horse as your own,' exclaimed the King.

The crook laughed and said, 'You can't prove anything because I was riding the horse and you just led it into town. So now go away and don't waste my time.'

Tapora was bewildered and didn't know what to do. Many people had gathered around them by now and one suggested, 'Why don't you take your problem to Birbal? He is the only one who can sort this out.'

Thus, both of them went to Birbal. Each told him his version of the story. Birbal listened intently.

'All right, just give me one day to sort this out. In the meantime, this horse will remain with me. You two can return to your lodgings.'

Immediately after they left, Birbal called one of his servants and said to him, 'Take this horse and follow close behind the two men. Then tell me who the horse follows, as a horse will naturally walk behind his master.'

The servant did as he was instructed and came back and informed Birbal what he had observed.

The next morning, when the two men appeared in front of Birbal, he took them to a stable where there were hundreds of horses. He then turned towards the two men.

'Your horse is here with the other horses. I am sure that the owner of the horse will be able to immediately recognize his horse amongst all the others.'

Sure enough, King Tapora went straight to his horse and untied him, whilst the crook stood bewildered. The horse also immediately recognized his owner and nuzzled against the King. Seeing this, the crook

immediately fell to Birbal's feet and begged his forgiveness.

The King thanked Birbal for his wise judgement, but did not reveal his identity. However, the all-knowing Birbal came up to him and whispered, 'I hope your Majesty will stay a few days as our honoured guest.'

'What? How in the world did you know my true identity?' asked the astonished King.

'Your Majesty, our spies immediately inform us about any stranger entering our kingdom. Apart from that, your confidence, gait and personality gave you away. I knew immediately who you were and that the horse belonged to you,' replied Birbal.

'But tell me how did you know the horse was mine?' asked the King.

'That was very simple,' said Birbal, 'Yesterday I asked my servant to follow both of you with the horse and he told me that the horse was following your footsteps. I already knew that the horse was yours. However, as I wanted to further confirm this, I arranged today's scenario, as only the rightful owner would be able to recognize his horse in a herd,' said Birbal.

The King was highly impressed by Birbal's wisdom and his act of justice. Birbal had handled the situation very wisely, without being partial to the fact that he was a King.

ACKNOWLEDGEMENTS

I feel like calling this book the 'book of chance'. It would not have been possible if the unforeseen and unpredicted chance meetings with the right people at the right time had not occurred. One fine day, I discovered a pile of audiocassettes in which, over the years, I had recorded short stories that I had heard from days gone by.

Why had I done this? To what purpose? Was it some half-formed dream to somehow preserve them and present them in a more permanent form for others to enjoy as much as I had enjoyed them—if so, then how did I hope to transcribe them and have them printed? So the search began. Initially I looked around among my circle of friends to help me in my effort. Thanks to Pamela Lander and Bron Lancaster for encouraging me, however they were obviously too busy to spare much time. Shirin and Majid's secretaries could not be spared. However, Annette and Dante made some print-outs of these tales, but this was time consuming. Nevertheless, I am grateful to all of them.

I had almost abandoned my plan, when by chance I met Diana Tattrikis at a party. She had read my book *Zelzelah* and inquired what I was doing these days. She had touched a sore point because I was so disappointed about not being able to transcribe my stories onto a disc in order to get them published and I poured out my heart to her. She offered to do this for me on her home computer and told me not to lose hope. True to her word, she worked for months, although she was a school teacher and a dedicated mother. She never complained, and we would often discuss the stories and change the script until they were all ready to be presented to a publisher.

Now I needed someone to make the illustrations. I wish to thank Seema Gargash for initiating the art work. A renowned artist, Tina Siddiqui, made some sketches but unfortunately these could not be used. But where could I find someone who would make illustrations for all the tales? Just by chance, one day on a visit to London, I entered a small store in Ealing to have some photocopies made of my stories. A charming young student of the theatre was at the counter and she asked what I intended to do with these. I told her my problem, and she, a complete stranger, told me, 'my dear, why don't you leave some of these stories with me and let me try to make some illustrations for them?'

At first I was hesitant, because I wasn't sure how much I could depend on a hard-working student who helped out in the family store, and who obviously wouldn't be able to spare much time. Also, she was a stranger to our ways and might not appreciate the eastern nuances of the tales. However, my young friend, Kerstin Meisinger, proved to be a *ferishta-e-Rahmat*, an angel from Heaven. Not only did she illustrate all the tales but she also designed the cover, and all this out of the goodness of her heart.

Now, at last I was armed with an attractive compilation, which I could present to a publisher. Then there was another chance occurrence. On a visit to Karachi, I mentioned to my cousin Siddiq if he could promote my book *Zelzelah* in Pakistan. Since most of the book is about my experiences in Karachi and Lahore, I felt it might be of interest there. He recommended that I visit Ameena Saiyid, the Managing Director of Oxford University Press, Pakistan—a woman in charge of such an empire! I was fascinated. And not only that, I discovered that almost all the editorial staff of OUP are women. Bravo!

Karachi has a sentimental value for my family and me. I have explained in *Zelzelah* why we made Karachi our home for several years. Here, among the joys and sorrows of that formative period of my life, I learnt the art of story-telling. I often regaled my little friends from the Fikree family with the stories I heard as a child. Later, I elaborated them for my grown-up friends.

Although *Zelzelah* was by-passed, to my delight my other manuscript was accepted. However, I was informed that a lot of work would have to be done on the stories and they would be on the lookout for someone to put them together.

Again, the hand of destiny intervened in a lovely form. Aquila Ismail, who did freelance work for the OUP, was posted to Abu Dhabi with her family and the publishers entrusted her with this work. Then miraculously, a ten-page story was artistically transformed into five pages without changing the essence and the style. She is an expert who feels the pulse, the culture and the congenial background of the East. Thus, there would be no *Heirloom: Evening Tales of the East*, without Diana, Aquila and finally, Imran Kureishi (another freelance editor in Lahore) whose touch has made all the difference.

From my family, I would like to thank my granddaughter Rasha, who read some of the stories and said to me, 'Grandma, I liked them. Go ahead and publish them.' What an encouraging reward! She has a lively imagination and a flair for writing herself.

I wish to express my heartfelt gratitude to Daleara of Oxford University Press and also to my friend and mentor, Chuck Grieve. My special thanks to Tina Ahmad who touched up some of the illustrations. Finally, thanks to my little Fikree friends, especially Munira, who is now a grandmother herself.

GLOSSARY

Aab ambar	water reservoir
Aajlab	ivory lips
Ab	father
Aab	water
Abayas	outer cover; *chadars* (Arabic)
Abra	boat
Al-Hamadolillah	all praise is for Allah
Allah Akbar	God is great
Vahy	revelation
Araq-i-bidameshk	herbal drink
Azaan	call to prayer
Baba	father
Bakhur	incense or sweet smelling fragrance
Behesht	heaven
Berkah	water reservoir
Bibi	A girl or woman; a term of affection or respect
Borki	dry nuts
Chaddar	long veil
Chowkidar	watchman
Darogha	sheriff
Deeg	large pot
Dervishes	saintly people
Dishdash	long dress for Arab men
Djinns	devils

Dooz	stitch
Edda	For widows after the husband's death, a period of isolation
Eid	A Muslim festival which occurs twice a year
Eidiya	Eid presents-usually coins
Eid-ul-Adha	Eid Qorban
Emam	Incharge of a mosque
Feel	Elephant in Persian and Arabic
Futoor	Iftar, breaking of fast during Ramazan
Goomi	Wake up or get up
Gorz	Club
Hader	Ready
Haji	A person who has performed the Hajj
Hakim	Doctor, philosopher
Halwa	Sweet
Halwa-sohan	Halwa, sweet dish
Hareesa	Shorba; porridge made by local Arabs
Henna	Natural dye made from henna leaves used by women to decorate their hands
Hil hilawi	Some one who bangs an empty tin to wake up people for Sehri

Houz	Pool
Imam	A Muslim well-versed in religious knowledge
Jallad	Executioner
Jarchees	Town criers
Kalagh Siyah	black crow
Kandooras	long dresses
Kaneezes	slave girls
Katchali	bald man
Khala Jaan	dear aunty
Khalifa	sultan, ruler
Caliphate	sultanate
Khoda Hafiz	Be in the protection of God; good bye
Khoosa-dozi	art work (badela)
Kondrok	locally made chewing gum
Kooza	clay urn for water
Mahajabeen	pretty face
Mahrams	close family members
Majlis	assembly, room
Majnoon	man mad from love
Maktab	school
Mashatas	hair stylists and beauticians who visit homes
Masjid	mosque
Maund(s)	A measure of weight
Mawa	A paste used on bread
Mehboob-e-Allah	The chosen one of Allah
Mehmane Khoda Hasteed	you are God's guests

Mehmane Nakhonda	uninvited guest
Mehtar	groom
Mokhada	large cushions
Monkhali	elder/respected
Mosafer khana	inn for travellers
Mossani	small courtyard
Mullah	a Muslim religious tutor who teaches the Quran to young children
Murtaz	recluse with psychic powers
Muttabak	type of bread made with eggs and sugar
Najis	not clean; impure
Nanwa	bread-maker
Neeki	good deeds
Noql	usually white marble-sized sweets
Pahlawan	champion
Pushti	huge hard bolsters
Qalyoon	hubble bubble pipe
Qawahs	coffee
Ramadan	the ninth month of the Islamic calendar, the holy month of fasting
Ramal	fortune-teller
Rangina	Sweet-dish made with dates
Regag nan	type of bread made on a griddle
Rooza	fasting

Sakoo	bench
Samovars	boiler for making tea
Shaela	veil
Shah-e-Chiragh	a saint's tomb in Shiraz, Iran
Sheer-e-pak Khorde	someone who has drunk clean milk
Sobhan-Allah	God be praised
Sofra	table cloth
Souq	market
Suhoor or sehri	the meal taken at dawn to initiate fasting
Sultan	ruler
Tanoor	Clay oven
Thobe	long loose dress worn over kandooras
Tokhma	nuts
Tumans	Iran's currency unit
Valinemat	benefactor
Waqf	dedicated
Vedas	Indian mythology
Vozoo	ablution
Wazir	minister
Zangardoon	group of women who go to invite people to weddings
Zelzelah	earthquake